ASH
&
LITTLE BEAR

A NOVEL

IAN J. HARRISON

MōZ
Press

Book Cover Design by Ian J. Harrison

1st edition 2024

International Standard Book Number: 979-8-9914062-1-5

In memory of Jared K. Harrison

We'll meet again someday… for the first time.

Book Cover Design by Ian J. Harrison

1st edition 2024

International Standard Book Number: 979-8-9914062-1-5

In memory of Jared K. Harrison

We'll meet again someday… for the first time.

<u>Acknowledgments</u>

This book has been a long, multi-year process, and, as no book is written in a vacuum, there are many people who share in the creative shenanigans needed to see it to completion. These are those people, who I will never be able to thank enough.

My dad, John Harrison and step-mom, Karen. You both have encouraged me from afar, especially when I needed it most. My brother Chris, who keeps things running smoothly at home, not an easy job. My mom, Reverand Jan Blackburn, who knows how to push me to do better, even when I'm convinced it's impossible. To Eric Hemion, one of the best, and closest friends a person could ever hope for. You understand the creative mind better than anyone. Oh, the stories we could tell! Thankfully, we don't have to.

To the staff of the Texas A&M Athletics Department, who supported me after the fire, especially James Duncan, Jae Fadde, Matt Watson, Brian Despain, Steve Miller and Coach Mike Sherman, you all helped me through one of the most difficult periods of time in my life. Oddly enough, had the fire not happened, I very likely wouldn't have begun writing in the first place.

To Quinn, who understands.

To my editor, Carrie Jones, who turned a loose conglomeration of letters and ideas into something far greater. Carrie is, without even the slightest hint of exaggeration, one of the most patient people in the world. Editors are the unsung heroes of the publishing world, without them, we would still be living in caves.

Finally, and most of all, to my twin brother Scott. You understand me better than anyone ever could. When I wanted to give up and delete everything, which was often, you encouraged me to keep going. There were so many times I wanted throw up my hands in frustration, quit trying so hard, and be done with it. But you wouldn't hear of it. When a person has someone in their corner who simply will not allow you to accept mediocrity, who refuses to let you throw in the towel, well, that is a wonderful thing. For me, that person is you. The world desperately needs more people like you in it. Thank you.

Undoubtedly, and unfortunately, there are those whose names don't appear here, and for that I apologize. If you don't see your name here, the fault is mine. Rest assured that your name is present, in invisible ink.

Ian Harrison
November 27, 2024

One

"Hey, half-breed!" someone with a deep, sloppy sounding voice shouted.

As if walking to school in the dead of winter wasn't bad enough, now some genius had to start yelling at people. Approaching the intersection ahead, I slowed my pace as snow crunched under my feet.

"Hey, half-breed, I'm talking to you."

Naturally the insults continued, further solidifying my opinion that very few decent people called this wretched city home. I could visualize the owner of the voice involuntarily spitting with every spoken word. They were almost certainly a horrifyingly loud eater, and I wouldn't envy anyone having to sit across from them when they ate.

It wasn't just the people of the city I loathed, though that would be enough. No, it was the color of the city itself. Gray, all of it. Every shade and hue of gray the mind could conjure was visible in just one square block. Any block, pick one. The streets, sidewalks, buildings, and yes, even the people, all various shades of gray. It was depressing.

"He ain't listening. Throw it, Pigs." a second, higher pitched voice called out.

I looked up, curious to see what the commotion was about, instantly recognizing the face belonging to the first voice to be Mike Pigliani. Big Mike, often just Big or Pigs, to his friends. He stood with his similarly attired friends, near the light post, under the crosswalk sign. Attending Yorktown High for only a short time, I had already learned to steer a very wide path around 'Big Mike.' At approximately six-foot-five, he was a giant. And not a skinny giant either, he was a broad-shouldered behemoth. Wearing a burnt orange hoodie, the sleeve cuffs stained with dirt, and blue jeans (only slightly less dirty), and a brand-new Seattle Mariners baseball cap tilted with obvious laziness to the right, he cast a threatening shadow without even trying. Earning the well-deserved reputation of bullies, Mike and his merry band of cohorts often had nothing but mayhem on their collective minds. I didn't care to imagine what he wanted that warranted my attention.

"Think fast, maggot." Mike announced through a threatening smile.

With no idea what he was talking about, I didn't have to wait long to find out. A brilliant flash of light flooded my vision as something cold and hard smashed into the left side of my face. Stumbling backward, I tried to discern what had happened while attempting to regain my sense of balance. Looking at the snow-covered sidewalk revealed the cause of my confusion: a snowball. No ordinary snowball, of course, this one contained in its center a rather large piece of jagged concrete. No wonder the impact had been so forceful.

"Oh, man, perfect shot. Pinpoint accuracy. I should be in the majors."

Mike's proclamation was followed by a loud cacophony of laughter from his tagalong friends.

Reaching up with my gloved left hand, I could already feel swelling under my eye, meaning there would be no way to hide this from my mom. Pulling my hand away from my face, my glove was already soaked with blood. Worse than I thought. When the mocking laughter stopped, I looked up to see another snowball arcing straight for my head. Instinct took over and I ducked, allowing the tiny frozen missile to sail over my head, landing harmlessly in the street.

Before I could formulate a response to the assault, Mike was running toward me, the evil grin never leaving his gigantic face. What now? As the lumbering giant approached, I imagined, with no small amount of hope, that he be struck by a passing meteorite or at least slip on the snow-covered sidewalk. To my profound disappointment, neither happened. Slowing his approach, sliding the last five or six feet, his crooked, yellow teeth seemed oversized, adding even more absurdity to his already odd caricature.

Why do bullies always have yellow teeth? Since time began, and likely before, anyone who has ever been bullied knows that bullies have yellow teeth. And yellow teeth almost certainly accompanied bad breath. Hopefully, I won't be exposed to the latter.

Neanderthal Mike, as I now thought of him, stood in front of me, and my eyes were level with the middle of his expansive, filthy, burnt orange chest.

He huffed, leaning forward.

"You little chicken shit half-breed. I didn't give you permission to duck."

Despite the difference in height, I still received a healthy dose of his putrid breath. I stifled a gag reflex, not wanting to wretch all over his decadent attire.

"You wouldn't happen to have any gum, would you? Something minty fresh?"

"What? Why would I have any gum? And if I did, why would I waste it on you? He wants to know if I have any gum."

He turned, looking for the validation of his friends, all of whom laughed as they were expected to.

"Never mind, it's not important."

"No kidding. You can stop talking now."

With that, he placed his gigantic right hand in the middle of my chest and pushed hard. With embarrassingly little effort, I landed with a sickening thud on my tailbone, the thin layer of snow offering little in the way of cushioning. Why was this happening? As if the freezing cold wasn't bad enough, why would he purposefully make matters worse? Life was already hard enough for everyone.

Having scratched the itch, he turned around and jogged back to his band of brothers, laughing the whole way as they crossed the street. Watching him go, I remained silent. There was nothing to say, and no one to say it to. With my left eye bleeding and swollen and a bruised tailbone, I picked myself up, dusted off the snow and shuffled over to the intersection where I waited for the crosswalk signal to give me permission to move. It seemed even the crosswalk signal was a bully. Even inanimate objects had to get their shots in.

Loneliness enveloped me, threatening to swallow me whole as I crossed the street. Well, loneliness and depression. Everything seemed to be stacking up against me; I was in a new school, had no friends because I didn't know anyone, the weather was awful, and now Yorktown High's most notorious bully had decided to pick me as his next target. Why did he call me a half-breed in the first place? How did he know?

It was true. After all, I was mixed race, my mom is Black, and my dad was white. Hating the term "half-breed," I much preferred the term "Mellado," But how did he know anything about this? It was none of his business I was the product of a mixed-race couple. I didn't understand people like "Neanderthal Mike," and chances were that I probably never would, which was a good thing.

Two

Arriving at school, I headed for the nearest bathroom to get a better look at the cut and swelling below my left eye. The bathroom smelled of cigarettes and cleaning chemicals, an olfactory combination that stays with you for a lifetime. Staring at myself in the mirror long past its prime, I was relieved to see the cut wasn't as deep as I had originally feared. With a wad of dampened toilet paper, I wiped off the dried blood, more clearly exposing the swelling. I really couldn't do anything about it, which meant having to explain what happened when I got home.

Exiting the bathroom, I set off for first period, US history, taught by Mr. Lewis. I've been a history buff for as long as I could remember; it was a subject I felt a closeness to, even though I felt like I had no discernible or definable ancestry of my own.

As I entered the room, Riley was already seated, looking as radiant as ever. It seemed she smiled for no other reason than she simply enjoyed it. Smiling suited her. Of course, everything wonderful in the world suited her. She wasn't pretty, she was gorgeous with her jet-black hair framing her perfectly symmetrical face and dark brown eyes. Hurrying, head down to my seat near the back of the room, I was eager to not make eye contact with her. In fact, I preferred not to make eye contact with anyone, lest they take notice of my damaged face. I sat, noticing the sound of the metal desk creaking as it accepted my weight. It was a sound unique to high schools far and wide and one I'd never heard in any other setting. It had become a sound I loathed as it reminded me of where I didn't want to be.

Mr. Lewis entered the room just as the first period bell rang. The creaking sound of desks across the room signified everyone in class adjusting in their seats, getting settled before class began. Almost tardy, I thought, not that I would ever accuse a teacher of such a thing. Still, I did have an inward chuckle as he walked to the front of the room. Dressed in blue jeans the style of which my mom would wear ("Mom jeans," I called them), as it was casual Friday, a red Polo shirt, and what everyone called gumshoes, likely purchased from the likes of an L.L. Bean catalog, he also wore a very expensive looking leather bomber jacket, complete with a scantily clad woman painted on the back. She appeared to be straddling a WWII era bomb and waving an American flag with her right hand. He removed the jacket and held it out with both arms extended, showing it to the class.

"Can anyone tell me what this is?" Mr. Lewis asked.

I knew exactly what it was but had no intention of speaking up. Being introverted and shy, I found making friends a difficult and tedious task and this extended to volunteering to answer questions in class. I was far more interested in immersing myself in books than anything else, cherishing the idea of getting lost in the places that books transported me to. Books were an avenue allowing me to leave behind the depressing gray world I lived in, shuttling me to an unlimited number of fantastic places existing only in my imagination. I mostly favorited science fiction but was gaining increasing interest in steam punk novels. These stories took place primarily in the Victorian Era but had many elements of technology that wouldn't be invented until decades later. They were an interesting combination of the old and the new, a mishmash, not unlike me.

Consequently, because I read a lot, I knew Mr. Lewis was holding a leather bomber jacket, the type commonly used by pilots and crews during WWII. Some of the characters in my steam punk novels were pilots and wore leather jackets of a similar fashion.

'Don't call on me! Don't call on me!' the voice in my head screamed as I quickly angled my head downward to not make eye contact with Mr. Lewis. The seconds ticked by in a slow-motion nightmare while my eyes bore holes into the desk as I attempted to make myself invisible. 'Fade into the woodwork! Fade into the woodwork!' my inner voice commanded. I could feel Mr. Lewis scanning the room, waiting for someone to answer his question.

Finally, he spoke, "Mr. Perrault?"

Shit. Shit, shit.

"Can you tell me what this is?"

I didn't dare look up, but I also knew better than to not answer the question.

"It's a leather bomber jacket?"

Answer in the form of a question, brilliant Ashley.

"I'm sorry Mr. Perrault, I couldn't hear you. Could you repeat that?"

Are you kidding me? How long would this new humiliation last? I could hear and feel the other students in the room shift in their seats.

"Umm, it's a leather bomber jacket. From World War Two I think."

There, that ought to do it. Done and done. I hoped.

"Mr. Perrault, could you please sit up straight, stop mumbling and answer the question loudly enough so the rest of the class can hear you?"

There was nothing to do but hope he wasn't looking directly at me as I raised my head.

"My God. What happened to your face?"

Thank you very much.

So, is this what it feels like when my nightmare explodes into reality? Every single person in the room had cast their gaze upon me. It was also the precise time in which I decided that teachers have no sense of tact and no concept that other people have feelings. My face was getting hot, indicating I was probably blushing, adding to my embarrassment.

Without thinking, I touched the swelling under my left eye.

"I got hit with a snowball. I think it had a rock in it."

No sense in lying about it.

"Well, it looks bad. Do you want to go to the nurse and get it looked at?"

Despite the freezing weather outside, I was beginning to sweat. When would this inquisition end? Everyone was staring at me. I was sweating and now Mr. Lewis seemed determined not to drop the subject.

"Not really. I'm fine. It's just a scratch."

What else could I say?

Surveying the room, I noticed Riley looking right at me, no expression on her perfect face. She probably thought I looked like an idiot. Now would have been a perfect time to get struck by lightning and completely vaporized.

I sat there, an embarrassed, humiliated, sweating mass of eye-swollen misery. Unfortunately, that seething, hot bolt of lightning never materialized. How, I wondered, could Mr. Lewis not know that singling me out in front of the entire class would be a thoroughly detestable experience? Didn't he think things through before opening his mouth? Apparently not.

"Mr. Perrault, I'd like to see you after class."

That figures, slinking down in my seat I sat there, resigned to my fate. The rest of the period passed without incident and by the time the bell rang signifying our dismissal, my heart rate had returned to normal, and I had stopped sweating. With haste, I shoved books and pens into my backpack and tried to scurry my way out of the room, hoping beyond hope Mr. Lewis had forgotten about our scheduled meeting.

"Mr. Perrault? Up front please."

Busted.

Stopping, I took a deep breath, turned on my heels and walked back to the front of the class as the other students made their exit. Riley, walking down the same aisle, but in the opposite direction, looked up and smiled sweetly as we passed each other, our shoulders ever so slightly making contact. The light breeze created by her passing carried with it the sweetest, most aromatic scent I had ever experienced. How could she possibly smell so good? It wasn't fair.

If she had to be so breathtakingly gorgeous, then she should, at the very least, be saddled with smelling horrid. Like a septic system or the dead rat that lived in the stairwell of my building. Mesmerized by her smile and wonderful aroma, I failed to watch where I was going, veered left and ran into a desk, banging my shin hard, adding to the list of wonderful things befalling me today.

Standing at the front of the room, Mr. Lewis rolled his eyes as I untangled myself from the desk, arms folded across his chest.

"So, Ashley, tell me what happened."

He had never addressed me as Ashley, and I took this as his way of trying to strike a friendly, nonthreatening tone.

"Seriously, Mr. Lewis, I got hit by a snowball as I was walking to school this morning. I look like this," indicating with my hand the small cut and swelling under my left eye, "because the snowball had a rock in it. I didn't see it coming."

He considered my answer, nodding slightly before inhaling. I could already guess what his next question would be.

"And who threw this rock-laden snowball?"

I knew right off the bat that telling him meant that in the eyes of many, I would be immediately considered a snitch. Honestly though, I didn't care. Nothing would come of it regardless, since I was new at Yorktown, and no one knew a thing about me. Neanderthal Mike being the obvious exception, who somehow knew I was mixed race. Besides, if anyone found out, and why would they, who was going to care in the first place?

"His name is Mike. Big guy, kind of looks like an oversized version of a Neanderthal man. Smells bad, looks worse."

I purposefully failed to mention Mike's half-breed comments, seeing no need to thicken the plot.

"Mm, hmm. Yeah, I know who you mean. Mike Pigliani. His friends call him Big Mike, sometimes just Big. I'd carve a wide berth when he's around if I were you. He's bad news. I'll talk to Assistant Principal Walker, see if we can get Mike to lay off."

While appreciating Mr. Lewis's offer of assistance, I knew I couldn't accept. If Mike learned I had ratted him out, he'd certainly and violently lose his cool, and I didn't want to incur his wrath any more than I already had.

"No, that's OK. I'm sure it was just a one-time thing."

"I doubt it. Mike is a bad seed and he's not likely to let up until he gets bored with you. You sure you don't want me to talk to AP Walker?"

"Yeah, I'm sure. No big deal. Thanks though."

I stood, waiting, hoping my answer had satisfied him. He remained silent, staring at me for an uncomfortable period, obviously pondering his next move.

"All right, get out of here." He waved his right arm toward the door at the other end of the room, signaling I was free to go.

I turned and walked out, thankful for the opportunity to leave the scene of my latest humiliation. The remainder of the day passed without incident. A few people asked about my swollen and bruised eye, so I told them the truth, I got hit by a snowball. When they asked me who threw it, I quickly changed the subject, knowing full well that if Mike heard I had been talking about him, things could get very nasty for yours truly.

Slowly, I navigated the dark corridors of the city, my only companion the windblown snow that continued falling. The darkness was pierced by traffic signals, street lights and car head and taillights, but I ignored them. All I noticed was gray. By the time I arrived home, I had a headache, my tailbone ached, and my shin hurt from running into the desk, courtesy of my own rather distracted nature. So, all things considered, it was a rotten day.

Three

Entering the lobby of my apartment building, I was thankful for the blast of warm air greeting me as I opened the door. Walking up to the small, metal post office boxes situated along the left wall, I retrieved the tiny key out of my left pocket, inserted it into the appropriate slot, and removed the day's mail. Thumbing through the standard stack of bills, credit card applications, and grocery store flyers, I found an envelope addressed to Koko Redfeather. I quickly surmised that Koko, whoever he was, was likely of Native American descent, it was as obvious as his last name. Evidently the mailman had inadvertently placed the envelope addressed to him into the wrong box. The addresses were only one number off, as Mr. Redfeather's apartment was directly above ours. I stuffed his mail into my jeans pocket, planning to return it to him later and headed upstairs.

After entering the apartment, I dropped my backpack on the couch and headed straight for the bathroom to determine what my face looked like. My left eye, more swollen than I had remembered, had a remarkably colorful bruise under it. There was no way to hide it from my mom, so I decided to not even try. She'd find out one way or another, as moms are prone to do. In the kitchen, I retrieved some ice, placing it in a Ziploc bag to reduce the swelling. She wouldn't be home for at least a couple of hours, so I busied myself with the day's homework assignments.

Just before finishing my reading assignment, the unmistakable sound of keys rattling alerted me, something my mom always did before inserting the key into the lock. The lock turned, the door swung open, and she emerged.

"Hey Ash. How was your day?"

Cheerful as always.

"Lousy, terrible, and worthless. I was hoping to get struck by lightning before lunch. Unfortunately, it didn't happen."

Busy removing her coat, she looked at me with a quizzical expression that rapidly changed to one of shock and puzzlement.

"What happened? Your face is swollen."

"You noticed that did you?"

"A blind alley cat would notice that."

"Thanks, that makes me feel a lot better."

She pulled out a chair and sat down at our 3rd or 4th hand dining room table, a genuine look of concern on her face.

"Tell me what happened."

I told her the story from beginning to end, omitting nothing. She sat silently, listening to my tale, nodding once or twice, but otherwise allowing me the freedom to vent my frustrations. I admired her patience and understanding as she could have immediately fired a barrage of questions at me, ones seething with anger that someone would blatantly and viscously attack her only son. But she was calm, her peaceful nature on full display as I recounted my dealings with Neanderthal Mike. As I finished my story, pain and concern were written all over her face as she furrowed her brow and pursed her lips.

I lowered my head, resting it on the open history book in front of me. I had been humiliated and injured, and this, I knew, would cause hurt to her. For that, I was ashamed. Inwardly cursing myself for not having the courage to handle the situation with Mike differently, I fought the urge to cry, as a lump gathered strength in my throat.

Sensing my pain, she lightly stroked the top of my head with her hand.

"You want something to drink? Hot chocolate?"

I nodded my head against the book, to upset to speak.

She busied herself in the kitchen, heating water in the microwave and adding powdered chocolate. As she finished preparing the tasty beverage, I closed my history book, reasonably confident I had read enough to get through Mr. Lewis's lecture on Monday.

"He called you a half-breed?" she asked, placing two steaming mugs on the table.

"Yeah, and that's what I can't figure out." I spoke. "I haven't the slightest idea how he would know anything about me. I mean, I've seen him around school a few times, but I don't have any classes with him, and I've never spoken to him."

"What did you say his name was?"

I thought for a quick moment, trying to recall how Mr. Lewis had pronounced Mike's last name.

"Umm, Mike. What is his last name, Mr. Lewis told me but …" I fought to put together the right combination of consonants, vowels and syllables. I looked toward the ceiling, hoping for a sign.

"Mike Pigli-something. His friends call him Big Mike. Pigliasi? No, that's not right."

My mom cringed, leaning forward slightly.

"It's not Pigliani is it?"

Lowering my gaze, I looked directly at her, confusion and disbelief registering on my face. I nodded slightly.

"Yeah, that sounds right."

She shook her head slowly, realizing something only she knew. I stared, waiting.

"Mom, what?"

Drawing in a deep breath, she let it out before telling me what she knew.

"There's a woman, another administrative assistant, that works for the Athletic Department, whose last name is Pigliani. At lunch a couple of days ago, we were talking about our families. I told her about you and your father, she must have said something to Mike about it."

Tightly closing my eyes, I bit my bottom lip and shook my head, not wanting to believe what I'd just heard. I felt like I had been betrayed by my best friend. Not that I had any concept of what having a best friend was like.

"So, I look like this …" I indicated with my left hand the swollen lump under my eye, "because you were talking to a friend at work?"

"Well, I wouldn't call her a friend. She's more of a friendly acquaintance than anything."

"Mom, I don't care!"

Instantly furious, my left eye began to throb as I stood from the table with such force that my chair fell backward. With my thoughts spinning in a million different directions and feeling the need for fresh air to clear my head, I marched for the door, opened it and stepped through, slamming it as I exited.

Quick stepping down the hallway to the stairwell, the sickening cracked and faded blue-green paint mocked my every step. Whoever selected this paint needed to have their eyes checked.

My desire for solitude drove me to the roof, the only place I could confidently expect to be alone. The stairwell to the roof smelled of body odor and weed, a sickening combination. Opening the dented and scratched, heavy, gray steel door to the roof forced upon me the chilling reality that I left the apartment wearing only jeans and a T-shirt. Perfect, just what I needed.

In a personal show of stubborn defiance, I stepped through the doorway despite the stabbing cold. Snow continued to fall, the fresh layer beneath my feet crunching like old brittle leaves in late fall. The wind, blowing much harder than it had earlier in the day, was painful.

Venturing further into the cold, I was assaulted by needle sharp snowflakes, every single one attempting to drive itself into my skin. Approaching the nearest edge, I looked down into the grayness, the daytime sun having long since faded into twilight. The sidewalk below was a white blanket of snow, not a footprint in sight. Few people would brave weather like this, with temperatures in the mid-twenties and the forecast calling for a low in the mid-teens by morning. I might well be the only person outside in the entire city, I thought. It would be so easy to jump, to end the misery. If only I had an ounce of courage. Resigned to the fact that the cold was much tougher than I could ever hope to be, I turned around and made for the door and warm shelter.

Reaching for the door, my ears detected a barely audible rhythmic, melodious sound through the stinging wind and snow. Following the sound, I wound my way around a hulking gray air-conditioning unit to see a figure bundled in a heavy, dark blue, puffy jacket, faded blue jeans, and a bright red, knit stocking cap pulled low over the ears, sitting motionless in the snow.

Placed before this person was what looked like an ancient pipe, the snow swirling and collecting around it, indicating he had been there for quite some time. Careful not to disturb him, I approached as quietly as the crunching snow would allow. But not quietly enough, as the rhythmic sound I now identified as chanting abruptly stopped. Slowly turning their head to the right to see who or what had interrupted this meditative state was a person I surmised could only be Koko Redfeather, my upstairs neighbor.

"Sorry."

I doubted he understood as I was shivering so violently, I was certain my teeth were going to rattle right out of my head.

Even through the fading light and blowing snow, the brilliant twinkle in his impossibly brown eyes was obvious.

"You must be Mr. Ashley. It is good to see you."

He knew my name?

Smiling as much with his eyes as with his mouth, he picked up the pipe, rose and walked silently toward me. The snow that crunched and shifted audibly under my feet was the same snow he walked on, yet he scarcely made a sound. How was this possible?

Stopping in front of me, he carefully placed the pipe under his left arm, reached out with both hands and with unrestrained enthusiasm, shook my right hand. His eyes were so deep brown, they appeared black. Even through the fading evening light and blowing snow and casting aside the fact that he smiled with his entire face, what struck me most was how genuine he appeared. He was genuinely happy to see me. In my entire life, the only person to display this trait was my mom.

I could not help but return his smile. It was the first time I'd smiled all day, and it hurt, with the muscles in my face stretching the swollen skin under my eye. I smiled anyway, through the pain.

He stopped shaking my hand, giving me a quick onceover, obviously noting I wasn't properly dressed for the weather.

"You are going to catch your death out here dressed like that. Inside ..." he pointed toward the door, "... get some hot chocolate. You need to warm up."

It wasn't a request, wasn't even a polite suggestion; it was more of a command. But it wasn't the stern, 'you'll do what you're told, and you'll like it' command I would expect from most adults. His was a heartfelt desire to help someone, and I saw no point in arguing about it.

He turned and began the short walk back to the steel gray door marking the entrance to warmth and the nauseating, colored walls. He walked as silently as a ghost, I crunched with every step.

Walking back to his apartment, I noticed his ramrod straight, perfect posture. About two inches shorter than I was, the top of his head remained level as he walked. Having removed the red, knit stocking cap, he revealed a head of mostly dark black hair, streaked in places with flashes of gray and gathered in the back into a neat ponytail.

Nearing his apartment, he slowed, turning toward me while fishing for keys out of the front pocket of his jeans.

"You have a black eye and a cut on your face. Why is this?"

"It's a long story. Well, not that long."

He began unlocking the deadbolts on his front door, all four of them, if my math was correct.

He opened the door and we stepped into an immaculate apartment adorned with many examples of Native American art. As he closed the door and locked the deadbolts, a soft meow called from the back of the apartment. Turning to find the source, a medium-sized, cinnamon-colored cat appeared, sauntered up to Koko and wrapped itself in figure eights around his legs, purring the whole time.

"Who's that?"

Koko bent down, gathered the purring cat in his arms, scratching it between the ears. The cat leaned into his hand, soaking up the attention with every scratch.

"This is Fred. Fred, say hello to my new friend, Ashley."

Fred gazed at Koko with a look of complete contentment but said nothing.

Fred? He named his cat Fred? I would have expected a name like Moon Shadow or Running Stream, but not 'Fred. Ok, I thought, Fred it is.

"I rescued Fred from a kitten mill that was shut down by federal authorities. Fred is a full-blooded Abyssinian"

"I thought we weren't allowed to have pets in the building?"

Koko's expression changed instantly, his smile fading as he clutched Fred a little tighter.

"You are correct, pets are not allowed. But could you say no to a face like this?" He held Fred out, away from his body to get a better look at him. Fred gazed at Koko, mewing softly, purring louder than ever.

"No, I suppose I couldn't. I've never had a pet though."

He looked visibly disappointed at my admission. It was as if not having a pet was a dreadful thing to consider. As much as I think I'd like to have a pet, there were some things I knew not to ask my mom for, and a pet was at the top of the list. New sneakers, candy when I was five, sure, those things were within the realm of possibility. A pet was not, and I instinctively knew it despite not having ever discussed it with her.

"Aren't you worried you'll get caught?"

Koko walked Fred to the nearest wall, placing him on a high shelf with a cozy, warm cat bed placed on it. Fred turned around three times, curled up, and closed his eyes.

"No, I do not spend any time worrying about such things. 'No pets allowed' is just an arbitrary rule. Sometimes, for the greater good, rules must be ignored."

"Ok, but what's the greater good in this case?"

"Is Fred not allowed a happy and fulfilling life? Am I? I smile every time I see him. He brings joy to my life, and I would like to think I provide the same for him."

I had to hand it to him, it made perfect sense. It was clear, even from the brief time I had seen Koko and Fred interact, that they had a special bond. To be honest, I was more than a little jealous. Perhaps, one day in the distant future, I might entertain the notion of having a pet. Right now, though, I have more pressing issues to deal with.

"Well, your secret is safe with me."

Pleased to hear this, his bright smile returned as his tense body language melted away as though it had never been there at all.

Koko turned and walked to the kitchen where I could hear him preparing the hot chocolate. I stood, just inside the door, looking around the apartment, amazed at the vast collection of artworks. On the wall to the left of the door was a large portrait of an elderly Native American man. Approaching the portrait, the intricate detail and innumerable array of colors displayed was astonishing. The man was staring straight ahead, his eyes, much like those of Koko, were those of a much younger man. His skin, wrinkled and deeply tanned, was reminiscent of a piece of old parchment. He wore an elaborate headdress adorned with many long black and white feathers and a breastplate made, I was guessing, of animal bone. The details were phenomenal and to me, the artist had captured the essence of the old man's character. He looked like someone that was not to be trifled with.

I took in the subtle detail of the vibrant colors. In the lower right-hand corner of the painting was a signature and date that read, very simply, "Koko, '99." Koko had painted the Native American man. My jaw dropped open as I stood, slack jawed at the realization.

Next to the painting, on a small, black shelf, was an earthenware bowl, about six inches high and four across, modestly decorated with two parallel grooves carved around its circumference, the top one red, the bottom, yellow. Curious if Koko had fashioned the pottery, I took a chance. Hearing him in the kitchen, the microwave humming away as it heated the water, I still looked over my shoulder, making sure the coast was clear. It was. Carefully picking up the pottery, I turned it over to look at the bottom, searching for a telltale signature. And there it was, scrawled in the center, an illegible name, but no date. Koko was not a potter as well as a painter.

Quickly returning the item to its proper resting place, I was careful in making sure it was perfectly centered. When I turned around, Koko was standing in the doorway to the kitchen, holding two steaming mugs of hot chocolate, smiling wide, something that seemed to come quickly and easily.

"I'm sorry. I was being careful, I promise."

"It is alright. Do you like it? My mother made it many years ago."

My eyes widened in response. Artistic talent ran in Koko's family.

"Yeah, it's amazing."

And I meant it.

Walking into the living room, he handed me a cup and took a seat in the leather recliner that sat catty-cornered to the left of the couch. He took a tentative sip, careful not to burn himself.

"She was an amazing artist. Some of her work is on display in the Smithsonian, in Washington, D.C."

"Impressive. You did that painting there? I saw your signature at the bottom."

He took another sip.

"Yes."

Looking around the apartment, I was taken by the sheer number of amazing works of art.

Gesturing with my free hand, I asked,

"Did you paint all these?"

"Most of them, though not all. Some I collected simply because I enjoy looking at them."

"Are they valuable?"

"I do not know. But yes probably. Which is why I have four locks on the door."

"Yeah, that makes sense."

As impressive as the art collection was, was the fact that many of the works were created by Koko's own hand. What treasures were hidden beyond the confines of his living room?

Leaning forward, he placed his hot chocolate on the corner of the coffee table and looked at me, pondering.

"So, Ashley. Tell me why you have a cut and bruise on your face."

Well, he doesn't beat around the bush. Despite the abruptness of his question, I did not feel as if I was being interrogated. His desire to know what happened was authentic.

Taking a seat on the couch, I gently blew on my cup before taking a sip, when it suddenly dawned on me how tired I was. The day had been long, stressful, humiliating and, at times, physically painful and this was the first time I had allowed myself to relax.

Koko leaned back in his chair, allowing me the freedom to begin my tale of woe only when I was ready. Seeing no reason for further delay, I jumped right in.

"As lame as it sounds, I got hit with a snowball this morning as I walked to school."

"A snowball did that?"

"Well, it wasn't an ordinary snowball. The guy who threw it packed a rock in the center. And he threw it when I wasn't looking. Then he and his friends laughed about it before he threw another one, which missed because I ducked. After that, he ran up to me, all pissed off because I ducked. He called me a half-breed and pushed me down into the snow. I bruised my tailbone."

I got it all out at once to keep the memory of the incident as short as possible.

Reaching forward, he picked up his hot chocolate, took a sip, and leaned back, deep in thought.

"What did you do next?"

"Nothing. What could I do? I picked myself up and walked to school."

"Hmm ... You did not retaliate?"

"No way. This guy is huge, probably six-foot-five and wide as a dump truck"

"Why did he call you a half-breed?"

My face was getting hot, meaning I was blushing. Koko didn't intentionally embarrass me, but his question, while a valid one, was very personal. Struggling to figure out the best way to answer him, I exhaled, deciding on the direct route.

"Because I am a half-breed. My mom is Black, and my dad was white."

Saying it aloud didn't make me feel better. People are fond of saying "Talk about your feelings, you'll feel better when you do." That's a bunch of baloney if you ask me. I had said it aloud and still felt horrible. Koko saw this immediately.

"I am going to let you in on a little secret. You are not a half-breed. You are not half of anything. You are a whole person, complete and unique in every way, regardless of what people say or how they treat you."

He was right, I supposed, but I still didn't know how to respond. What was maddening is that he wasn't just trying to blow sunshine up my keester to make me feel better. He believed every word.

Sensing the heaviness in the room, he deftly changed the subject.

"How is your hot chocolate?"

"It's great, best hot chocolate I've had in a long time."

He smiled. I figured he would smile at the drop of a hat if given the opportunity.

"A good cup of hot chocolate in the dead of winter will cure almost anything."

Where he produced that little nugget, I have no idea, but it was hard to argue with such profound logic.

"What are you going to do next?" he asked.

"I have no idea. Nothing. I don't think there's anything I can do. I can't fight him. He'd happily squash me like bug without even trying."

Closing his eyes, the old man tipped his head back, angling his face toward the ceiling. He remained silent, his lips moving imperceptibly, giving the appearance of him conversing with someone unseen. When Fred jumped down from his shelf and trotted across the room to leap into Koko's lap, he didn't move a muscle. Finally opening his eyes, he took his time looking around the room, thoughts turning around in his head.

"I need to give this situation of yours more consideration," he said, pausing briefly. "This is a complex problem, one which must be given a considerable amount of understanding."

My guilt was immediate as I had no intention of unloading my burdens on him.

"You don't have to do that." I implored. "It's my problem, I'll deal with it. I'm sorry, I didn't mean to burden you with all of this."

I hung my head in shame.

Koko raised his hand, palm out.

"This is not a burden to me. You are my friend, and I will help you. No, you will not face this alone."

So touched by his support, a lump began forming in my throat. He didn't know me from a stranger on the street, so why would he go out of his way to help? Why would he call me his friend when we barely knew one another? There were more questions than I had answers for, and I didn't want to offend him by asking. Instead, I sipped my hot chocolate, wondering how he could possibly be of assistance. Not to belabor the point, but he was an old, slow-moving man. He would be no more able to physically stand up to Mike than I could, not that I would ever expect him to, which, of course, I wouldn't. How he planned on approaching my problem was a concept my brain failed to grasp. My gut was telling me he didn't know either.

Four

I finished my hot chocolate, set the empty mug on the spotless coffee table, and got up to leave, figuring my mom would probably be worrying about me.

Koko carefully picked up Fred, gently placing him on the floor before standing up. Fred looked around the room, then up at Koko as if he couldn't understand why his slumber had been so rudely interrupted. Koko looked down at Fred, shrugging his shoulders.

"What?"

Fred turned, and looking right at me, meowed loudly.

"Don't look at me."

Fred walked over to me, tail high, and began walking figure eights between my legs.

"Ah, see, Fred likes you. Now you have two new friends."

I bent down and scratched Fred between the ears, something he seemed to enjoy immensely. Hearing Koko say that I now have two new friends pleased me greatly. Oddly enough, even though my situation regarding Neanderthal Mike hadn't changed, I felt much better than I did storming out on my mom. Whatever magic he weaved seemed to have worked. Or maybe he spiked the hot chocolate, I'm not sure.

"I have to get going. My mom is probably sending out a search party to find me."

"Yes, I understand."

"Thanks for the hot chocolate. It was good. Oh, I almost forgot ..." I reached into my jeans pocket, retrieving the letter addressed to him. "This is yours, but it ended up in our box. Sorry about that."

"You are welcome and thank you for returning the envelope." After unlocking the deadbolts, he opened the door, allowing me to step into the hallway where I turned to face him before walking away.

"See you later, OK."

"Yes, I will see you soon." Smiling, he closed the door, locking the deadbolts in turn as I walked the dingy hallway toward home. Pondering my mom's reaction when I arrived left me feeling heavy with guilt. More than likely, she would apologize, but beyond that, I didn't know how she would react.

Opening the apartment door, the smell of fresh cookies baking in the oven signified a truce, and her desire to make me feel better. I couldn't help but wonder if Mike's mom ever did something similar for him. Very unlikely, I thought, which might explain his abrasiveness to everyone he encountered. Freshly baked cookie deprivation will turn just about anyone into an asshole, I deduced. It's pure science.

With the door closed, I slammed home the single, forlorn deadbolt. With no pristine works of valuable art, one pitiful lock was all that was necessary. Old, worn-out furniture and a tired, color-tube TV summed up our pricey belongings. Not that I was complaining. Compared to many people, we were blessed beyond words. Keenly aware of never really needing anything, my mom saw to it that I always had enough food to eat and clothes to wear. Hearing the door open and close, she walked into the living room, wiping her hands with a small red dishrag. The painful look on her face served to make me feel even guiltier. Moms, I decided, were experts at this, however unintentional.

"I'm sorry I stormed out like that."

"That's OK honey, I understand. How are you feeling?"

A headache, bruised tailbone and a sore, swollen face didn't make for a happy Ashley, but mostly I was tired.

Physically and emotionally, I was wrung out, ready for the day to end.

"More than anything, I'm just tired. A little sore from this morning, you know, a headache and my face hurts."

"That's not surprising," she said. "You want some aspirin? Might make you feel better?"

"Yeah, that's a good idea. Thanks." Always looking out for me, baking cookies, and making sure I had aspirin for my aches and pains, she did it all. Despite the dreadful day, I recognized how fortunate I was.

While she retrieved two aspirin and a glass of water from the bathroom, I noticed the chair I knocked over had been picked up and my history book and backpack placed on the coffee table in the living room. I found it amazing how she handled my childish tantrums with such grace and peace.

"You want some cookies? They should be done soon," she asked, handing me the aspirin and water.

"Yeah, sure. What kind are they?"

As if that mattered. In my entire life I don't think I've ever turned down an offer of freshly baked cookies. I might be more timid than a church mouse, but I'm not stupid. Besides, a church mouse wouldn't turn down freshly baked cookies either.

"Chocolate chip with pecans. Where'd you go by the way? You were gone for a while."

"Up to the roof. I felt like I needed to clear my head. Know what I mean?"

She returned from the kitchen with a plate of piping hot, chocolate chip cookies.

"Yup, been there, done that. Got the certificate and everything. Crap, I forgot something. Hold on a minute, don't move a muscle," she instructed, running back into the kitchen.

"You said crap. I'm telling on you."

I was teasing of course, a not-so-subtle way of letting her know that I was, in fact, doing OK despite the day I had. She returned holding two tall glasses of milk. I smiled. She never missed a beat.

"Yeah, I know. Me and my potty mouth. I forgot the milk. A fresh plate of cookies without a tall glass of milk is a plate of cookies not worth eating."

"You're right."

She was right on the money, and I recall her telling me more than a few times what my dad was famous for saying," Pay attention to the details, for they are always important,"

She took this advice to heart, and it showed.

"Pay attention to the details for they are always important," I announced.

She smiled, raised her glass of milk, and, looking at mine, nodded gently. Immediately getting the message, I raised my glass, and we toasted Dad. Nothing else was said about what had happened, nothing about my run-in with Mike the Neanderthal, nothing about my mom confiding in her co-worker who happened to be Mike's mom. Her intuitive feel for people and knowing just what they needed and when they needed it was remarkable. There would be time, tomorrow, to deal with the trappings of conflict and conflict resolution. Right now, it was quite enough for us to simply enjoy each other's company.

Five

Saturday morning greeted me with a brilliant, cloudless blue sky. Considering the previous day, I felt reasonably well. My tailbone ached and the area under my left eye was quite sore to the touch, but my headache was gone. The bathroom mirror exposed decreased swelling but significantly more bruising under my eye. Could be a lot worse.

For reasons I'll never fully understand, I stared into the mirror wondering what Mike was doing at this very second. Probably robbing a convenience store and beating up the clerk. Possibly hijacking a bus? A bus full of nuns? Who really cared what he was doing? Why did I concern myself with such things? The Neanderthal, I'm sure, wasted no time thinking about me.

A note on the refrigerator informed me that Mom had left to get her shopping done early, so I ate breakfast while getting the day's homework out of the way. Two hours later, keys rattling in the hallway were a sign she was home, so I put my books away and helped her unpack and put away the groceries.

"I just ran into your friend from upstairs, the Native American man. He says hi and wanted to know how you were feeling."

"Oh, yeah. Mr. Redfeather. Well, he goes by Koko. Cool, yeah, he seems like a nice guy."

"Yeah, that's what I thought. How are you feeling by the way?"

"Pretty good. My face and tailbone are sore, but that's to be expected. Other than that, I feel fine." And I did feel fine, though I still had some lingering feelings of humiliation and embarrassment from yesterday's encounter.

"Good to hear."

"Is it alright if I head out later to catch a movie?" I asked. "There's a new sci-fi that just came out, it starts at two I think." I didn't bother asking if she wanted to come as I'd learned long ago that science fiction held no interest for her.

"That's fine. You caught up with your homework?"

"Yup. I'm ahead now, ready for Monday."

She didn't miss a trick. If I was going out, I knew ahead of time she was going to make sure I had my homework finished first.

With time to kill before leaving for the movie, I holed up in my room and got lost in a book of science fiction. With the movie theater only a few blocks from the apartment, I got up twenty minutes before showtime and readied to leave.

"I'm leaving now" I said, slipping into my jacket and gloves.

"Okay. Have fun stormin' tha' castle!"

I had to laugh. "Have fun stormin' tha' castle!" a quote by Miracle Max in the film The Princess Bride, one of our favorite movies was recited often in our house.

Stepping into the frigid December air, a light breeze flitted about just enough to make things interesting. Turning right from my building, I walked in the direction of the movie theater, passing large piles of garbage accumulating along the sidewalk, threatening to spill into the street. Despite the sub-freezing temperature, I nearly gagged from the stench and hoped the city's sanitation department ended their strike soon so the cleanup could begin. Going out of my way to walk in un-trampled snow, closer to the buildings and away from the stinking piles of refuse, I was curious if I could replicate the noiseless way Koko walked from last evening. Crunching and sliding with every step, I wasn't even remotely successful. Walking silently in the snow was difficult to the point of hilarity. Imagining Koko watching me with mock disappointment, gently shaking his head, made me smile. How did he do it? His movements seemed effortless. It was as if he didn't have to think about it. Trying as hard as I could, which must have been an odd sight to the other pedestrians on the sidewalk, I couldn't take a single step without making noise. It must be my imagination, no one could walk on snow and do it silently.

At the theater, I paid for my ticket and entered, thankful for the blessing of warm air. Removing my gloves, I looked around, trying to locate the theater my movie was playing in. That was when I saw her, Riley, in all her enchanting glory. Dressed in jeans and a large puffy, white jacket, wisps of jet-black hair danced around her ears from the stocking cap she wore to fend off the cold. She was the only person I had ever seen capable of wearing a stocking cap and making it look stunning. No one in the history of civilization looked cuter in a stocking cap than Riley. I wouldn't tell her that, of course. With my bruised face, it would only come off as creepy and awkward. The wisest course of action was to courageously duck into the theater before being spotted.

Lingering a moment too long, I took one step toward the theater when she saw me. Waving, she walked toward me, so I did what any reasonable person my age would do, I panicked. With no reasonable way out, I waved back and walked toward her. God, she was so pretty. She even walked pretty. How was that possible?

"Hey Riley."

She stopped in front of me, smelling of flowers and all things wonderful. How did she do that? I decided right then and there, it had to be a conspiracy, all pretty girls smelled good, and they did it to throw the male of the species into a tailspin from which there is no hope of recovery. I was heading straight for the ground, tail-spinning like crazy.

"Hey Ash, what's up?"

Even her smile was riveting, damn it.

"Umm, not much really. You know, it's Saturday."

It's Saturday. Who says that I wondered.

She giggled, smiling even wider, if such a thing were possible.

"So what movie are you going to see?"

A perfectly valid question.

"That new sci-fi one with what's his name?"

I knew exactly what his name was and the title of the movie, but would my brain connect with my mouth to say those things? Of course not, that would make sense.

"Umm, the one with Bruce Willis?"

"Yeah, that's the one, the one with Bruce Willis. What are you going to watch?"

The same movie, I hope.

"Oh, the new Jim Carey movie, I can't remember the title. It's supposed to be funny."

"Oh, cool."

"So, what happened to your face? I heard you got punched by a cop."

"Oh, ha-ha. No, nothing like that. No, I got hit with a snowball, that's all. It had a rock in it which is why I look like this."

"Oh, OK. Who threw it?"

Should I have lied, told her I didn't know who threw it? No, nothing good came from a lie. Besides, how could I lie to such a pretty face? There had to be a law against that somewhere. If I told her, did that turn me into more of a snitch? Why was I protecting Mike Pigliani? He was the one who did something wrong.

"You know Mike Pigliani? Big guy, face like a dump truck."

She thought for a moment, tilting her head and narrowing her eyes.

"Yeah, I know him. Well, I don't know him, I know of him."

"You're not missing anything. Anyway, he threw it."

So far, I had managed to not start sweating or say anything dreadfully stupid, but we were now at the point in our fledgling conversation where the awkward silence made its debut. A woman I didn't know approached, saving me from certain self-inflicted humiliation.

"Oh, hey honey. I Couldn't find you."

"Oh, hey Mom. Mom, this is Ashley, he's in a couple of my classes."

"Hi, Ashley, I'm Sara."

Reaching out to shake my hand, she noticed the bruise on my face.

"What happened to you?"

"Oh, nothing really. I got hit with a dump truck yesterday."

Imaginary face palm.

"I mean a dump truck with a snowball in it."

This is not a better answer.

"A dump truck threw a snowball."

Smooth. Take a deep breath.

"Someone threw a snowball at my face."

And the plane has finally landed.

"A snowball with a rock in it" Riley added with emphasis.

Riley's mom cringed. "That must have hurt."

"Yeah, it didn't feel good. Gave me a pounding headache."

"I'll bet it did. Riley, we need to get going, I don't want to miss the trailers. The trailers are the best part."

She was right, the trailers are the best part.

"Okay. See you later Ash."

And with that, they were gone. So, I had a completely semi-literate conversation with Riley and didn't burst into flames. That's what I call progress. Despite the slip-up near the end, the whole encounter left me feeling pretty good. Smiling the whole way, I walked to the theatre, wondering what more good fortune I had in store.

Though the movie had its share of plot holes and some questionable science I wasn't buying, overall, it stood up well. As part of the unwritten movie-going code, I exited the theater and went straight to the bathroom. Donning my stocking cap as I exited the theatre, it occurred to me that I didn't pull off the look as successfully as Riley. In that regard she was a pro, and I, a mere amateur.

Dusk had arrived as I left the theatre, the elusive time between daytime and dark, bathing the city in strange, ethereal, and muted tones. Reflecting on this, it seemed dusk, and I had a lot in common. Dusk wasn't daytime, but it wasn't nighttime either. I'm not entirely white, but not entirely black. Laughing to myself, I considered that I was muted sometimes, preferring to stay quiet until I had something worth saying. The ethereal part though, I hadn't mastered yet.

Six

My world, in fact my entire existence, became a mass of confusion and unrelenting pain. So many unfamiliar sounds and smells. Was that rubbing alcohol? Why was I in such incredible pain? My ribs were on fire, and I was sure my head would soon explode. Maybe if my head exploded the pain would end. What happened? Where was I?

Slowly opening my eyes, I found myself surrounded by bright lights and fuzzy shapes. Ghosts? Were the fuzzy shapes ghosts? Was I a ghost? Unlikely, as ghosts didn't feel pain. The fuzzy images floated around as if drunk, lightly bumping into one another. In time, the shapes resolved themselves into people, crisp, clean and in focus people. None of them were familiar, and I was too disoriented to even think about conjuring up a healthy sense of panic.

A woman, wearing a strange, blue shirt and a stethoscope around her neck approached. A doctor, perhaps a nurse? Crap, I'm in a hospital. Great. What had I gotten myself into this time?

"Oh, hi. You're awake, that's good."

Her voice bounced up and down like a yo-yo, the pitch rising and falling to unnatural levels. Shielding my eyes against the bright lights, with my left hand, took my breath away as pain jolted throughout the length of my arm. My useless arm dropped to my side, allowing me an obstructed view of the IV sticking out from the inside of my elbow joint. My first IV, and I didn't like it.

"How do you feel? Can I get you anything?" Her sing-song voice now more level in pitch.

"Lights"

She looked up.

"Oh, yeah. I'll turn them down."

Walking out of my field of vision, the lights miraculously dimmed, allowing me to relax a little. She came back into view.

"How's that?"

"Better. Thank you." My throat was dry as a chalkboard. I had never been this thirsty in my life.

"I'm Dr. Albermarle, but you can call me Meg if you want."

Okay. Meg, huh? Maybe I'll stick with Doctor or Doctor Albermarle. Looking around the room, with Dr. Albermarle on my left, to my right stood a large, black man wearing similar clothing as the doctor. Smiling wide and towering over me, I pictured him in a football helmet and shoulder pads. He was enormous, but his size seemed at odds with his relaxed, confident nature.

"I'm Greg."

"Football?"

Why this was my first question, I have no idea. More than anything, I wanted to know why I was in a hospital in such pain and when I could see my mom, but what came out of my mouth was 'football.'

Chuckling, Greg's eyes widened as my question caught him off guard.

"Yeah, I played football. Linebacker at Harvard. You're perceptive."

Despite an intimidating physical presence, his demeanor was warm and welcoming, I liked him immediately.

"I'll be right back, OK?" Dr. Albermarle said.

Speaking, as painful as it was with my dry throat, I nodded. Greg stood silently smiling as Dr. Albermarle left the room.

"Can I have a glass of water?"

Greg looked at the door and back at me. "Let's wait for Dr. Meg to get back and see if she thinks it's OK. I'm sure it will be, but I'd rather her make the call."

Nodding my understanding, I closed my eyes, too tired and foggy headed to keep them open any longer. When I opened them again, Mom was sitting in a chair to the right of the bed, gently holding my hand. I squeezed her hand; she squeezed back, a faint smile at each corner of her mouth. A single tear fell from her right eye, rolled off her cheek, and landed softly on the back of my wrist. Seeing the pain in her eyes was more than I could take, and I began to sob. Perhaps crying was a sign of the obvious but unspoken bond she and I shared being acknowledged. She leaned in and stroked my hair with a gentleness only a mother could provide.

"That's OK, honey. It's OK to cry. Your dad used to say, 'A man that won't allow himself to cry, isn't really a man at all.' So, you go ahead and let it out."

Her smile widened with the memory of my father. I did cry, for the love of my mom, for the loss of the father I never knew, and for knowing that whatever had happened to me, I was safe now.

Greg returned a few moments after I stopped crying. Whether his return was by design or coincidence, I couldn't say, but I knew what my suspicions were telling me, and I silently thanked him for it.

"Dr. Meg said it was OK for you to have some crushed ice. Let's get you propped up a little and see how you do. Okay?"

Walking around to the side of the bed my mom was sitting, he picked up a small remote control, the wires of which snaked over the railing and out of sight.

"Going up. First floor, socks, locks, and ladies' underwear. Whoa, where did that come from?" He laughed.

For a brief second, I laughed along with him, but the pain it caused was too great, so I stopped. Wiping a tear from her face, Mom looked at Greg and smiled, turning her attention back to me a moment later.

"Where are we?"

"St. Peter's Hospital, downtown, near the waterfront. You can see it from the window."

Looking to the window, I wondered what the view was like. Thankfully, the blinds were drawn as I doubted my eyes could take any direct sunlight. Not that I had any inkling of what time it was. Greg raised the bed enough for me to reach a semi-sitting position, just enough to see no sunlight peeking around the edges of the blinds.

"Here you go partner! Take it slow at first OK." With patient deliberateness, he lifted my right hand, placing a small cup of ice in the palm. Painfully reaching into the cup, feeling the frigid, crushed ice slip and move around my fingers, I grabbed a small handful and placed them in my mouth. The ice quickly melted around and over my tongue, dribbling down my chin. Paying it little mind, it was the most glorious ice I had ever tasted.

"What happened?" I asked, looking at my mom.

"Well, we were hoping you could shed some light on that."

With no more idea what happened than the man on the moon, I didn't know how to respond. I remember watching a movie and then waking up in the hospital, whatever happened in between those two moments was anyone's guess.

"I have no idea. The movie ended, I went to the bathroom, then I woke up here," I said. "How long have I been here?"

She hesitated before answering, preferring to lean in, stroking the side of my face. Her smile fading, another tear escaped, slowly tracking down her cheek.

"Mom, how long?"

"Almost three days." Her words were barely audible.

Three days! I was stunned. That meant today was Monday. Or was it Tuesday? Do you count the day you arrive at the hospital, or do you start counting on the first full day? Of all the unknowns in my life, I was questioning this? All the thoughts bouncing around in my head only served to increase the pain. Realizing I'd lost three days for completely unknown reasons was enough for me to start crying again. Perhaps, knowing whatever control I thought I had over my life had been nothing more than an illusion was all the incentive I needed. My life, now a chaotic storm of uncertainty and pain, was a mess.

"It's OK, Ash, we'll figure this out. We don't have to do it right now. Just get some rest, OK?" On very rare occasions she called me Ash, which meant she was severely rattled.

A light knock on the door sounded as a face wrinkled and weathered with time, a face I confidently felt could tell a thousand stories without slowing down, appeared. The face of my friend, Koko. Seeing him there, in the doorway to my hospital room made me happier beyond words. His demeanor, one of well-defined concern, was written all over his kind face and carried in his body language. It was the first time I'd seen him not smiling. If I didn't know any better, I'd have guessed that Koko looked to be in as much pain as I was.

"May I come in?"

The kindness in his voice was palpable.

"Yes, please come in." Mom replied. Walking around the bed, he stopped next to my mom, holding a small, brown paper bag tightly with both hands.

"You look terrific," he lied.

I smiled at his sarcasm. Based on how I felt, I could imagine I looked hideous.

"No, I don't."

"No, not really. You look rather awful."

"Koko came to the hospital with me on the first day, and he's been here every day since." Mom stated.

This fact surprised me quite a lot, something Koko seemed to do with growing regularity. Why he had taken a keen interest in me, I couldn't guess. While I appreciated his interest, I didn't understand it.

"Why?"

It was a legitimate question, but certainly not one I would have asked under ordinary circumstances. Vaguely aware that I was almost certainly under the influence of heavy-duty painkillers, I silently hoped I wouldn't say something stupid.

Koko smiled, which made me feel better, I didn't enjoy seeing him with such a pained look.

"It is simple, Ashley. I am concerned for your wellbeing. We are friends and friends are there for each other no matter the circumstance."

His answer was delivered sternly, but also with a smile. He meant every single word, making it clear he took friendship very seriously.

"Thank you, Koko."

With fatigue taking over, I still had questions that needed asking.

"What's wrong with me? I mean, how am I?" Based on the pain I was in, I was pretty banged up, but still had no idea how bad it was.

"Well," she said, "you have three broken ribs, a small fracture near your right eye and Dr. Albermarle is certain you have a severe concussion as well."

So, not good. Only then did I realize I wasn't seeing particularly well from my right eye. Lightly touching the right side of my face, even through the bandages, I sensed a considerable amount of swelling.

Stepping forward, Koko reached into the small, brown bag, the paper crinkling lightly in his weathered hands.

"I brought you a small gift."

Reaching forward, he placed a small, smooth object into my hand. A small, red bear, carved out of marble, or perhaps granite, sat in the middle of my palm. The bear, red, had thin, gray swirling bands along its surface. Despite the freezing temperature outside, the bear was warm to the touch, having spent time in Koko's hand and pocket. My intuition understood this tiny bear to be something incredibly special, very personal. Though small, the bear had a significant heft to it. I also noticed it had an undefinable gravity of importance.

"It is a representation of the Kodiak. The fiercest bear in the land. This one was carved by a friend of mine who lives on the Blackfoot Reservation, in Montana."

"I love it"

It was a heartfelt and thoughtful gift, and for me, a treasure. Determined not to let it go, I held it tightly. I looked at my mom, she smiled at me, then at Koko.

"Okay, Ashley needs his rest, but you can all come back tomorrow," Dr. Albermarle announced, entering the room.

I was profoundly relieved hearing her announcement. I was exhausted and fading fast, my eyes getting heavier by the second. Leaning in, Mom brushed a few strands of hair from my forehead as Koko folded the small, brown paper bag a few times, placing it into his jeans pocket.

"I'll be by in the morning, OK?"

"What about work? I don't want you to get into trouble."

"The athletic director is giving me as much time off as I need, so it's no big deal. Don't worry about it."

"May I come back tomorrow too?" Koko asked in the politest way imaginable.

"Of course." I replied.

As I fought to stay awake, Mom said something before leaving, but I was unable to understand any of it. Nodding, I gave her a brief smile before fading off to sleep.

Seven

The following morning greeted me with a colossal headache, light-headedness, and an overwhelming need to go to the bathroom. Fast asleep one second, the next, I was trying to figure out how to get to the bathroom, clear on the other side of my room. From the bed, the bathroom looked to be about a mile away, and I had no idea how I was going to make it work. Looking around, I figured I was going to have to solve this little puzzle by myself.

Hyper aware of the IV in my arm, I propped myself up on my elbows and swung my legs over the side of the bed. With ribs exploding in pain, I scrunched my face in silent protest, gritting my teeth while waiting for the pain to subside. With the pain fading to a tolerable level, the rubbery squeak of sneakers on the floor told me someone had entered the room. Having been caught, I hung my head, waiting for an admonishment I knew was coming.

"Whatcha' doin'?"

It was a female voice, one belonging to the attractive nurse who at that moment was walking around to the side of the bed I was trying to extricate myself from. Her shoulder length, auburn hair framed a face with delicate features and a sprinkling of freckles along the length of her nose. Standing five-foot-two and quite pretty, she still wasn't the vision of beauty that was Riley.

"Oh, umm ... I need to go to the bathroom. Like, bad."

I was going to ask her to help me, but she beat me to the punch before I could even get the words out of my mouth.

"Sorry mister. No can do. See this?"

She lifted a strange, dark blue, plastic bottle hanging from the railing and showed it to me.

"Yeah…"

"This is your bathroom. Well, it is if you need to do number one. If you need to go number two, then you use this, it's called a bedpan."

She picked up a triangle shaped, shiny metal can with a cavernous hole in the middle. It didn't take long for me to get the picture of how this was supposed to work.

Looking toward the bathroom, over a mile away from where I sat and back to my nurse overseer, the distinct feeling that pleading my case with her was going to be a lost cause flooded my brain.

"Nope. Don't even think about it. I'll help you swing your legs back into bed and get you situated. I'll skedaddle for a while so you can go to the bathroom using either one, or both, of these."

Lifting both bathroom receptacles in an exaggerated manner and having obviously been through this scenario in the past, she'd anticipated my upcoming argument and was having none of it.

Her height was irrelevant; she might as well have been General Patton. Outmatched, I would lose every argument with her, and we both knew it.

"Fine."

Gently helping me swing my legs back into bed, an experience so painful it took my breath away, she again picked up both containers and showed them to me.

"You seem like a smart guy, so I think you can figure these out, but if you have any questions, don't hesitate to ask, OK? My name is Marnie. If you need anything, just push this little blue button, OK?" she said, pointing to the same controller that raised and lowered the bed.

Spinning on her heels, Marnie left the room, leaving me to contemplate another attempt at crossing the mile wide chasm between the bed and bathroom. With the memory of my first adventure firmly implanted in my mind, I chose instead to rethink my plans. Going to the bathroom while still in bed is not a natural feeling. And, despite being the only person in the room, it was humiliating as well.

After completing my business, at some point I fell asleep, waking only when Marnie entered the room to check on me.

I yawned. It hurt.

"How do I turn on the TV?"

"Oh yeah, sorry about that." Picking up the remote control that moved the bed up and down, she pointed to the appropriate button.

"Right here in the middle of the controller is the on/off button and next to that is the one that changes the channels, below those is the volume control."

"Cool. I need one of these for home."

As she attended to her duties, I busied myself with figuring out the remote and its various functions, making the rounds through the channel selections, settling on Sports Center. I preferred to watch a movie, something light and funny like The Princess Bride, but with limited choices, it was either sports or news.

A light knock, and my mom's head poked through a gap in the door. She looked much better than last night, appearing more relaxed as she entered the room.

"Are you awake?"

"Yeah, come on in."

Koko entered the room next, also looking better. Although he looked better, I couldn't figure out how. More than likely, he was a chameleon, or some kind of shape shifter. A shape-shifting chameleon? Finally coming to my senses, I accepted the fact that Koko was an elderly Native American and no matter how hard I tried to understand him, no matter how many questions I asked, there were elements of him that would forever remain mystery. And I was OK with that.

Walking to the right side of the bed, Mom pulled up a chair and sat down. Though another chair was available, Koko chose to stand.

"How do you feel? Did you get enough sleep last night?" she asked.

"Yeah, but it seems like all I do is sleep. I mean one minute I feel fine, well not fine exactly, but OK, and the next minute I can't keep my eyes open. I don't get it."

"Your body is doing everything it can to heal itself. That takes a lot of energy; it'll wear you out. The pain medication plays a role, too."

"Yeah, I guess so."

It annoyed me knowing I wasn't in complete control of the way my body responded to all that had happened.

"I brought you some things to read. Textbooks, some novels, stuff like that." She smiled, placing a tote bag full of books on the bedside table.

"Oh, thanks. I've been dying to read something, anything really. I can only take so much TV before my brain begins to shrivel."

Being handed some of my textbooks brought into sharp focus the realization that I had a lot of catching up to do. It also made me wonder, surprisingly for the first time, how long my hospital stay might be.

"Oh, there's this too. A get-well card from, well, about the whole athletic department at school. Everyone signed it, coaches, staff, everybody."

She handed me a bright red envelope with "Ashley" written on the front in large, black script.

"Cool!" Opening the card, the inscription read,

Ashley,
Wishing you a speedy recovery and best wishes!

Sure enough, the inside of the card was filled with signatures and well wishes, with scarcely a blank space remaining. Humbled and surprised by this gesture, I had no idea so many people even knew I existed or cared enough about my wellbeing to personally sign a get-well card. I didn't know what to say, much less how to react and the increasingly all-too-familiar lump in my throat gained strength. Sensing my emotional predicament, Koko intuitively stepped forward.

"Fred and I were talking last night, and he mentioned that you have not been by recently to say hello. His feelings can be easily bruised, as you can well imagine."

Though sounding serious, Koko relayed this information with a wry smile. Knowing Fred had mentioned me and was missing my presence warmed my heart.

"Tell Fred I'm sorry I haven't been by in a few days. I miss him too."

"Fred?" my mom asked, turning to look at me.

"I'll tell you later."

I winked at Koko, letting him know the secret of Fred was safe. He smiled even wider, as if that were possible, and nodded his thanks. Secrets between friends were a matter to be taken seriously, as I'm sure he would agree.

"I talked to a detective from the police department last night. He said he's going to stop by later today to get a statement from you," Mom said, changing the subject.

"I don't know how much help I can be. I've been wracking my brain trying to remember anything about what happened, but I keep coming up blank."

Honestly, I was a little surprised the police would be interested in me at all.

"You never know. He might ask questions that jog your memory. It can't hurt to talk to him. I wrote down his name and phone number. I think I've got it here somewhere." She dug through her purse.

"Yeah, I suppose it can't hurt."

There was no point talking to the detective as I didn't see what good asking me bunch of questions could accomplish, I didn't remember a thing.

"Ugh, I can't find it. Sorry Ashley."

"That's OK, no worries."

The three of us spent some time talking about unimportant things, nothing of significant consequence, watching TV, and enjoying each other's company, thankful for the time we had been given. It was nice.

Less than a minute after they left, I fell asleep, confirming what Mom had said about a healing body, it takes a lot out of you. Sleep was welcome, allowing me to stop questioning what had happened to put me in the hospital, as well as freeing me of the burden of dealing with the constant pain.

Waking sometime in the early afternoon, I flipped through every channel on TV only to turn it off, thoroughly bored. With plenty of schoolwork to catch up on, I reached for my history textbook and got started.

A chapter and a half later, Greg appeared. The room took on a different air with his presence, changing things for the better. His being in the room left me confused, but not in a bad or unwelcome way, more of knowing I needed to pay attention.

"Hey there, Ash. How are you feeling?" His voice was a deep baritone.

"Hey Greg. Feeling OK, I think. My ribs are sore, but that's not surprising."

"No, it's not. Especially considering what you went through. You remember what happened?"

"Not a thing."

"Don't let it get to you. Sometimes not remembering can be a good thing. Whatever it was that happened to you the other day wasn't pretty. You might as well consider it a blessing."

"That's one way of looking at it."

I hadn't considered that not remembering could be a good thing. Did I really want to know? He might have been right.

"Same thing happened to me a few years ago. I was in a serious car accident and woke up in the hospital a day later not remembering a thing. I still don't. I only learned what happened from being told. Turns out I got hit by a drunk driver."

"That's not good. But you made it through, right?"

"I made it through, only by the grace of God himself did I survive. The guy that hit me wasn't so lucky, he died instantly."

It was clear the memories of his accident still affected him greatly, even years later.

"Hey look at that. Did you get a get-well card?" he asked, looking at the bright red card sitting on the small square table next to my bed.

"Yeah, all the people that my mom works with signed it. Pretty cool huh?"

"Yeah, that's great. Can I look at it?"

"Sure. Go ahead" His request surprised me.

Picking up the card, which appeared like a postage stamp in his giant hands, he looked at it, obviously surprised.

"Look at all those signatures. You have a lot of people that in your life that care about you, that's for sure."

"I guess so. Honestly, I'm kind of shocked so many people took the time to sign it."

"Don't be too surprised Ash. People have been visiting you every single day since you arrived. Starting with your mom. She loves you more than life itself, that much is clear."

"Other people? What other people? You mean people other than my mom and Koko?"

I was shocked.

"Yeah. Your history teacher was here on day one. What's his name?"

"Mr. Lewis?"

I had trouble believing he had been here.

"Yup, he was here. So were your principal and assistant principal. Oh, and a cute girl and her mom, they were here too."

My eyes widened as far as the swelling would allow, which was painful, but at that point, I didn't care. To say I was shocked would be a gross understatement. Riley and her mom, here, in this very hospital room? Impossible. Absolutely impossible. How did they know I was here? I had so many questions, I didn't know where to start.

"They were here? The cute girl and her mom were here? In this room?" The surprise on my face couldn't have been more obvious.

He giggled at my obvious disbelief.

"Yeah Ash, right here in this room."

"You're pulling my leg, aren't you? Just kidding around, right?"

And I honestly thought he was. I was sure Greg was just trying to get a rise out of me. But if he was just kidding around, then how would he know anything about Riley and her mom? Maybe he was telling the truth.

"No, I'm not. I don't kid around when it comes to the ladies. Women have enough of a tough time when it comes to dishonest men in this world. I don't need to make it any worse."

He was serious.

"If I woke up tomorrow with my head sewn to the carpet, I wouldn't be more surprised than I am now," I said.

Bending at the waist, Greg howled, laughing so hard, tears rolled down his face.

"Christmas Vacation, I love that movie!"

He was right, I had just quoted a line from the movie Christmas Vacation, starring Chevy Chase.

"I quote that movie all the time and so far, you're the first person that ever got it."

"Oh, I got it alright. I haven't heard that line in a long time."

Unsure what to think, I was as surprised he had correctly identified my obscure movie reference as I was knowing that Riley and her mom had visited me in the hospital.

Though still amused, he managed to stop laughing and regain his composure.

"Why are you surprised?"

"I don't know,"

I lied.

"Yeah, you do. Don't try and kid a kidder."

He caught me with nowhere to hide. Lying, or even telling a half-truth, wasn't going to work this time. Lying was never tolerated by my mom, but somewhere along the line I had unknowingly convinced myself that lying about how I felt about me, was perfectly acceptable. Intuition told me that lying to Greg would not only be wrong, but he would take it as a personal insult. So, for the first time in longer than I care to admit, I decided to play it straight about how I felt about Ashley.

"Honestly, I thought no one cared. I'm biracial, a half-breed, not all white and not all Black either. Why do you think I don't have any friends?"

I used the same hate filled moniker Mike had skewered me with only days before.

Surprise and hurt registered on Greg's face, neither of which I understood. So, I have a low opinion of myself, so what? Why did he care? I made my case abundantly clear, whether he agreed with it or not was none of my business.

"First of all," Inhaling deeply, he sat in the chair next to my bed, "Half-breed, let's start there. You'll be doing me, and yourself, a huge favor by not using that term ever again. Ever. You're better than that."

He was as serious as anyone I'd ever seen.

"Second," he continued, "You're biracial. Yeah, and? Who on planet earth isn't? Look at me, I'm Black, right?"

"Yeah, I guess so."

I was completely blind to where this was leading.

"Don't guess, this isn't multiple choice and it's not a test. My outward appearance is Black, but there's much more to me than that, far more than the color of my skin. My ancestry is Scottish, Italian, and unbelievably, Cherokee. My skin is just a color, same as yours. Don't give color power over how you perceive yourself. It's just a color, that's all. No one looks down on a violin just because it sounds different than a piano or a saxophone, do they?"

"No, that would be kind of ridiculous."

"Exactly. A sound is just a sound, and a color is just a color. They're no different than taste or touch. A color only has power if we give it power. It took a long time for me to understand that attaching an emotion to something like the color of my skin, or anything else for that matter, is just wasted energy."

"But some people see the color of my skin and they automatically hate me for it. I didn't choose this."

"No, you didn't choose your skin color any more than I or anyone else did. You had no control over that. But you do have control over how you feel about it. How other people feel about the color of your skin is not your responsibility. Some people will see that you're biracial and they'll hate you because of it. But that's what hate is, people see a certain color and they attach an irrational emotion to it."

Everything he said made perfect sense, and as I lay there in the hospital bed my head was spinning, but not because of the drugs or the pain. It was spinning because my world view, the view that I'd held onto with a vice-like grip for as long as I could remember, had been turned upside down in an instant.

"Think about it like this," he continued. "A member of the KKK, and I say member because there are both men and women in that vile organization, a member of the KKK walks into a convenience store and buys a chocolate bar, OK?" he said, not taking his eyes off mine.

Nodding to my understanding, I became mesmerized by how easily and clearly, he explained some of the crippling obstacles in my life.

"So, the person gets into their car and eats the chocolate bar. Why did they do this?"

"I don't know. You've lost me, sorry about that."

I felt bad admitting I was lost, apologizing because deep down I felt certain I'd already failed him, that I'd disappointed him.

"It's OK. No harm, no foul."

Detecting my disappointment, he gave me a reassuring smile.

"They did it because they love chocolate. But the point I'm getting at here is, even though the chocolate bar and yours truly are identical in color, the KKK member loves the chocolate bar, but hates me."

My eyes widened as I gained a clear understanding of what he meant. I couldn't help but smile. He had altered my worldview for the second time in a matter of minutes.

"It all comes down to choice, Ash. The KKK member, man or women, it matters not, chose to love the brown chocolate bar and just as equally, chose to hate and judge me based on what I look like, based on the color of my skin."

"But there's a big difference between a person and a candy bar."

I had contemplated not saying this because I felt like I was defending prejudiced and bigoted people everywhere.

"Sure, there is. But the choice to like one and hate the other is the same, identical in every way. People, regardless of color, do terrible things, right?"

"Yeah, absolutely."

I knew the power of this fact just as well as anyone. Neanderthal Mike was white, but that didn't make him a saint.

"Right. Well, have you ever heard of anyone getting steaming mad at a chocolate bar?"

"No, of course not."

I was beginning to get that lost feeling again.

"Everyone on planet earth loves chocolate, that's indisputable. But no one ever condemns and ridicules and murders a chocolate bar because it gave them a cavity or made them gain weight all the while being the same color as me. There are bad qualities in chocolate just like there are bad qualities in people. Yet chocolate, despite its color and the cavities and the weight gain, gets all the praise. You see what I mean?"

"Yeah, I do."

How did Greg, I wondered, in the span of one conversation, bring sense and clarity to a dilemma that had been plaguing me my entire life? I still had questions, plenty of them, but I also had a greater measure of understanding than I had before.

"See, a candy bar doesn't aspire and feel; it doesn't have dreams of a better life. People have all those things and yet chocolate is revered and people, often, are not."

"It doesn't make much sense when you put it like that."

"No, it certainly doesn't. But, let me be clear about something else; it isn't just a problem for people of a certain color. There are many people of color, whether they're black, yellow, or red or whatever, filled with just as much hate as that prejudiced member of the Klan that loves candy bars. Prejudice is colorblind."

It was his last sentence that blew me away. 'Prejudice is colorblind' might have been the most powerful words I'd ever heard in my life. They were also the truest. I had never considered the possibility that people of any color could be filled with hate and prejudice. The whole conversation had been one huge eye-opening experience.

"Where did you come up with all this stuff?"

"Well, it's taken me a long time to understand, and it didn't happen overnight. I'm still working on it. I've got a long way to go because I'm learning new things every single day. But a whole heap of credit must go to my parents. They constantly encouraged me to be curious, to ask questions. I have a feeling your mom is the same way."

"Yeah, she is. She's terrific. I mean she can really be a taskmaster that's for certain, but she's made sure I have everything I need. I always have enough food to eat and clothes to wear. And she listens when I have questions about anything"

"That's a whole lot more than a lot of people have. What about your dad?"

It was a fair question. I'd been in the hospital for days now and I'm sure Greg wondered why he hadn't seen my father yet.

"He died right before I was born."

"Oh, man. I'm sorry. Hey, if you don't want to talk about it that's cool with me."

"No, it's OK, I don't mind. He was a Navy SEAL stationed out in California. Anyway, he was walking back to base one night when he got jumped by a bunch of gang members. You'd think a Navy SEAL could handle a bunch of gangbangers, but there were a bunch of them. My mom told me once that they shot him first and then beat him to death."

"Really? That's terrible"

"Yeah. She doesn't mind talking about him, but she seldom talks about how he died."

"That's understandable. It had to be tough on her seeing you laid up like this." With a wave of his arm, he indicated the hospital room.

Greg's statement forced me into an immediate, and figurative, face slap as I hadn't put the two together until he mentioned it. Here I was, beat up and broken in a hospital bed, having survived an attack like the one that had killed my father. How must that have affected her? Reflecting on how strong and resilient she was left me feeling acutely selfish. While I was stuck in a hospital bed wracked with pain, she was hurting as well. My pain was obvious, hers? Completely invisible.

"Yeah, you're right. I honestly can't imagine what she's going through. I wish there was something I could do for her."

But I didn't have any answers, and the more I thought about it, the more I realized I didn't even know what questions to ask.

"The best thing you can do for her is to be the best version of yourself that you can. That's something my dad tells me even to this day," he said.

"Hey, I've got to finish my rounds. Think about what we talked about. Let it roll around in your head for a while. You have any questions, anything you want to talk about, just let me know. Okay?"

"Yeah, sure. Thanks, Greg."

"No problem, Ash. That's why I'm here." With his trademark smile, Greg turned and strode out of the room, one of the kindest, most understanding people I've ever met. My conversations with Greg were of the kind that changed my reality, but I still had a lot to learn, especially about how other people love and value me as a person and how I could also learn to value and love myself. Lessons like that aren't learned overnight, but over a lifetime. At least that's the way it seemed to me. It didn't take long before I fell asleep again.

Eight

Paper gently rustled me awake, sounding more like brittle, brown leaves blown across the sidewalk on a brisk fall breeze. Marnie stood by my bed, carefully considering the information in front of her.

"Hi, Marnie." I groaned, in the middle of a yawn.

She smiled and looked up.

"Hi, Ash. How do you feel?"

"Umm, not too bad really. I can't get over how much I've been sleeping though."

"Well, you took a severe blow to the head. That'll take the starch out of just about everybody."

"Hey, do you know Greg? Really big guy, played football at Harvard?"

"Yeah, I know Greg. Why?"

"What does he do here at the hospital? I mean, he's one of the most genuine people I've ever met, but I don't know a whole lot about him."

"Greg is one of the most genuine people you'll ever meet. He's a teddy bear, he really is. He's a resident here, which is a fancy way of saying he's a doctor in training. I think he's got a year left and then he'll leave to work on his specialty."

"Huh, I didn't know that. I talked to him for quite a while earlier today; he's smart"

"Yup, very true. One of the smartest, that's Greg. But what sets Greg apart from everyone else is how he relates to people. He's good with people. The rare thing about him is that he's wise beyond his years."

A moment later, a tall, sharply dressed man walked into the room carrying a Manila folder overflowing with dog-eared papers. His dark slacks, light blue button-down shirt and purple tie had me immediately wondering if he might be color-blind. He was also not wearing a jacket, which I thought was remarkable considering how cold it was outside. Realizing that I was, perhaps, judging him unfairly, I let the matter slip from the folds of my brain. His black hair, lightly feathering to dark gray around his ears and temples bestowed on him the dignified air of someone approaching middle age. Or someone who no longer cared what people thought of him. Confidently walking to the end of my bed, his face expressionless, he flipped opened the folder and began to read, not acknowledging Marni and my existence.

"Can I help you with something" Marnie politely asked, approaching the purple tie wearing man.

"No. I'm just here to ask ..." at this he looked down again at his papers, "Mr. Ashley Perault, some questions."

"Visiting hours will begin in an hour. What's your name?"

Marni was clearly annoyed by the interloper.

"My name," he said with emphasis, casting his gaze upon Marnie, "is Detective Sharply. I'm going to ask Mr. Perault some questions."

This was a declaration; he wasn't asking for permission.

"Yeah, I don't think so. You can come back in an hour, *Detective*." Marnie replied, crisply enunciating every syllable in 'Detective.'

Detective Sharply rolled his eyes, making no attempt to hide his annoyance.

"I'm not going anywhere," he said, leaning forward slightly to look at the name tag clasped to left side of Marnie's shirt just below the shoulder, "Nurse Marnie."

Enunciating each syllable in her name and title, the tension in the room went from a mild simmer to a rolling boil in about a second and a half. I sometimes wondered what it looked like when a rock meets a hard place. Now, I knew. I'd have left the room to give them some space, but that wasn't going to happen.

The diminutive Marnie, all five-foot-two of her, made her stand and marched right into the personal space of the much taller detective.

"You!" she said, forcefully poking an index finger into Detective Sharply's chest. "Are going to turn around and sashay yourself and that hideous tie out of here and return in an hour!"

Her jaw quivered as auburn hair fell across her eyes. I wasn't the only one to notice the tie.

Taking a deep breath and slowly exhaling, the detective altered his approach. I expected yelling, faces turning red, a pull no punches argument by two obviously strong-headed individuals. That's not what happened.

"I am going to take a few minutes, that's all, to ask Mr. Perault some questions."

His voice was even, his tone neutral and non-threatening, as calm as a lake in winter.

Marnie wasn't buying it.

"I'll be right back. Ashley, don't go anywhere."

She pushed Detective Sharply aside, quickstepping out of the room. Marnie was on a mission.

Detective Sharply laughed.

"Whatever. Wow, she's a little firecracker, isn't she?"

"Looks that way. Though I can't imagine where she thinks I'm going to run off to. Or how."

I didn't know much about Marnie, but I could surmise, based on my limited time with her, she was not to be trifled with.

"Excellent point. Ok, as you may have already guessed by now, I am Detective Sharply. I just need to know what happened on Saturday. Late afternoon, was it?"

"Yeah, late afternoon. I don't think I'll be able to help you very much though. I don't remember a thing."

Having never spoken to a police officer before, much less a detective, I was a bit nervous. I shouldn't have been, but there you go.

"Well, let's start with the last thing you do remember. What might that be?" he asked, unclipping a pen from the edge of the manila folder.

"The last thing I recall is putting my gloves on in the lobby of the theater. What happened after that, I haven't a clue."

He scribbled on a piece of paper resting on the top of the folder.

"Did you notice anyone following you? Someone eyeballing you as you put your gloves on?"

They were good questions, ones I would certainly expect to be asked, but they didn't get either of us closer to an answer.

"No, I didn't. I walked to the theater alone, didn't see anyone following me. I didn't see anyone in the lobby of the theater after the movie either, at least no one I knew."

"What about enemies? Anyone that might want to hurt you?"

"No. This is my first year at Yorktown, so I don't know that many people. I keep to myself anyway."

And then I remembered Mike. While I didn't know Mike per se, I knew about him. We'd never spoken to each other, aside from the snowball incident and I'd only seen him in school on a handful of occasions. Though I felt certain my interaction with him amounted to nothing, it might be worth mentioning.

"There was something that happened last week."

"What's that?"

He flicked his pen rapidly back and forth through his fingers, a nervous habit from someone who appeared supremely confident.

"I was walking to school on Friday morning when I got hit in the face with a snowball, it had a rock in it, which explains the bruise," I said, indicating the mark under my left eye.

"Okay, tell me what happened."

"Another snowball came flying at me, so I ducked, and it went sailing over my head. This big guy that goes to my school comes running up, pushes me down because he said he didn't give me permission to duck."

"Did he say anything else?"

"Oh, yeah. Right before the first snowball came flying in, he called me a half-breed."

I felt stupid having forgotten that detail … a reminder that as much as the snowball to the face hurt, being labeled a half-breed was far more painful. Whoever coined the saying 'sticks and stones may break my bones, but words will never hurt me,' never had to endure racial insults.

"You know this guy's name?"

I knew the question was coming but was still nervous of what might happen if it was made known that I'd talked to the police, divulging the name of my assailant. Still, I had no intention of defending Neanderthal Mike and his bullying tactics.

"Mike Pigliani. He's a junior I think, big guy, like six-foot-six or there about."

"Do you know anything else about him?"

"His nickname is 'Pigs' from what I understand. Oh, his mom works with my mom at the university. That's all I know."

I added the last part about our moms working together not knowing whether it mattered.

Mike would blow a gasket if, and perhaps when, he learned that I'd mentioned his name to the police. Well, it's too late now. Besides, I still had no idea who attacked me. What were the chances it was Mike? My guess, it was just a random attack.

"Well, I'll investigate it. He might be involved, and he might not. It's strange though that you weren't robbed. We found $15 in your wallet. Was that all the money you had?"

I had to think about it for a moment as I wasn't completely sure.

"Yeah, that sounds about right. I don't remember exactly how much it was, but $15 seems close."

"Look, I might be reaching here, but something isn't right. For one, you weren't robbed, and two, whoever knocked you out, kicked you after you went down. It just doesn't add up."

"That's hard to argue with."

He looked around the room as if searching for a way out.

"Okay, well that's about all I've got. So far, it seems like we don't know much. The people that found you said they didn't see anything either. We think they found you shortly after the attack."

"Who found me?"

My curiosity was getting the better of me.

Looking down at his paperwork, the detective leafed through the pages searching for a specific bit of information.

"Oh, here it is. Looks like it was Sara and Riley MacAlister. It's a good thing they found you when they did, it was frigid that night."

With his face buried in the folder, he failed to notice the look of shock on my face. So, Riley and her mom found me lying unconscious on the sidewalk. Besides surprise, I wasn't sure how to feel about this new revelation. I was glad they found me when they did, as there was no way of knowing how long I might have lay in the snow.

"Yeah, I guess so."

"Okay, I've got to get going before Nurse Battle Axe comes back with an angry mob."

"Yeah, that might be a good idea. No one needs an angry mob."

"No, no one needs that. If you remember anything, just give me a call, OK?" he added, handing me his business card.

Just as Detective Sharply turned to leave, Marnie stepped into the room, followed closely by who I surmised was a hospital administrator. She was boiling mad and had no intention of letting anyone, a police detective of not, dictate how things were going to run in her hospital. I didn't envy the detective at all.

"Nurse Marnie. How are you?" Detective Sharply queried, in his most condescending tone.

"You know exactly how I'm doing. You're going to leave, and I mean right now. You can come back in an hour."

"There's no need to get snippy."

Finding the incident rather amusing, the detective turned toward me and winked. Seeing no need to muddy the waters any more than it already was, I made no attempt to acknowledge the wink, nor his jab at Marnie.

"Get out! Out, out, out!" Marnie barked, again jabbing a finger into the middle of the detective's chest.

"Now Marnie, the detective is leaving. Let's give him room to do just that." The administrator chimed in.

Detective Sharply put on his brightest smile, practically strutting out of the room. Marnie watched him go, exhaling quickly upward, blowing the hair from her eyes.

"What an asshole."

While the administrator and I both displayed surprise at her remark, Marnie did not.

"Marnie, really? There's no need for that."

"Hmph! Thanks for backing me up on that one Phil."

Marnie's response landed with a thud as she stormed from the room. The administrator followed a second later without a word, leaving me and the hospital room walls the only witnesses to a decidedly odd several minutes.

With nothing left to do, I picked up a novel, immersing myself in the fantastical world of science fiction. And then I fell asleep. Again.

Nine

I woke exhausted and hungry, craving hospital food that had a notoriously bad reputation. I just didn't care, feeling sure I'd eat anything put in front of me.

Marnie walked in carrying a tray of food to the right side of the bed.

"Hey Ash, how are ya? Hungry?"

"Hi Marnie. Yeah, starving. That's a good sign huh?"

"Oh, yeah, it's a great sign. I think we'll be able to take that IV out soon. It's up to Dr. Albermarle when it comes out, but I think tomorrow probably."

The IV felt more like having an anchor chained to my arm and I couldn't wait to be rid of it. Wherever I went, the IV followed. When I forgot about it, which happened often, the IV tube would pull and threaten to rip itself from my arm. The IV was inconvenient, cumbersome, and painful.

"Great, I can't wait to be done with it."

"Here's your dinner, don't eat it all at once."

While she may have been kidding around, if given half a chance I think I could have inhaled the entire plate of food, utensils, and all, without even trying.

"Don't tempt me."

"I'm sorry you had to see me be all mean and ugly with that detective earlier. I'm not usually like that."

"It's OK. He had it coming."

"Yeah, I guess so. But I should have handled it more professionally, and I didn't. I mean, I could have just as easily let it slide. We often do that for the police, but he walked in here with such a holier-than-thou attitude."

"Yeah, he did. He was having a bad day or something, you never know."

"Could be. Or he was unhappy with his tie. Oh, Dr. Meg is going to stop by tomorrow, in the morning, to go over your test results. That way you'll have a better idea of when you might get to go home."

"Cool, I can't wait to go home. Not that I don't mind being here. Well, maybe a little. I just don't want you to take that the wrong way," I said with a sheepish grin.

"No, it's OK. I understand. You don't like me. No, really, I get it," she alleged, trying to stifle a giggle. Seeing someone I hardly knew pulling my leg, joking around with me just because, felt good. Things like that don't happen often in my life and I couldn't help but laugh.

"Well, it's not you, it's me. No, seriously. There are just SO many women in my life. They see all the good times you and I have had recently and they're getting jealous. I see it all the time."

I tried not to laugh but couldn't help myself.

"Well, that makes more sense. I don't feel so bad. But, you know, that hurt and I'm not sure if the pain will ever completely go away Ash. It's quite a burden to bear though, I'm sure. All those women."

She wiped an imaginary tear from her eye. At that point neither of us could hold the laughter back any longer. Marnie doubled over in fits of giggles while I tried to keep myself from laughing altogether, such was the agony it caused my ribs. I laughed despite the pain.

Before the laughter stopped, two people I had never in a million years expected to see walked into my hospital room. Riley and her mom. They both looked fabulous as I tried to play it cool and not look surprised. My attempt, a dismal failure if ever there was one, proved pointless as my eyes widened and a large smile enveloped my face.

"Mm, hmm." Marnie quietly uttered, nodding at me over her left shoulder as she left the room, giggling all the way down the hall. I would have to thank her later for ignoring the visiting hour rules in this case.

Both were fashionably dressed, Riley wore a red and black, tweed overcoat gathered at the waist with a black belt and blue jeans while her mom sported black slacks and a puffy white jacket. Being stuck in a hospital bed left me feeling starved of sensory input, I just didn't realize it until now. With no warning, my senses were overloaded. Not that I was complaining.

"Hi Ash. Wow, you look a lot better than the last time we saw you. You remember my mom, right?" Riley asked.

"Yeah. I mean, yes. Hi Mrs. MacAlister. How are you?" I nearly stuttered, trying to get the attention off me.

"Oh, we're doing fine, Ashley. The more important question is how are you doing?" Mrs. MacAlister asked, smiling.

"A lot better than I was the other day. My ribs are sore, and I have a constant headache. I've also been sleeping a lot. I mean it seems like all I do is sleep."

I still couldn't believe I was talking to Riley and her mom.

"Yeah, we heard you might have a problem with headaches. The doctor said after the hit you took, headaches would be likely," Riley added.

"I talked to a detective earlier and he said it was you that found me. I want to thank you for that. I don't know what it was you did for me that night, but thank you," I said with as much honesty as I could muster.

"Oh, it's no problem at all. We called the police and stayed with you until they arrived. They wouldn't let us go with you to the hospital; we would have if they had let us," Riley said. The disappointment in her voice was still raw with emotion.

"I'm so glad you found me when you did. There's no telling what would have happened if you hadn't."

"Well, we're glad to see you doing so much better. You didn't look so good when they loaded you into the ambulance. The paramedics said you took a severe blow to the head," Mrs. MacAlister said.

"Yeah, that's what I've been told, too. It's why I'm still here actually. They did a bunch of tests on me today, an MRI, a CT scan, and more x-rays. They want to be sure nothing else is wrong. I guess if I hadn't been out cold for three days I might be home already."

"Yeah. But you'll be back home in no time," Riley added, smiling.

She reached into her overcoat and removed a large, light blue card with 'Ashley' written across the front in black ink. She stepped forward and handed it to me, remaining there, not taking a step back.

"I got you this card and had a bunch of people at school sign it. I hope you like it."

Her smile was one suggesting she was a little unsure of how I might take this gesture of kindness.

"Really? You didn't have to do that. I mean, I appreciate it."

I was, to put it mildly, not sure what to say or even how to react. This was the second time since I'd been in the hospital, the second time in my life that I had received a get-well card.

The large blue envelope wasn't smooth like normal paper, having a rough texture to it, like what you might find when handling an orange, only less pronounced. It had been dutifully sealed, and, as I brought it closer to my face to go about the task of opening it, I noticed the ever so slight aroma of Riley attached to it. I knew right away she had not brazenly sprayed a dash of perfume on it. That would have been out of character and much too forward for her to have even considered. The aroma was barely discernible, clinging to the envelope due to whatever or however it is some women have the uncanny ability to smell divine. Regardless, I noticed the subtle scent almost immediately and my head spun for reasons I still don't understand.

Carefully and purposefully opening the envelope to not unduly tear this new and precious treasure as Riley and Mrs. MacAlister looked on, I separated the card inside from its blue envelope and looked at the cover. On the outside, against a light green background, was a picture of 'Miracle Max' played by the comedian Billy Crystal in the film The Princess Bride.

'Miracle Max' had his mouth open and was pointing with his right hand. The caption at the top, above his head, read …

"You rush a miracle man; you get rotten miracles."

One of my favorite movie quotes of all time. When I saw the picture of 'Miracle Max' and read the quote, I was stunned. How did she know? I laughed aloud as I gazed at the picture and corresponding quote. The inside of the card had been signed by as many people as had signed the card my mom gave me. The school's principal, assistant principal, Mr. Lewis, some of my other teachers and a whole host of classmates had signed it. In the middle was the neat, cursive flow of Riley's hand…

"Ashley,
Get well soon! Anything else would be "Inconceivable!"
-Riley

"Inconceivable!" she wrote. The significance of the word was immediate, a statement uttered many times by the character, Vizzini, played by Wallace Shawn in the same movie.

"Inconceivable, That's great." I said, quietly.

She had taken the time to write something personal, something she felt might bring a smile and joy to my life inside these hospital walls. With one simple get well card, a card I never expected to receive in the first place, Riley had given me

tangible proof there were people out there in the world who cared about me. More to the point, I realized, it was not the first-time people had displayed to me that they cared, it was the first time I believed it for myself.

Riley and her mom both took this as a positive sign and smiled at each other. I took a few moments to scan the signatures and well wishes. A vast majority of the names I knew, but some were unfamiliar. My brain searched for reasons as to why people I didn't even know would take time out of their day to do something kind and thoughtful for me.

At the very least, I was overwhelmed. Much had happened in a short span of time, most of which would take effort for me to wrap my head around. A solitary tear began forming in the corner of my left eye, and before I had a chance to react to its presence, it slowly made its lonely journey down my cheek. I knew I couldn't hide it, to do so would have been unfair… unfair to the tear, unfair to Riley's thoughtfulness and care, and, most importantly, unfair to me. This tear had been earned … a solitary tear followed shortly by a few of its friends, tears who, it appeared, preferred to travel in pairs. Riley and her mom looked at each other, their smiles fading slightly.

"Are you OK Ash? Did I do something wrong?"

"Yeah, I'm OK," I replied, sniffling a little. "No, you didn't do anything wrong. It's just that this is more than a get-well card to me. I mean, it took a lot of time for you to get all these people to sign this," I said, holding the open card aloft.

"Honestly, it's one of the most thoughtful things anyone has ever done for me. I had no idea this many people even knew I was in the hospital. Thank you."

"Ashley, I think everyone at Yorktown knows you're in the hospital," she said, using my full name for the first time. "And you're welcome. It's the least I could do."

"How did you know about The Princess Bride? It's one of my favorite movies."

"Your mom told me. It was either the night you got here or the day after that. I don't remember exactly. We were sitting in the waiting room, and she talked about how you and she often quote the movie to each other. She told me that it's one of your favorites. It's one of my favorites, too."

Before I could gather my thoughts, my mom and Koko walked into the room. I was pleased to see them and about to make the customary introductions when I realized everyone already knew each other.

Riley and her mom made room for my mom and Koko at my bedside as hellos and "how are yous" were exchanged. It created a disorienting feeling, watching two distinct groups of people that orbited my tiny universe interact with one another. These two small groups of people greeting each other like it was no big deal at all, each one happy to be in the presence of the other, was heartwarming.

Leaning in, my mom kissed me on the forehead.

"I love you, honey."

"I love you too, Mom."

I'm pretty sure I blushed.

"Hello Ashley, you look better today." Koko said, edging closer.

"Hey, Koko. Thanks. How are you?"

"I am well, Thank you. Fred sends his greetings."

It felt good seeing four people I cared about in the same room together. They were here for me, their presence a clear display that my well-being was important to them.

"Mom, look what Riley did for me. She got a card and had a bunch of people at school sign it," I said, handing her the card.

She took the card, smiled at the cover, immediately understanding the significance of Miracle Max. Opening the card and reading the inscription, she unconsciously covered her mouth with her left hand, inhaling deeply. The care and thought Riley had put into selecting a card that had meaning and significance was plain to see, and in that moment, I realized the card held significance and meaning to her as well. She looked at Riley and, with tears streaming down her face, stepped forward and gave her a hug of thanks and understanding. She then gave Mrs. MacAlister a hug, too, for good measure.

The remaining visiting hours we spent talking about whatever happened to come up. I talked about my MRI and CT scans and the added x-rays. Riley and I talked about what was going on at school while my mom and Mrs. MacAlister chatted about whatever moms' chat about. Koko stood silently taking it all in, not bored at all. He never stopped smiling, looking, quite simply, like someone who was happy to be alive. Looking around the room at the people gathered around my bed, I was beginning to understand how he felt.

Ten

After everyone had left, my mind raced, filled with the memories of the day and the thoughts those memories provoked. I slept, but only in short bursts. Something was tugging, reaching for purchase at the back of my mind and try as I might, I couldn't identify the whispery feeling, as whatever tendril of thought it held would not, now, free itself of entanglement.

The morning dawned with another colossal headache, not as severe as its predecessors, but still a significant annoyance. An unfamiliar nurse came in and took my vitals, checked my IV, asked me how I was feeling and promptly left. Not much for small talk. Sometime later, Dr. Albermarle arrived carrying my breakfast. I was excited to see her as I found her friendly and easy to talk to. I also felt a little trepidation as I knew her visit brought the possibility of learning what my current condition was and when I might get to go home.

"Morning, Ash, how are you feeling?" she said, placing my breakfast on a tray and rolling it over the bed so I could eat.

"Hi Dr. Meg."

I chose to use her first name instead of her full title, just to see how I felt about it.

"I feel OK. Not terrific, but not awful either. What's bothering me the most right now is the headache. It's not as bad as it was yesterday, but it's still there."

I carefully spread cream cheese on what felt like a stale bagel.

"You're going to have those from time to time I'm afraid. It's not unusual for people that have suffered a head injury like yours to have intermittent headaches for months sometimes. I wouldn't be too worried about it. But we'll keep an eye on it just to be on the safe side."

"Yeah, OK. My ribs are feeling a bit better, which is nice. But my whole chest feels tight, like it's being squeezed."

"There are a couple of reasons for that. One is that you've been lying in this bed for a long time, so you haven't had the opportunity to stretch yourself out and get blood pumping. The second is that broken ribs are exceedingly painful, so you haven't been taking any full, deep breaths. The muscles in your ribcage and around your chest are getting stiff because you haven't been using them as you normally would."

"That makes sense."

"I know it's painful, but the more you move around, the more you'll feel better eventually. I'd suggest starting slowly, occasionally focus on taking as full a breath as you feel comfortable with."

"Okay, sure."

I waited patiently to hear the results of yesterday's tests.

"So, I looked at your test results from yesterday and I'm happy to tell you that everything came out negative, which is great. I didn't see any evidence of bleeding in your brain, and you won't need surgery for the fracture near your right eye. Your ribs are already showing signs of healing as well, which is nice to see."

Until that moment, I hadn't fully comprehended just how much worried energy I'd spent thinking about the possible ramifications of the test results.

"When can I go home?"

"Well, I don't see why you can't go home later today. It'll take some time to get your discharge papers ready, but we can start working on that right away," she replied. "I don't know exactly how long that'll take, but I think you should be out of here sometime after lunch. How's that sound?"

Terrific was the word that sprung to mind. As a reserved and introverted person, I don't often appear outwardly excited, but at that moment, had my ribs and face not been broken, I would have started doing cartwheels.

"That is exactly what I needed to hear."

I smiled a painful smile, so excited I couldn't hold it in.

"I thought you might say something like that," she said, returning my smile. "What you need to be aware of, though, is that I want you to take it easy for a while. No heavy lifting, no long jogs in the park. And please, no boxing, mixed martial arts, kickboxing, hockey, football, or jumping out of planes. I added the jumping out of planes thing only because that truly scares the crap out of me."

"Sure, so lay off the contact sports and falling from a great distance is what you're saying?"

"Yup, that's what I'm saying."

"When can I go back to school?"

"I'd really prefer it if you took the rest of the week off, give yourself a chance to rest and regain your strength. You should be fine to go back on Monday. Cool?"

"Yeah, sounds like a plan."

"Okay, then. I've got to get going, more patients to see, stuff like that. But I'll be by before you get discharged."

"Alright."

Dr. Meg casually walked out of the room to see her other patients. Lying in bed, in the still and silent room, I couldn't stop smiling. Finally, I was going home. Desperately, I felt like I needed to tell someone, to shout it at the top of my lungs. The intervening hours were glacially slow as I tried to watch TV and read some of my history textbook. Neither distraction worked, so I switched to a sci-fi novel. That didn't work either. I was bored and restless, feeling as if I hadn't had this much energy in ages.

My mom arrived at one o'clock, looking just as excited as I was about my impending discharge.

"Ready to go home?"

"I can't wait, let's get out of here."

The same nurse that had checked on me in the morning returned and she and my mom worked together to help me sit up in bed so I could make the necessary preparations to leave. The nurse, Amy, as indicated by the I.D. card affixed to her shirt, was still in no mood for chitchat. She concentrated solely on the job at hand, her demeanor, while professional and competent, made me miss the time I spent with Marni, Greg and Dr. Meg. While I didn't know them very well, or for very long, I still considered them friends and missed their presence.

Having spent the day concentrating on going home, I was surprised when these feelings surfaced. The time had arrived, and I felt a pang of guilt realizing I had been thinking only of my wants and needs. Not once did I consider the time and effort of the people that made it their duty to care for me. They did care, to them I wasn't just a nameless patient in need. I was Ashley and to Dr. Meg and Greg and Marnie that was important. Suddenly, I was incredibly sad.

"Okay, ready to stand up?" Amy asked.

"Yup. More than ready."

With Amy on one side and my mom on the other, they cradled my arms in theirs, and gently helped me to my feet. Though slow and painful, standing up felt wonderful and when I felt stable enough, they each let go and I stood unassisted, smiling like a little kid at his first sighting of Disneyland.

"Hey, you're doing good. Think you can make it to the bathroom?" Mom asked.

"Yeah, I think so."

She handed me the change of clothes she brought with her.

Slowly and methodically, I shuffled my way to the bathroom, and someone closed the door behind me. Slipping out of the hospital gown was straightforward, as was sliding into my underwear and jeans. My shirt, however, proved far more difficult. Moving my arms and chest in ways I hadn't tried since I had arrived at the hospital was painful. I opted to put my sweater on after I exited the bathroom, figuring that in this instance there was no shame in asking for help. Stepping into my shoes, I found that I couldn't tie them without flashes of stabbing pain shooting through my ribcage. No problem, I thought, I'll just ask my mom to tie them. She'd tied my shoes countless times before I learned how to do it myself, a few more certainly wouldn't hurt. I opened the bathroom door and shuffled out, purposefully trying not to step out of my untied shoes.

"Well, I got there most of the way. I just needed help with my sweater, and I couldn't get down far enough to tie my shoes. Sorry."

"Sure, no sweat. No need to apologize." She smiled, eager to help, bent down and tied my shoes and assisted me into my sweater and coat. It would do no good to get discharged only to freeze solid on the way home.

Nurse Amy had left and returned with a wheelchair. I looked at her, puzzled.

"I don't need a wheelchair. I can make it just fine."

"Yeah, I know. It's hospital policy though. We'll just wheel you down to the lobby, no big deal."

Resigned to my fate, I sighed. All bundled up, I eased myself into the wheelchair and said a silent but cheery goodbye to my hospital room. The trip to the lobby was uneventful, but I was saddened that I didn't get to see Greg, Dr. Meg, or Marni one more time. That is until we rounded the last corner leading to the lobby and all three were standing near the sliding glass door that opened out into the sprawling city beyond, waiting for me.

Nurse Amy brought the wheelchair to a halt near the lobby door, making sure the brakes had been engaged as Dr. Meg approached.

"Take care of yourself Ash. Stop by the hospital every now and then, just to say hi, OK? Your mom has my business card, so call if you need anything," she offered. "Oh, and no bungee jumping. At least not for a few weeks." She gave me a gentle hug after I stood up.

"A few weeks? OK, I can wait that long."

Marnie approached next, also taking care to hug me gently.

"So, Mr. Ladies' Man, leaving us already?"

"Yeah, I guess so. It's not that I want to leave, but, you know, my adoring public awaits."

She smiled and laughed.

Greg stepped forward as I extended my right hand, expecting a firm handshake. I got something altogether different when he bypassed my extended hand and very gingerly gave me what can only be described as a bear hug.

"Remember what we talked about." He instructed, taking a step back.

"I remember. I'll never forget it. Thank you, Greg."

"You ever need anything, anything at all, you just let me know, OK?" he told me as he handed me his business card. "I mean it."

"OK, I'll do that."

Mom and I stepped through the sliding double glass doors of the lobby and onto the sidewalk where a cab sat, waiting to shuttle us home. It felt good to be surrounded by the sights, sounds, and smells of the city again, especially after having been confined to the four walls of a hospital room for more days than I cared to count.

Eleven

The cab ride home was normal, but for some reason it felt new. It was as if I had never ridden in a car before. The colors of the city were more vibrant, the smells more pronounced, even the sounds seemed crisper, more alive. I didn't know why these stimuli, these elements, made the city what it was seem as if they had, in some way, been transformed. The city I had resided in before my unfortunate stay in the hospital certainly hadn't changed, but for some reason it seemed altogether different. The transformation was subtle, yet profound, and I couldn't fathom why it had occurred.

One thing that hadn't changed was the cold, and I was thankful the cab driver had turned the heat up to its maximum setting, making the car warm inside. Still, despite the heater working its hardest, it was easy to imagine the frigid winter air making every attempt to break into our tiny cocoon of warmth.

On the way home, we passed the bundled masses as they made their way to destinations known only to them. Some, I imagined, were doing their Christmas shopping, making their way to Macy's or Neiman Marcus, stores I'd never even thought of entering. Some appeared to be either going to or coming from business meetings, dressed in dark shades of black or blue, most of them wearing long, black, London Fog style overcoats that were the fashion trend this year.

Delivery drivers rushed through the cold, making their rounds all over the city, looking like multi-colored versions of the Michelin Man in their puffy winter jackets, pushing or pulling their red, or yellow, or black hand trucks stacked with boxes of goods the public would soon snatch up with all their hard-earned money. So much hurried activity, I thought. I wondered about it all. Did all this chaos, all the hustle and bustle of the city, did it all go on before my hospital stay? How had I not seen it? I had noticed the color of the hand trucks used by the delivery drivers as well as their puffy multi-colored winter jackets. Surely, all these things weren't coated in muted shades of black and white before? Of course, they were in color. Right?

The cab wound its way through the city, finally coming to a slushy, sliding, wet stop in front of the building we called home. My mom got out and hurried around to my side to help me exit the cab and pay the driver. In the frigid, early afternoon breeze, I detected the distinct aroma of freshly brewed coffee. Looking to my right, the bright red neon sign of a coffee shop hanging above the door, perpendicular to the sidewalk, beckoned. The shop was right on the corner, less than a block away. It must be new, I thought, as I'd never noticed it before.

"Mom, when did we get a coffee shop? Is it new?" I asked, pointing with my gloved left hand.

My mom, now on the sidewalk, stopped and turned to look in the indicated direction.

"Mm, no, I don't think so. I'm quite sure it was there when we moved in."

"Huh. Guess I must have missed it."

We made our way across the snow shoveled sidewalk, a sidewalk I traversed with great caution to not slip and fall, and into the welcoming warmth of the lobby of our apartment building. I still didn't appreciate the faded color on the walls, but it did feel good to be home. We took the elevator to our floor and walked the short distance to our tiny sanctuary. As soon as my mom opened the door, my nose immediately alerted me of the presence of recently baked cookies. They smelled fresh, likely baked this morning. Stopping a few feet inside the apartment, I took a breath, not nearly as deep a breath as I was normally capable of, but deep enough I think to make Dr. Meg proud.

"Cookies. I smell freshly baked cookies."

"Yup, baked just for you this morning. Chocolate chip with pecans. But you don't like cookies, so I'll just have to eat them myself."

"No, you're right. I don't like cookies or anything with chocolate in it, or pecans for that matter. Vile things, cookies."

"That's what I thought. Let me put this stuff away and I'll get a plate ready. And a couple of glasses of milk too, don't want to forget that."

Slowly, I shuffled to the couch and sat down, a painful process that forced me to catch my breath once I had myself situated. Nothing about the apartment had changed and I found the familiarity remarkably comforting. It dawned on me that during my time in the hospital, my mom had to sleep here alone, something I felt certain she'd not done since my dad was killed. How hard this must have been for her, I don't know, but it couldn't have been easy. My admiration of her grew, and I became acutely aware, now more than I ever had before, that the crosses she had to bear, the loss of my father, raising me on her own, my recent attack and hospital stay, were crosses she bore silently and without complaint. Simply put, she was remarkable.

She exited the kitchen carrying a plate of cookies, placing them on the edge of the coffee table nearest me so I could reach them easily without having to move too much. She went back into the kitchen, returning with two tall glasses of cold milk. Slowly, and very deliberately, I reached forward to grab a cookie when she put up her right hand, palm out.

"Hold on. You can't start yet." She said, walking across the room to turn on the TV and DVD player. After returning to the couch, she sat down and pressed play on the DVD player's remote control.

"Okay, now you can start."

The TV popped on, revealing the opening credits to The Princess Bride. At that moment, I knew I had it all. Warm chocolate chip cookies with pecans of course, a tall glass of cold milk and a mom that made it all happen. I was one lucky kid. With a cookie in one hand and a glass of milk in the other, I settled in for what was one of the most contented and happy moments I'd ever experienced.

I couldn't guess how far I got through the movie, but I woke up sometime in the middle of the night, stretched out on the couch and covered in blankets. The soft warmth of the blankets was a blessing, and threatened to lull me back to sleep. The TV was off, the cookies and milk put away, and the light in the hallway still on, casting a warm glow into the living room. I surmised that my mom left the hall light on in case I woke up and wanted to go to my room and the bed that I had missed so much during my hospital stay. I slowly walked to my room, dragging the blanket behind me and with great care, gingerly folded myself into bed, falling asleep in no time.

Twelve

The next morning was defined by considerable pain as my head ached and my ribs and face hurt. Added to all that was fatigue. I was so tired I wondered if I had slept at all the night before. With reluctance, I climbed out of bed and walked to the bathroom to brush my teeth and take a painkiller. I wasn't thrilled about having to take a painkiller, but I saw no alternative. It was a choice between taking a pill to lessen the pain, and thus endure its dulling effects on my brain, or suffer through it. I saw no point in suffering any more than I had to, but I also failed to see the logic in the term "painkiller." With my limited experience with pain reducing medication, I hadn't once had the pain "killed." The medication served to reduce the pain, but it never came close to totally extinguishing it.

Much of my day was spent trying to catch up with schoolwork and sleeping. Occasionally, I grabbed a bite to eat, usually a cookie, sometimes two, if I'm honest. As the day soldiered on, I slipped into a deepening cavern of darkness and depression. Unable to figure out why my mood had dropped so precipitously, I tried to lie down and get some sleep, but restlessness prevented it. Yesterday I was on cloud nine, today I found myself lying in the gutter, staring up at the bottom of my own shoes. What was wrong with me? I was home, had cookies, milk, and access to my own bed, yet I was completely miserable.

I was watching TV, lost in my own depressed thoughts when my mom walked in.

"Hey, Ashley. How are you?"

"Not doing so good to be honest. I was OK this morning, but as the day drags on, I just keep getting increasingly depressed. I don't get it, I'm miserable. What stinks is I have no idea why."

"Hmm," she said, sitting next to me on the couch. "Well, think about it this way. Yesterday was filled with a lot of anticipation and excitement, right?"

"Yeah, I couldn't wait to go home."

"Exactly. You spent a good part of the day getting all psyched up to leave the hospital," she said, looking at me. "Well, now you're home, and all that anticipation and excitement is gone. It's like you were on a rollercoaster slowly going up the steepest part of the ride, then suddenly you get that awesome adrenaline rush as the coaster crests the top and you go screaming down the hill at incredible speed. Eventually you're going to reach the bottom and that can be a huge disappointment. Ashley, right now you're at the bottom of the hill. Don't be surprised that you're depressed. But trust me, it won't last."

Depression wasn't new for me, but the depth and completeness of this bout was somehow different. The letdown following all the excitement and anticipation of yesterday was inevitable, I suppose, but I had a feeling there were also other factors at work, ones I hadn't yet identified. Instinctively, I knew that pinpointing these factors was going to be a monumental struggle, one I wasn't looking forward to.

"I hope not. I'm getting sick of it fast."

I was in the middle of reaching for a cookie when someone knocked on the door, two quick wraps, and then silence. With an inquisitive expression, I looked at my mom and shrugged my shoulders slightly, not enough to induce pain, but close.

She rose from the couch and walked to the door, looking through the tiny peephole in the middle to see who it was.

"Oh, hi Koko. Just a sec."

She unlocked and opened the door.

"Hi Koko, come on in."

She stepped back to allow Koko to enter. He walked into the apartment with his customary smile firmly in place, casually dressed in blue jeans, a light blue t-shirt, and white tennis shoes that looked like they had seen better days. The salt and pepper hair he usually wore in a ponytail was hanging loosely, nearly touching his shoulders. He looked, quite simply, extremely comfortable. I was happy to see him.

"I hope I am not disturbing you."

"No, you're not disturbing us at all," Mom replied as she closed and locked the door. "How are you?"

"I am doing well. Thank you."

"Ashley, how are you feeling? You look well rested," he asked as he sat in the recliner next to the couch.

"Okay, I guess. This morning was rough though, I guess from all the moving around I did yesterday. But right now, I'm doing well."

"Ah, that is good to hear."

"Koko, would you like some cookies?" my mom asked.

"Yes, that would be great. You will never hear me turn down the offer of cookies," Koko replied, his eyes twinkling.

He turned his gaze to me. "When are you going back to school?"

"Dr. Albermarle said I could go back on Monday. She wants me to take it easy until then."

Returning from the kitchen with a plate of cookies, Mom placed them on the coffee table whereupon Koko leaned forward, took the nearest one and began eating.

"An excellent cookie."

Mom smiled. "Thank you, I appreciate it."

"Ashley, I have something I would like to talk to you about if that is OK."

"Yeah, sure. What is it?"

"It is a ..." he hesitated, looking briefly at the ceiling, searching for the right word, "... ceremony, I would like to talk to you about."

"Uh, OK. What kind of ceremony?"

"A warrior ceremony, a ceremony of blessing, you might say."

As he said this, his smile disappeared, melting away like snow on boots after you step out of them just inside the front door.

He wasn't sad or upset, but the smile I was so accustomed to seeing was noticeably absent. To Koko, this ceremony was clearly especially important. I didn't know where he was going with this conversation, but I was curious to find out.

"If it is OK with your mom, and you feel up to it, we will go up to the roof to perform the ceremony. Is that OK?" he asked, turning to look at my mom.

"Sure, it's OK with me. If you both bundle up. It's cold tonight."

With the vague description about the ceremony and its purpose, I was surprised by her reaction. She didn't even bat an eyelash and I couldn't help but wonder why. I concluded that despite my belief that I had my mom totally figured out, occasionally, she had the distinct ability to surprise me.

"Okay. I'll get my jacket."

I retrieved my coat and stocking cap from my room and as I entered the living room, Koko stood up, grabbed another cookie, holding it aloft.

"One for the road."

"Great idea."

I snagged one for myself.

We exited the apartment, silently walking down the hall, each finishing our last cookie.

"I need to stop at my place first to get something. Do you have the small red bear that I gave you?"

"Yeah. Right here in my pocket."

"Great. We will need that."

We took the elevator for the short ride up to Koko's floor.

"Koko, you know that coffee shop down the street, the one on the corner?"

"Yes. They make a fabulous caramel latte. I go there often."

"How long has it been there?"

Koko stopped to think, fishing for keys out of his pocket as the elevator doors opened.

"Hmm, I need to think about that one. Six years, I think. That sounds about right."

Six years? We had moved in a few months ago, but still I had only just noticed the coffee shop was there. What was wrong with me?

"Six years? I can't believe I'd never noticed it until yesterday."

"That is not surprising at all, Ashley."

His tone was level and understanding, without surprise or ridicule.

"Huh?"

How could he interpret it in such a matter-of-fact way, I simply couldn't understand.

Koke stopped in front of his apartment door and began unlocking the four deadbolts, starting at the top and working his way down.

Once inside, he disappeared into one of the small bedrooms, returning a few moments later (with Fred in tow), wearing the same jacket, stocking cap, and gloves he wore the first night I met him on the building's roof. Walking to the far wall of the living room, he retrieved the long ceremonial pipe, lifting it with great reverence and care. We exited the apartment, and I waited in the hallway as he relocked the four imposing deadbolts, this time working from the bottom and moving his way up. With great difficulty, I remained silent on our way to the roof. Despite my curiosity, I instinctively understood to keep my questions unasked.

I followed Koko up the short flight of stairs leading to the thick metal door that opened to the roof.

"One, two, three, four, five and six," I counted.

"Were you just counting?" Koko asked as he stopped at the door.

My face flushed as I realized I had been counting out loud.

"Uh, yeah. I count stairs. I usually count silently in my head, but every so often I forget and end up counting aloud. It's stupid. Sorry."

"It is not stupid at all. It is unique and part of what makes you an individual." He turned toward me and smiled. "My mom did the same thing her whole life and both of my brothers do as well."

"Really? I thought I was the only one. Huh, that's surprising."

"Keep at it. Embrace that which makes you, uniquely you."

"Okay, I guess."

He waited for a beat before continuing.

"Where were we? Oh, right, warrior ceremony. Okay, since it is so cold outside, I will briefly illustrate to you what we are going to do right here. The less time spent outside, the better. It is too windy to light the pipe, but there is nothing that can be done about that. Know that it is important to have the pipe anyway. Okay?"

"Sure. That makes sense."

Even though it didn't.

"This is an ancient Blackfoot Warrior ceremony my ancestors have been performing since the first moon rose. This ceremony asks the Gods to bless the Blackfoot Warriors, bless their weapons. It is a way to ask the Gods for courage in the face of evil, to face the fears inherent in all of us. This special ceremony is a solemn time to find peace in one's mind and calmness in one's soul before going into battle."

"Koko, I'm sorry, I don't understand. I'm not a warrior and last time I checked, I don't have any plans to go into battle."

The words were out of my mouth before I realized I may have insulted him.

"Things will be made clear soon. We must first perform the ceremony. Are you ready?"

"Um, I don't know. I have no idea what's going on. Honestly, I'm confused. You're talking about warriors, weapons, and battle. I'm just a kid in high school."

"It will be OK. You will understand at the proper time. You still have your bear, right?

It was clear I wasn't going to get any more information out of him, so I let out a nervous sigh of resignation and nodded. What on Earth was I getting myself into?

He swung the door to the roof open, and we were immediately blasted by a frigid wave of below freezing air. The air stung the inside of my nose as I consciously reminded myself to breathe, such was the cold. With the frigid wind swirling around us, we walked past the now familiar air conditioner to the location where I'd first seen Koko meditating.

When we reached the right spot, he stopped, taking a moment to carefully survey his surroundings. All I saw were the buildings that surrounded ours, most of the windows had lights on, and some had Christmas trees visible. Not sure what he was looking for, I followed the arc of his gaze. Perhaps, I considered, this was a vestige of the ancient ceremony where the participants would make sure the area around the ceremony site was free from danger. Whether or not this was true was anyone's guess. Nonetheless, I decided against asking him about it as I didn't want to interrupt the ceremony, which I wasn't sure had even started. Satisfied, he walked to a predetermined spot, known only to him, and stopped.

"Please stand here," he instructed.

Carefully, I walked to where he indicated and stood next to him. He turned, looking at me with eyes I'd never seen on anyone in my life, a combination of serious and solemn. He turned around 180 degrees, walked away from me, stopping about eight feet away. After a brief pause, he began chanting, starting at just above a light whisper and at the proper moment, turned to his left and began a slow rhythmic jog, arcing away from me. Holding the ceremonial pipe aloft, high over his head with both hands, every few seconds he would lower the pipe to just above waist level where it remained for a brief time before being lifted once more above his head. One quarter around the arc, he stopped, held the pipe high over his head, and, in a booming voice, exclaimed something unintelligible, to the heavens. He continued along the arc, chanting and stopping three more times along the path, each time another quarter, finally stopping at the exact point at which he had started. With me at the center, he had completed a circle. At this point, I surmised he had likely stopped at the four cardinal points on a compass, North, East, South, and West.

Though the pipe wasn't lit, Koko nonetheless inhaled. Casting his eyes to the heavens, he exhaled, waited two or three seconds, closed his eyes and slowly lowered his head. After opening his eyes, he walked to the center of the circle where I was standing, extended his arms and, without speaking, instructed me to mimic his actions with the pipe. In that moment I felt silly taking part in a ceremony I had no claim to. As far as I knew, I had no Native American blood in my ancestry, making me little more than an imposter. But I knew that by refusing the invitation, he would be personally insulted.

He stood there, waiting, having not moved a muscle, so I took the pipe and did as he had silently instructed, handing the pipe back to him when I was done. He turned to his right, walked a few steps, and placed the pipe on a nearby air conditioning unit before returning.

Facing me, his black and gray hair blowing gently in the frigid breeze, our eyes locked for an awkwardly prolonged period. His face was like stone, eyes unblinking, as long hair blew around his eyes. Right before I mustered up the courage to ask him if the ceremony was over, he took a small step back.

"The bear, please."

Reaching into my jeans pocket, I retrieved the bear, carefully handing it to him. He backed up to the spot he had previously been standing when he made the circle with the pipe, repeating the process. He chanted, as before, but I could tell some of the words had changed. Throughout the arcing circle he held the small bear aloft, lowering and raising it just as he had done with the pipe. The meaning of the rhythmic chant was completely lost to me, though I had no doubt it was significant and ancient.

Having completed the circle's second navigation, he stood, as before, facing me. He took a moment to retrieve the pipe and crossed into the circle. With the pipe in his left hand and bear in his right, he closed his eyes, extending both arms, reaching as high as he could. He recited more words from the ancient language, a recitation continuing, unbroken, for what I guessed was over two minutes. Upon completion, he opened his eyes and smiled.

"We are done. Normally, a warrior blessing ceremony is performed around a large fire and will last many hours. The ceremony typically begins at dusk and continues into the night. Because we are in the middle of the city, we could not perform the ceremony around a fire. We could also not have continued after nightfall; it is much too cold for that."

"Why did we do this?" I asked.

"We should go inside to warm up. I will explain things then."

We walked back into the building, ridding ourselves of the bone chilling temperatures on the roof.

Thirteen

Arriving back at Koko's apartment, he went into the kitchen to prepare some hot chocolate while I sat down on the couch and marveled, yet again, at the amazing array of artwork displayed in his home. As I sat taking everything in, I felt a pressure against my left leg and looked down to see Fred staring up at me with copper-colored eyes. He meowed, jumping onto the couch next to me, stepping forward to give me a firm headbutt on my left shoulder. Having no experience with cats, I took this gesture to mean he wanted me to pet him. Extending my left hand, I lightly scratched him on the top of his head, right between his large ears. He leaned into my hand and began to purr before crawling into my lap to soak up all the attention. Koko returned from the kitchen holding two large mugs of steaming hot chocolate, placing them on the small coffee table.

"Look at that, he likes you. Fred is very particular about who he considers a friend. This is very unusual behavior for him. He is an excellent judge of character," Koko informed me as he sat down in the recliner next to the couch.

"I'm honored. I don't have any experience with cats. In fact, I have no idea what I'm doing."

"You are doing fine by the looks of it. Fred thinks you are a pro."

Fred did seem to be enjoying himself, his purr increased in volume, and he began kneading my jeans. He stood up, turned around three times, and curled up into a ball on my lap. Not sure what to make of this, I sat still and looked at Fred, amazed. He was such an intriguing creature, a furry ball of purring happiness.

"Do you know why we performed the Warrior Blessing Ceremony?" Koko asked, changing the subject.

I didn't know how to respond. My instinct was to shrug my shoulders in resignation, acknowledging the fact that I didn't have an adequate answer. I decided to go with blunt honesty, which I felt he would respect more than no answer at all.

"Honestly, I have no idea. In fact, using the words 'warrior' and 'blessing' in the same sentence seems like a contradiction to me."

"Why do you say that?"

"Well, warriors are all about violence, chaos, and death. Blessing, to me, is all about happiness, forgiveness, and devotion."

"Hmm, you know, you are right. I had not thought about it like that before."

Knowing I had the ability to surprise him caught me off guard as I was under the distinct impression there was nothing that I, a sophomore in high school, could offer that would be of any value to someone like him. He had wisdom and knowledge about life I couldn't understand, so how could he learn anything from me?

"I suppose we could rename the ceremony, but that would take a considerable amount of time and contemplation. We will revisit this idea later."

"You don't have to change the name just because I had an observation. I'd prefer it if you didn't. I mean the name is fine with me. I was just thinking out loud."

Had there been a hole in the floor, I would have crawled into it.

"Hmm … The Warrior Blessing Ceremony …" Koko continued, "… is one the warriors would perform before they went into battle. The ceremony would commonly be held the night before the conflict. Sometimes the confrontation was a full-fledged battle in every sense of the word. Other times it might be a small raiding party, or a similar small group would go out on a scouting mission to assess the strengths and weaknesses of the enemy."

"Okay, I understand all that. But what was the purpose of it all? I mean, why would a warrior need a blessing in the first place?"

"Those are excellent questions, Ashley. A warrior typically asks the gods to bless his or her horse, that he may run swiftly, his weapons that they remain strong, sharp, and true. But more than anything else, a warrior asked the gods to give him the courage to face his enemy, to face everything he fears and, despite these fears, to rush into battle. To face his fears with courage and strength is the primary goal of a warrior."

"What would a warrior be afraid of? Why would a warrior ask for courage? I thought warriors weren't afraid of anything."

I sipped my hot chocolate, eagerly waiting for Koko's answer.

"A warrior is, in every conceivable way, just like everyone else, Ashley. A warrior has the same fears, concerns, worries, and anxieties as you and me and everyone on the planet. There is, however, one thing that separates the warrior from the masses, just one thing." He paused. "Do you know what that one thing is?"

I thought about it briefly, squinting my eyes in concentration.

"No, I don't. I'm sorry, but I'm drawing a blank."

"There is nothing to be sorry about, Ashley. It is OK. The warrior will consciously recognize these fears, concerns, worries and anxieties and will move forward despite them." He leaned forward even as he said, 'forward.'

"Huh, that makes sense."

Koko had the remarkable ability to make complex problems appear ordinary.

"When a warrior knows she or he is going into battle against a formidable foe, do they turn around and run away in the other direction? No, of course not. Your father was a Navy SEAL, right?"

"Oh, OK. Yes, he was a Navy SEAL."

"It would be inconceivable to consider your father backing down from a challenge, correct?"

"Well, I never actually knew him. But, yeah, from everything my mom has said, he always attacked challenges head on. Full steam ahead, my mom would say."

"Exactly, full steam ahead. That is a terrific way to put it. Here is what most people fail to consider when it comes to warriors. Most people think that to be a warrior you must know how to shoot and fight and kill people. Warriors have, for thousands of years, been thought of as physically strong and intimidating characters. Am I right?"

"Yeah, that sounds about right."

"An individual does not need to do or be any of these things to be a warrior. A person does not need to know how to shoot and fight and kill people. One does not need to be physically strong and intimidating to be a warrior."

"I'm not sure I follow. I mean, how can someone be a warrior without being tough and intimidating?"

"Ultimately, what being a warrior really boils down to is this," he said, and paused again. "A warrior must face his or her fears. Despite everything else, if a warrior faces these fears, stares them down, even in the face of incredible odds, they can never be defeated."

He looked as serious as I had ever seen him.

"A warrior must face his fears? That's it?"

"Yes, that is it. It may sound remarkably easy, but do not be fooled, it is exceedingly difficult. The most demanding thing a person can overcome. Think about it, Ashley, really take time to consider how fear rules the lives of every person on earth."

"I never really thought about fear. You really think it rules our lives?"

"Yes, without question. It is a sad truth, but fear dominates the lives of nearly everyone. Some people are so controlled by it that they fear, fear. They are afraid of being afraid. People will not apply for a job they really want because they are afraid, not only of not getting the job, but they are afraid of getting the job as well. If they get the job, they are afraid of not being good at it, they are afraid of failure. A man will not ask out a woman he finds attractive because he is afraid she might say no."

"I asked Riley out to the Christmas dance last week and she did say no."

"That is great Ashley!"

"What? How can that be great?"

"When you were thinking about asking her to the dance, when you were considering it in your mind, did this make you nervous?"

"Yeah, sure. I was extremely nervous."

"And yet, filled with nervousness and anxiety, you approached her and asked her to the dance. Am I right?"

"Sure, I guess so."

"No, do not guess. Know. A warrior is either sure or isn't. In between is where mediocrity lives and thrives. In that precise moment, when you approached her and asked her to the dance, you had the mindset of a warrior. You faced your fear, the fear that Riley would reject you, but you forged ahead anyway. This is what I am talking about."

"Yeah, but she said no."

"Yes, but that is not the point. Remember, Riley is not the enemy, despite the unfortunate outcome. The true enemy is fear.

In this instance, you were victorious. You were a warrior!" he said, shaking a balled-up fist into the air.

His enthusiasm made me smile. I knew he was right just as much as I knew that I did, in fact, need to spend some time thinking about the role of fear in my life. He was unquestionably right about one thing; I was nervous about asking Riley to the dance. But I did it anyway.

"Consider this, Ashley ..." He paused, before continuing, "Fear precedes action. But, once the action starts, fear melts away as if it had never been there at all."

"I'm sorry, what?"

"As an example, you were nervous about asking Riley to the dance, correct?"

"Yes, very nervous."

"But once you began talking to her, were you still nervous? Were you still operating from a position of fear?"

His question hit me like a bolt of lightning as my eyes widened and I stared at the floor replaying in my mind's eye the interaction between Riley and myself.

"Oh, wow! You're right. I remember now. As I talked to her, I felt pretty good about myself. That almost never happens."

"See? That is how it works. Most people don't realize this, and those that do, often forget it."

"Wow. I think I get it. I mean, I need to spend some time tossing it around in my head. But wow."

I was dumbfounded.

"So, can anyone be a warrior? My dad was a warrior, and my mom is a warrior too. What about Mike, the guy that hit me with the snowball? What about the person who attacked me? Can they be warriors too?"

Koko wasted no time responding to my rapid-fire questions.

"Your parents are most certainly warriors. As far as Mike and the person who attacked you? My answer is no, they are not warriors. They are bullies who operate out of fear. This is an important distinction to make. A bully is afraid of the same things everyone else is afraid of, but instead of facing their fears, as a warrior would do, they lash out to create fear for those around them."

"So, you don't think Mike is a warrior? Because he won't face his fears, because he is too afraid?"

"Yes, exactly. I have no idea why he does the things he does. I do not know his history, what his life story is. I only know that he does not face his fears, therefore he cannot be a warrior."

"What does it matter what his life story is? Who cares?"

"Ashley, it is a significant matter. A warrior needs to understand his or her adversary, whether that adversary is the fear of rejection or an actual person. A warrior who understands the history of his or her enemy has already seized the advantage."

"I would have thought the less I know about Mike, the better."

"It is the exact opposite. Why does he lash out? Why does he mistreat people the way he does? There are answers to these questions and they are important. What is it that Mike is so afraid of that he would attack someone?"

I didn't have the answer to any of those questions. In fact, the more I thought about it, the more questions I had. It had never occurred to me that Mike would be afraid of anything.

"Do you think he is afraid of me?"

"I do not know what he is afraid of. It could be he is afraid of what you represent. He does not know you, nor I suspect, does he understand you. I think we can safely say there are things in his past that contribute to his behavior."

"Okay. What about this? If a bully can't be a warrior, can a warrior be a bully?"

Koko looked at me, tilted his head to the right ever so slightly, and smiled.

"I must say Ashley, you ask very thought-provoking questions."

"Thanks."

"So, if a bully cannot be a warrior, can a warrior be a bully? The answer is yes. A warrior can be a bully. It has happened many times throughout history. Many warriors have acted in ways that are contrary to the way a warrior is expected to behave. When a warrior crosses that line, they cease to be a warrior. The warrior has become the bully. Bear in mind, it happens most often to individuals, but it does not stop there. Countries have, many times in the past, been the bully on the block. Nazi Germany is a perfect example. But it is not just countries with their armies and navies that have the power to be bullies. Many businesses are bullies. Some of them will stop at nothing to amass more money and power. Religions are not exempt either, untold numbers of people have been killed because they were not the 'right' religion."

"Well, can a warrior who has turned into a bully then become a warrior again?"

"Yes, that is possible. A warrior turned bully can certainly change their behavior. But the warrior will never be able to erase the title of bully, just as he cannot erase the harm he caused when he was a bully."

That made a lot of sense, I thought. It's nice to know that people can change, that they can better themselves. But Koko was right again, a change of behavior doesn't change the past, it doesn't erase it.

"Why are you telling me all this?"

Leaning back in his chair, Koko took a long sip of hot chocolate.

"I am telling you this because of what happened to you, because of the attack you suffered. You may not realize it yet, Ashley, but your life has changed. You are not the same person now that you were before the attack. Right now, you are in a period of transition as you grow into the person that you are to become. The old Ashley is gone. In a manner of speaking the old Ashley has died. A new Ashley is emerging. It is like a birth. A new Ashley is being born from the old one. This is often a difficult transition to make. I would like, if you will allow me, to help you during this time."

"Sure, I don't mind."

I couldn't help but wonder why he would want to help me, but I didn't ask. Instead, I said, "Sure, I don't mind."

"I am also telling you these things because I believe in paying it forward. Many years ago, one of the tribal elders did a similar thing for me. I, too, had experienced trauma in my young life, and he took it upon himself to see me through it."

His gaze drifted to a time long since passed.

I quietly nodded, though I doubt he noticed. We sat silently for the next several minutes as each of us rolled around in our head things only we could know.

"Do you remember asking me about the coffee shop down on the corner?"

"Yeah, I remember. It's been there for years, but I only just noticed it."

"Yes. It there anything else you have noticed since you were attacked?"

"Umm ..." I paused to consider it. "Yeah, there is. On the way home from the hospital, I noticed all the people that were walking around. It's not just the people that I noticed either, I noticed what they were wearing, what color their clothes were, what they were doing. I even noticed the color of the hand trucks the delivery people were using. I noticed smells and colors. I wondered about where the people who were walking on the sidewalk were going. I never used to notice or think about that stuff."

"You see," he said, smiling. "It has already begun. You left the hospital and entered a whole new world. This is part of the transition I was talking about. It is likely you will notice more of your life, more of what makes up your world, changing. It can be an exciting time, but it can also be frightening. You are going to see and experience things that may be unfamiliar to you. I can help you with this if you will allow me."

"Sure, I mean, if you don't mind. I need all the help I can get."

I did need all the help I could get. Not knowing what the future held for me was one thing, no one really knows what will come, but I was doing it now with a newfound awareness. It was a disconcerting feeling to be sure.

"Why did you use my bear in the ceremony?" I asked, finishing the last of my hot chocolate.

"The bear is a representation of your courage and the resolve contained within you to face your fears. Bears are not fearless creatures like many people would have you believe. A bear is extremely intelligent and will choose her battles only when she knows she has the advantage. A bear, even the mighty Kodiak, has no desire to engage in a battle in which they are outmatched. The bear will of course, but only if he or she has no choice. A cornered bear will fight their way out despite being afraid and will not cower in the hope that the threat will go away."

"But there's an enormous difference between a bear and a person. A bear is huge, has big teeth and claws, and can run fast."

"All of these things are true. But there is no difference in the fear the bear experiences and the fear that a person feels. The fear is the same."

"Huh. I never thought about it quite like that."

"Keep your bear close to you, Ashley. When you are feeling anxious or nervous, or when you feel the weight of a situation is more than you can handle, hold the bear, feel the weight of it in your hand, remember what it represents. The bear will help you face whatever fears are placed before you."

I didn't know what to make of Koko's heartfelt instructions. I knew he meant well and that he believed very deeply in what he had said. But I didn't know if I believed it. Did I believe the bear would miraculously pull me out of any future tough situations? No, not really. But I was willing to give Koko the benefit of the doubt.

"Okay. I'll try it."

I left Koko's place and headed home, one floor down, certain in the knowledge that I had a lot to think about. The problem I now faced was where to start. Koko had given me much to consider, and I had trouble making sense of it all. The next few days were an uneventful blur. I slept a lot and did a bunch of homework in an attempt to catch up. I didn't see Koko, Riley, or anyone else from school. I stayed inside and kept to myself. Simply put, I was lazy.

Fourteen

Early Sunday afternoon mom answered a knock on the door to find Koko standing there, smiling as usual.

"Hi Koko. What brings you by this neighborhood?"

"I stopped in to see if you and Ashley might be interested in getting some coffee."

"I'm not really into coffee, thank you for asking. I'm just going to stay here and read. But Ashley might be interested." She turned to look at me, tilting her head to the right. "What do you think?" She asked.

"Yeah, I'm game. It'll be good for me to get out of here for a while."

"Great. Coffee with friends is always more enjoyable than coffee alone."

Gathering up my jacket, gloves, and shoes from my room, I returned to Koko munching on a cookie, one of the few remaining from my return from the hospital.

"You sure you don't want to go, Mom?"

"Yeah. I'm sure, thanks though. Have a good time."

The wind was light and crisp and, mercifully, snow no longer fell as Koko, and I exited the lobby of the apartment building. Half a block away, I could already smell the warm aroma of coffee escaping from the coffee shop. The prospect of discovering a new (to me) coffee joint and determining if they could produce a nice hot cup of Joe had me more excited than I normally would have expected. While my mom wasn't a fan of coffee, I was a self-confessed junkie, and while we hadn't yet reached the coffee shop, I began to feel better.

The sidewalk outside had been thoughtfully covered with small salt rocks, allowing easier passage on the slick surface. Entering the coffee shop, appropriately named The Java Coast, we were engulfed in an envelope of freshly brewed coffee nirvana as the aroma emanated from every corner. However, it wasn't just the smell of coffee there. I detected scones, cinnamon buns, and other distinct types of pastries.

The small shop on the corner was moderately busy with a sprinkling of people scattered about, most of them talking to friends or reading quietly. Tastefully decorated with a comfortable mix of tables and couches, the shop décor was an interesting collection, none of which really matched. The couches were eclectic and in reasonably good shape while the tables and chairs were an assorted bunch that exuded their own distinct brand of character. There was a bar at the back of the shop where the cash register was located, alongside which was a motley crew of fashionable t-shirts with the shop's logo and large coffee mugs of various sizes and colors. I liked the place immediately.

Koko motioned for me to order first. The menu, placed high on the back wall just behind the bar, had a dizzying display of choices. Selecting at a coffee shop, especially one that you've never been to, is a matter not to be taken lightly, not rushed. Methodically, and with careful consideration, I scanned the menu, settling on an item called a Snickers latte. I figured, rightly of course, that if it tasted anything like a Snickers candy bar, it had to be good. Koko stepped up and wasted no time ordering a caramel latte. Since he had frequented the coffee shop before, I wasn't surprised.

I pulled my wallet out to pay but Koko waved me off.

"No, please Ashley. Allow me."

"Okay. Thanks Koko."

The cashier completed the transaction, informing us that she would bring our beverages to us when they were ready. I turned around, looking for a place to sit, only to notice that Koko was already a step ahead of me. He headed straight for a small, round table at the front of the store and the expansive window overlooking the sidewalk outside. He shrugged out of his jacket and took a seat to the right while I did the same and took the opposite seat on the left. It was comfortably warm in the coffee shop, but I could feel the wintry weather outside trying to intrude through the window. The mix of comfortable warm air inside opposed by the freezing temperature trying to force its way inside made for an interesting combination. Not too warm, but not too cold either.

"This is my favorite table; I sit here whenever I get the chance."

"It's a great spot," I agreed.

"I like it because I can sit here with my coffee and watch the world go by. People driving by in cars and walking past the window, you never know who or what you might see."

His eyes glimmered.

"Do you come here a lot?"

"Yes, quite often. Two or three times a week. Sometimes more, sometimes less."

"Wow, that is a lot. I like it here. I could see myself coming here a lot too."

A few moments later, a server approached with our lattes, placing them on the table. I picked up my Snickers latte and, holding it just under my nose, inhaled deeply. The aroma was divine. Koko dove right in, sipping his caramel latte. I sipped mine next and was met with an intoxicating delivery of flavors, akin to drinking a cup full of joy. The Snickers latte became my new instant favorite.

"Oh man, this is the tastiest latte I've ever had."

"I am glad you like it."

We sat for quite a while, not saying anything as cars and pedestrians passed by the window and people came and went from the coffee shop.

The peaceful afternoon was shattered when I saw something that made my blood run cold. Two exceptionally large individuals lumbered by the window, one bearing a striking resemblance to Neanderthal Mike. My only recourse was to sit there and pray that if it were Mike, he would continue on his way, and I could forget I ever saw him. Mike and his companion shuffled their way past the window and out of my line of sight, leaving me a short span of time to contemplate what might happen next. Just as I felt certain enough time had elapsed for them to pass, the small bell that hung inside and above the door tinkled rapidly, announcing to everyone that customers had either entered or exited the building. Mike and his companion sauntered toward the rear of the shop with relaxed bravado, seemingly without a care in the world.

Inhaling sharply, I instinctively knew without even looking that they had entered.

"Ashley, what is wrong? You have the appearance of a ghost," Koko asked looking over the edge of his latte.

"You see the two guys that just walked in? One of them is Mike, the guy that hit me in the face with a snowball and called me a half-breed."

Koko gently set his coffee on the small table and looked past me to the individuals that were now walking to the bar at the back of the coffee shop.

"Which one is Mike?"

"I don't know. The big one," I said, quickly realizing how ridiculous that sounded.

"They are both big. In fact, they are both huge."

"Yeah, I noticed. I hope they don't see us."

My reaction was more visceral than I had expected upon seeing Mike for the first time since the snowball incident. Despite my proximity to the window and the freezing air trying to force its way in, I was starting to sweat, and my heart felt like it was beating a mile a minute. Despite knowing better, I was well on my way to a full-fledged panic attack.

"Ashley, I want you to look at me and take a deep breath," Koko said in a calm, reassuring tone. He could sense my panic as well.

Only I didn't react to his advice, I continued to stare at the backs of the two behemoths who had just walked in.

"Ashley!"

My head whipped around to see Koko staring at me intently, still smiling.

"Ashley, please take a deep breath. Exhale slowly, inhale slowly, and drink some of your latte."

Only then did I realize that I had, in fact, been holding my breath. I exhaled, letting out a considerable amount of barely contained panic. Closing my eyes, I inhaled as deeply as my injured ribs would allow and slowly exhaled again. When I opened my eyes, I felt marginally better.

Koko gestured with his right hand toward the latte I had momentarily forgotten. With a considerable amount of conscious attention, I picked it up, and with both hands visibly shaking, took a nervous sip. I lowered the latte from my lips and looked at Koko, the definition of calm as his eyes twinkled and the smile never left his face.

"Ashley, did you notice the smell of the pastries when we walked in a little while ago?"

"Umm, yeah."

I stole a glance toward the back wall where the two giants stood.

"Ashley, please look at me."

I allowed my observation of Mike and his companion to hover for a moment more before returning my attention to Koko.

"Ashley, I want you to focus your mind. Do not focus on the two gentlemen at the cash register. You have no control over what they will or will not do. You do have control over how you react to it though."

"Okay, sorry. Did you ask me a question a second ago? Sorry, I wasn't paying attention."

"There is no need to apologize. I understand what you are going through. I asked if you noticed the smell of the pastries when we walked in a little while ago."

"Yes, I did. I'm pretty sure I could smell cinnamon buns and scones, among other things. Why do you ask?"

"Would you like a pastry?"

"Uh, I guess so. If you don't mind."

"I do not mind at all. What kind would you like?"

"A scone. Cranberry if they have it. I love cranberry scones."

Koko could no doubt sense the nervousness in my voice.

"Then a cranberry scone it shall be. I am craving a cinnamon bun. They make excellent cinnamon buns here. I will be right back."

Koko rose and peacefully walked to the rear of the coffee shop where he patiently stood behind Neanderthal Mike and the other giant. I sat, mesmerized by it all, for a few seconds before realizing that he had nothing to fear from Mike. Unlike Mike and I, he and Mike had no history. Not wanting to attract Mike's attention, I returned to contemplating my newly discovered latte.

Staring into the latte's infinite depth, I purposefully tried to concentrate on anything but Mike and my growing fear, but I couldn't help it. As much as I tried to think about other things, my mind steered itself back to him and what he had done and said to me. I tried to focus my thoughts into performing a Jedi mind trick, only instead of trying to control the mind of another person, as Obi-Won Kenobi had done in the first Star Wars film, I tried to see if I could get Mike to spontaneously explode.

Explode! Explode! Explode!

I opened my right eye and took a brief side-glance to see Mike still among the living. He had not exploded. He was still standing at the register, a dwarfed Koko behind him.

Opening both eyes, I turned back to my latte and stared into its muddy brown depths. No oracle of fate stared back at me offering to solve all my problems. But when a shadow slowly crept across the floor toward the table, I assumed Koko was returning with the pastries. The shadow continued its path and eventually covered the table in darkness. Reluctantly, I lifted my head to see Mike towering over me. Had we been outside, he would have blocked out the sun.

Unlike my recent observations of people walking the city sidewalks during my cab ride home from the hospital, I didn't notice what he was wearing. Two things registered in my brain when my gaze met his. The first was the smell, Mike's body odor; he smelled awful. Had I not been on the verge of a full-fledged panic attack, I would have passed out from the stench. My suddenly overburdened olfactory senses detected sweat and cigarette smoke, odors that fell from him in waves so strong I'm surprised they weren't visible.

When I was certain things couldn't get any worse, I noticed teeth. His mouth was contorted into a smile that can only be described as sinister and he held back a set of teeth that were more yellow than white. Mike's commitment to personal hygiene was nonexistent.

"Half-breed, hey man, it's been a while. You don't look so good," Mike said, leaning in and slapping his gargantuan hands onto the table hard enough to rattle the drinks into spilling over their edge. The sharp sound was loud enough to attract the attention of many of the coffee shop's customers.

My eyes narrowed at the sound of his insult while his considerable size prevented me from getting an idea of where Koko was. My attempt to look around him only got harder when another massive individual walked up and stopped, blocking out even more light.

"My name is Ashley."

At some point I had retrieved the small, red bear from my pocket, though I don't remember having done so. Under the table I turned the bear over and over in the palm of my hand, feeling its weight and the smoothness of its surface, remembering what Koko had said to me. The bear was a representation of my courage. A cornered bear would not cower in fear and hope that the threat would just go away. He would, if left no other choice, fight his way out.

Though I certainly felt cornered, I knew that fighting my way out of this current situation was simply out of the question. Physically, there was no way I could stand up to Mike without being squashed.

"Your name is whatever I say it is."

"Hey Mike, who's your little friend?"

"Dad, this is half-breed. Remember? I told you about him, he's the one that ratted on me to the police."

"So, you're the little asshole snitch, huh?" Mike's dad asked, sneering through teeth surprisingly more yellow stained than his sons.

The elder Pigliani was slightly shorter than his son, but his potbelly indicated that he outweighed him by a considerable amount. He had an ever-present bit of moisture gathered at the corners of his lips, enough that I was surprised he didn't have a trail running down his chin. I surmised he stunk to high heaven, too, but Mike's divine aroma overpowered everything in the vicinity, including the coffee.

"I didn't rat on anyone. The police asked me some questions, which I answered."

My voice, smooth and even, belied the fear threatening to explode within me.

"Well, half-breed, you shouldn't have. You made a big mistake when you mentioned Big Mike's name to the police." It was then I noticed the two rippling scars across the landscape of Mr. Pigliani's face. The smaller of the two crossed just below the bridge of his nose, while the larger one spanned from the middle of his forehead just below his hairline and stopped just in front of the top of his right ear. Both scars appeared to be quite old, likely standing out only when his blood pressure rose with his anger. At this point, the evidence of both wounds was easily visible.

"Well, maybe Big Mike shouldn't have hit me with a snowball and pushed me down."

I locked eyes with Mr. Pigliani.

"You know, somewhere along the way," I continued, "someone didn't teach him to mind his own business."

It was a deliberate and ill-advised dig at Mr. Pigliani, but I was angry, and the screaming threat of dire consequences was rapidly fading to a whisper. My display of bravado far exceeded my feelings of the same.

The tension in the air rose higher with every passing second, and it was obvious that Mike and his dad were angry. The relaxed nature with which they entered the coffee shop was gone, replaced with body language that displayed seething, muscle contracting rage. Again, I tried to see past the mass of humanity in front of me, looking for Koko, and a way out of the situation.

"Oh, it's not the snowball thing that I'm pissed about," Mike shot back, stepping forward, decreasing the distance between us. "The police wanted to know where I was when you got attacked. They called my mom's house, called my dad at work. They even showed up at the house asking all kinds of questions."

He was shouting now, as a line of spittle shot out of his mouth, landing on his chin. He took no notice, allowing it to remain.

I became aware of the other customers in the coffee shop, many of whom were staring, having taken notice of Mike's enraged outburst. The din of conversation in the room ceased completely.

"Then why did you attack me outside the theater?"

Asking such a direct question was a calculated risk; my aim was to get him to answer me quickly before he had time to think about what he was saying.

"Be..." he blurted. "No way half-breed, I'm not about to fall for that one. You think you're smart, don't you?"

A sliver of light, color, and salvation revealed itself between the hulking bodies of Mike and his father. In that small vertical space appeared the distinctive silhouette of Koko.

"Excuse me, gentlemen," Koko said, smiling up at Mike and his dad as he squeezed his way between them.

The two leviathans instinctively parted, allowing Koko to pass. As soon as he had cleared their personal space, the part closed like two giant dungeon doors. No way out, I thought. Koko placed the cranberry scone and cinnamon bun on the table and sat down. Immediately, the smell of the pastries temporarily relieved me of the deadly aroma surrounding Mike.

"Well, who's this? You Indian or something?" Mike's dad asked, his face twisted with judgment and contempt.

"Yes, I am Blackfoot. The Blackfoot tribe is in Montana and Southwestern Canada. Beautiful country."

"I don't care where you're from. You're a half-breed just like him." Mike's dad replied, pointing a thick, calloused finger at me.

"Ashley is not a half-breed, and neither am I."

"You are what I say you are."

"Ashley is not half of anything. I am not half of anything. Each of us is one whole person. One may be a small number, but it is the most important." His voice and delivery were the definition of calm, his countenance even and neutral.

"Don't spew your philosophical crap on us. If Pops here says you're both half-breeds, then you're both half-breeds."

Mike looked to his father, searching for reassurance.

Koko slowly rose to his feet and turned to face the two hulking men.

"It is time for the two of you to leave."

Koko's statement was firm, his voice never rising above that of casual conversation. He didn't shake his fist or point a finger, but his point was clear. Game time was over.

"Oh really? Mike, can you believe this guy? He's asking us to leave."

Mr. Pigliani chuckled, nudging Mike in the shoulder with his elbow.

"It was not a request," Koko replied, making his point perfectly clear.

At that moment one of the coffee shop employees approached, concern written all over her face.

"Is there a problem here? Can I help anyone?"

Mike stepped toward our table, leaning in so far, our noses touched. His huge head consumed my entire field of vision as the odor oozed from his clothes and skin in sickening, overwhelming waves. Anger and hate charged the air between and around us, threatening to boil over.

"Talk to the police again half-breed. Please, I dare you. Talk to them just one more time, for me."

His voice was barely a whisper as he uncoiled and stepped back, standing even with his father as the sinister yellow smile returned to his face. His father's face twisted and quivered with rage as he seemed consumed with hatred and anger. Inexplicably, and without another word, they turned in unison and walked out of the coffee shop, leaving Koko and I and the employee to ponder what had taken place.

"Well, that was strange," the employee said as she turned around and walked back to the cash register.

I sat in stunned silence, no longer interested in my Snickers latte or cranberry scone. Not knowing what to say or think, I leaned forward in my chair, burying my head in my hands. Shame and confusion swirled in my mind as my emotions fought for control. Equal parts of me wanted to cry, scream out in anger, or hide in a corner, none of which would have accomplished anything.

"Ashley?"

Lifting my head, I reached for my latte and took a sip of the still wonderful elixir, taking a moment to look at the warm cranberry scone waiting for me on the small table. If the scone could talk, what would it say about the scene that just unfolded, I wondered. What advice would it give me?

"Ashley, are you OK?"

"You know, those are two very unhappy people."

Koko smiled at my revelation.

"Yes, they are exceedingly unhappy." He paused. "A sad thing to see. They are poisoned by their own hate."

"They are, aren't they? I never would have thought to put it like that. They are poisoned by their own hate."

Suddenly, I felt a profound sadness for both Mike and his dad. Had someone told me I would one day feel sadness about Mike, I never would have believed it. And yet here I was, pondering what had just transpired and feeling whatever trials I was going through in my life, at least I wasn't filled with poisonous hate.

"What was it Mike said to you when he leaned forward? He spoke so quietly I could not hear it."

"He dared me to talk to the police again. He practically asked me to."

"That young man has many issues."

He sipped his latte.

"What do you think I should do?"

"Well, I think if the police contact you again, you have an obligation to talk to them. Mike will not like this, but that is not your responsibility."

"I don't even know what I would say to the police. I mean, Mike didn't specifically threaten me."

"No, he did not threaten you. Not openly, not blatantly. But make no mistake, the threat was there, and it was real. If the police ask, I think you should tell them."

As much as I didn't want to talk to the police, I was inclined to agree. If, and when, the time came to speak to Detective Sharply, I would relate to him the events of the day. Would Mike find out? Possibly, but only time would tell.

"Ashley, I must say you handled that situation extremely well."

He smiled.

Returning his smile, I raised my left hand to show him the bear I had been holding during the encounter. His smile widened as he reached out to take the bear from my hand.

"It is an amazing thing. So small, yet also powerful."

"It is amazing. But it's not small, at least not to me."

He beamed at my exclamation, turning the bear over in his hand to gaze upon it from every conceivable angle.

"I don't even remember reaching into my pocket to get it. Suddenly there it was, right in my hand."

The fact that I didn't remember retrieving the bear left me astounded. The more time I spent with Koko, the more I found myself in various states of astonishment. He had that effect on people.

"It is not surprising you do not recall reaching into your pocket. The mind has ways of helping us through tricky situations. How and why it happens is not for us to always question. The bear was there for you when you needed it, that is the important thing to remember."

"You know, I just have a feeling this whole thing with Mike isn't going to end well."

"That is a natural thing to think. None of us can know what the future holds though. Maybe in the future, you and Mike will become friends."

"Yeah, I don't think so."

"Hmm, me either."

Fifteen

Stiff and sore, especially the area surrounding my ribcage, I nonetheless woke up early Monday morning, happy to face the day for the first time in ages. Though still not completely caught up with my schoolwork, I was looking forward to going back to school.

Three times before I left the apartment, I checked myself in the mirror to get a better feel for how I looked. It wasn't pretty, but it could have been worse as the swelling under my left eye had gone down considerably. Still visible though, was the bruising caused by the snowball and imbedded rock Mike had fired at me.

The right side of my face was a different matter altogether. My eye wouldn't fully open due to the swelling while the bruising completely encircled my eye extending halfway down the side of my face. I had the appearance of prizefighter that had gone ten rounds and lost by unanimous decision. There was nothing I could do about my appearance, and I knew it.

On my way to school I became acutely aware of everything around me, every footfall from passersby, every car as it glided past on the street. Paranoia was rapidly taking hold and it seemed like every sight and sound triggered a panicked response from the inner workings of my brain. Despite being only a couple of blocks from school, I stopped and leaned against the nearest building to calm my frayed nerves. I wondered about the building that currently held me upright; if the building could talk, what would it say? What amazing stories could it tell of its time in the city? Reaching into my pocket, I removed the marble bear and stared at it intently. I couldn't feel its smooth surface through my thickly padded winter gloves, but I could appreciate its weighty heft. The bear's small size belied its solid feel. In my mind, I reviewed the things Koko had taught me about courage and fear. Fear controlled the lives of almost every human being on earth, he had said. I didn't want to be one of those people, being paralyzed by fear was a trap I didn't want to fall into.

Having spent some time re-training my thoughts and calming down, I put the bear back into my pocket, stepped away from the building, and continued my journey to school. The small detour had done the trick, and I began to feel better. The bitter cold had caused my ribcage to tighten up, so I ascended the tall steps to the front door of Yorktown High School with much care and patience, counting every one along the way. Upon entering, I was greeted by a fellow student, one I'm certain I didn't know.

"Hey, you're back. So happy to see you!"

His enthusiasm surprised me.

"Thanks. Yeah, I'm back."

On the way to my locker, I received half a dozen similar greetings and well wishes. Some of the people I knew, or at least recognized, some of them I didn't. Upon reaching my locker, I noticed the front of it had been decorated with bright blue letters with yellow trim that said,

Welcome Back Ashley!

My mouth hung agape as I pondered how an unknown student like me could garner such attention. Whoever the mystery decorator was, they had put a lot of time and effort into making this happen. All around me were students, from freshmen to seniors, retrieving books from their lockers, mingling with friends, and ambling toward the first class of the day, and I had to look around to make sure that I was, in fact, at the right locker.

The outpouring of support I had already received was by far more than I had expected, which was none, and the day had just started. The rest of the morning was much the same as teachers and students approached and expressed their feelings, some saying they had prayed for me, others expressing they were glad to see me on the mend and back in school. It all got to be quite overwhelming. I reasoned I was getting a brief taste of what it must feel like to be one of the 'popular kids' in school.

While appreciating the well wishes from everyone, it left me feeling a bit uncomfortable since I was used to passing through the halls and classrooms unnoticed, a ghost among the living. I was a ghost no longer. Everyone in my orbit treated me like I was an actual living, breathing person: a bruised and battered, living, breathing person, but a person just the same.

At 11:30, I stopped by my locker to drop off some textbooks, pick up different ones for my afternoon classes, and grab my lunch before slowly walking to the cafeteria. The cavernous lunchroom was the usual chaotic mass of students, some coming, some going. The cafeteria had a distinctly unique smell, a combination of odors from the lunch line: pizza, boiled and overcooked vegetables, taco meat, along with what I could only guess were a various array of fluids used for cleaning the floor, tables, and counters. They were all smells I didn't recall noticing before. Walking to the far back corner of the large eating space, I settled into the same spot I always sat in for my solitary lunch experience.

Opening the small, brown lunch bag my mom had prepared the night before, I removed its contents. An apple, peanut butter and jelly sandwich, and a small zip-lock bag full of cheese crackers, all placed with care. As I was pulled out the cheese crackers, a small piece of paper, folded neatly in half, fell onto the table. Unfolding the paper revealed, in her neat flowing script, a message from her that read:

Ashley,
I hope you've had a great day so far! Enjoy your lunch! See
you later this afternoon! Maybe we can make cookies?
Love, Mom

I knew that my mom loved me very much, but this was the first time she had ever placed a note in my lunch bag. The note was a very touching gesture, one that took little time to compose, but would have a lasting impact. The last week of my life had been difficult, not just for me, but for her as well. I read the note one more time before folding it up and putting it in my pocket. A vaguely familiar voice sounded behind me as I began to eat my sandwich.

"Do you mind if we sit with you?"

Slowly and deliberately turning around, I faced the smiling, angelic image of Riley MacAlister. With my eyes wide and mouth hanging open, I don't think I could have appeared more shocked. Riley was genuinely asking if she could sit with me in the cafeteria? In front of other, living people?

"Uh, yeah, sure."

"Does that mean you do mind, or it's OK if we sit with you?"

It was a legitimate question.

I shook my head in frustration, clearing out cobwebs of confusion, having realized the uncertain nature of my response.

"No. I mean, yes…"

So flummoxed by Riley's presence I couldn't even formulate a coherent reply. I tried again.

"I mean, please do. You can sit here if you like."

Riley and her friend walked around the end of the table, placing their lunch trays down, sitting directly across from me. I took a quick glance around, wondering if the entire lunchroom had come to a grinding halt, awestruck at the spectacle they were seeing. To my surprise, everyone behaved in much the same way they had before Riley and her friend sat.

Riley was a vision of beauty with a red ribbon tied into a bow through which her dark black hair was pulled into a ponytail. Her off-white knitted turtleneck sweater came to a stop just under her chin.

"Ash, do you know my friend Niki?" Riley asked.

"Yeah, we're in the same English class, right?"

"Yeah, that's right. I knew I recognized you from somewhere," Niki replied.

"I don't know how you could recognize anybody when they look like this."

With a wave of my hand, I indicated the colorful bruising on my face.

"It's not that bad." Riley said, perhaps to make me feel less self-conscious.

"Thank you. I feel like I look hideous, to be honest."

"You don't look hideous at all. You look a lot better than you did the night my mom and I found you unconscious on the sidewalk."

"Wait, you and your mom found him?" Niki asked, obviously surprised.

"Yeah, remember the night I asked if you wanted to come with us to the movies?"

"You never tell me anything. What else are you hiding?" Niki asked, chewing her pizza while looking at Riley.

"Thank you for that, for staying with me until the police and paramedics arrived. And for the card that you got me, it really means a lot."

"Sure, it's no problem at all," Riley said as she began eating her lunch, a rectangularly shaped segment of pizza more closely resembling a thin piece of cardboard with a few bits of cheese hastily placed on top.

"Do they have any idea who attacked you?" Niki asked.

"No, not yet. I talked to the police a few days ago. They asked me a few questions and said they'd get back to me. But so far, I haven't heard a thing. Hopefully, I will soon."

"Yeah, I hope so," Niki answered.

"So, how are you doing? Feeling, OK?" Riley asked.

"Yeah, better than a few days ago. I still get headaches periodically and the freezing weather makes my ribs tighten up and ache."

"What's wrong with your ribs?" Niki asked.

"Oh, three of them were broken. The police think I was kicked after I got knocked out."

"Oh, wow. I hadn't heard that," Niki replied, wiping her mouth with a napkin.

"Hey, did you see my locker? Somebody decorated it. It looks amazing."

Riley smiled, a coy, mischievous smile if there ever was one.

"Yeah, I saw that. I wonder who the responsible person might be?"

"Did you do that?"

Riley smiled and shrugged her shoulders as if to say, "Maybe I did, maybe I didn't."

I decided not to press the issue any further, happy that someone, whoever that person was, thought to do something nice for me.

We sat in silence for a bit, each of us concentrating on our respective meals. I was still having trouble believing that Riley had asked, on purpose, to sit with me at lunch.

"Hey, did you guys know that male goats pee on their own face in order to attract a mate?" Niki blurted out. "Apparently the girl goats find it irresistible."

"Yeah, I don't believe that for a second. Every time I try it, the girls all run away, and I end up getting arrested. I'm telling you, it doesn't work," I answered.

Riley and Niki both stared at me for a second and then fell into fits of uncontrolled laughter.

"Whew. That is the funniest thing I've heard in a long time!" Riley said, wiping tears of laughter from her face.

I opened my mouth to ask Riley how her pizza tasted when I noticed she had stopped laughing altogether. Her eyes grew wide as the color drained from her face. She was staring at something or someone behind and above my left shoulder. Niki had a similar look on her face as she stopped mid chew, staring behind me.

"Half-breed. What's up?" Mike asked, striking the side of my head with an open hand. The open-handed blow stung, but the more severe damage had been done to my pride. I was sitting, having a very pleasant lunch with the girl I happened to be smitten by, when my arch nemesis appeared out of nowhere to accost me yet again. Why was this happening?

I let out an exasperated sigh.

"Ashley. My name is Ashley."

My statement sounded far braver than it felt.

"Whatever."

Plopping down in the seat beside me, the distinct smell of body odor and cigarette smoke invaded my personal space, instantly extinguishing my appetite.

"Whatcha' eating?"

It was more of a statement than a question as he reached over to snatch the apple sitting in front of me. I made a halfhearted attempt to take it back, but he was too fast.

"That's not yours."

"See, that's where you're wrong half-breed, it is mine."

He took a large, yellow-toothed bite out of the middle of the apple, causing juice and pulp to dribble down his chin. He swiped the mess from his face with the back of his hand before wiping it clean on his jeans. The smell of apple juice fought a pitched battle with Mike's body odor, a battle it had no chance of winning.

My face grew red as I stewed, again, in humiliation. The incident with the snowball was bad enough. This was far worse as it was happening in front of my lunch guests. Riley and Niki, sitting as still as statues, not eating, not moving a muscle, wore shocked looks on their face. I took this to mean they were fearful of what might happen next.

"Never mind. I don't want it anymore."

"Why not? You think you're too good for this apple now?"

He took two, huge slurping chomps. If he was going to steal my food, he should at least have the decency to not sound like a rooting pig while eating it. The smell of apple was rapidly losing its appeal.

"No, not at all."

"No? So, what is it?"

He leaned in, closing the distance between us.

"I'm asking you a question half-breed!" he shouted, pushing my shoulder with a giant hand. My ribs reacted to the push with instant, stabbing pain. I bit the inside of my lip, not wanting him to see me in pain.

"Mike, I think you should leave now." Riley said.

"I think you should shut your mouth!" Mike yelled at Riley, pointing his right index finger into her face. She recoiled from the invasion of her personal space.

As much as I tried, I couldn't figure out how to defuse the situation. Students at surrounding tables were now turning to stare at the escalating dispute, their attention diverted by Mike's increasing volume.

"Come on Mike. Seriously? You're going to yell at her too? She's not a part of this."

He redirected his attention back to me.

"It's sad when a tiny little girl like that has to stand up for you. Huh, half-breed?"

The cafeteria was now uncomfortably silent as more students became aware of the growing confrontation. Having every pair of eyes in the huge room trained in my specific direction was one of the most unpleasant feelings I had ever experienced.

"Remember what I told you, half-breed. Talk to the police one more time, tell 'em what happened, I don't care. I'm begging you to talk to them. If fact, I'm daring you."

His voice was a whisper as he leaned in, his face and ruinous, yellow-stained smile only inches from mine.

What could I say to placate this hulking mass of bad attitude?

"I'm not sure you're aware of this Mike, but his name isn't half-breed, it's Ashley. Wait a second … are you hard of hearing? Do you have peanut butter stuck in your ears?" Riley asked, tilting her head slightly to the right.

"Is there a problem here?"

It was Mr. Lewis. He had been made aware of the growing tension in the lunchroom.

"Yes, there is," I said.

"Ashley started it. He tried to take my apple, Mr. Lewis." Mike said, barely able to keep himself from laughing.

He stood up straight, backing away from the table, his eyes locked on mine the whole time.

"Don't forget our little agreement. Okay, buddy."

He turned and walked away without another word.

The tension in my body melted away with every step Mike took in the opposite direction. I felt exhausted and ashamed, a combination of the healing process from my injuries and the abrupt withdrawal of adrenaline coursing through my system. My shame was, no doubt, due to my inability to stand up for myself in the face of Mike's vitriol. The fact that Riley and

Niki were there to see the incident only compounded the feeling. Why did Mike have to treat me like this? I had done nothing to cause his hatred of me. My every existence was enough.

"Ashley, what was that all about?" Mr. Lewis asked.

I waited a few moments before answering, preferring to sit with my head down, staring at my sandwich, but not really seeing it. Then the strangest thing happened, I thought of my dad, deeply wishing he were here. Despite having never known him, I intuitively felt he would know exactly how to handle the situation. Sitting in the cafeteria, surrounded by people, and feeling completely alone, I realized for the first time in my life that you could miss someone you never even knew. I missed my father.

"I don't know. He just won't leave me alone. This is the second time he's dared me to talk to the police. He knows I mentioned him to the police once before, and he is begging me to do it again."

"It's not my place to offer you advice, Ashley, but I'm going to anyway." Mr. Lewis said, blowing out a large sigh. "I think you should talk to the police again. Mike is a loose cannon, and eventually, he's going to go off and people are going to get hurt."

"Yeah, I know. But I can't help but think that if I do talk to them, the situation is only going to get worse."

"Well, I'm going to talk to Principal Watson and Assistant Principal Dover, see if they have any bright ideas on how to handle this."

"Don't bother, it won't do any good."

Mr. Lewis turned and walked out of the cafeteria as I faced Riley and Niki. The looks of pity on their faces were soul crushing. The last thing I needed was pity. What I wanted was to talk to someone that understood what I was going through.

No one fit that description, at least not presently. I briefly entertained the thought of making a rapid exit from the cafeteria so I could slowly simmer in my misery alone. But that would accomplish nothing, and it seemed akin to running from my problems and fears instead of facing them head on as Koko had advised.

"Sorry about that," I said, shrugging my shoulders as I looked at Riley.

"Ash, there's nothing to be sorry about. You didn't create this problem with Mike, he did."

"Yeah, I guess you're right."

"That guy's an asshole," Niki proclaimed.

Despite my surprise at Niki's abrupt declaration, I was inclined to agree with her. He is an asshole. But I recalled a piece of advice Koko had recently given me, that of knowing the history of your enemy. While I most certainly didn't like Mike Pigliani, and I didn't understand him or his actions, I knew there were, more than likely, episodes and circumstances in his past that contributed to the person he was. As much as I didn't want to feel sorry for him, I did anyway.

"Well, that's true. But, you know, we don't know anything about him. We don't know why he is the way he is. I'm not defending him, and I'm not excusing his behavior, but I think to understand him, we need to understand his history."

It wasn't remotely what I would characterize as an original thought, and I felt a little guilty about owning it and not saying anything about its origin when I looked at Niki, busy chewing on her cardboard style pizza, and then to Riley who had the most peculiar look on her face. She was smiling, but not completely. Her head was tilted a little to the right and she was staring straight at me. I didn't know what to make of her reaction, so I nervously picked up my sandwich and began to eat.

"I could care less about his history. He's still an asshole," Niki said in between bites.

Riley continued to stare at me for a moment or two more before turning her attention back to her lunch.

Sixteen

The rest of the day passed without further trouble as I received many greetings and well wishes from students and teachers alike. Aside from the incident with Mike at lunch, the day was remarkable. Before today, I had convinced myself that I was the most invisible person in the entire school. Now, surprisingly, I knew this to not be true.

The walk home from school had me feeling a bit on edge as I half expected Mike to jump out from an alleyway or from behind a car to harass me again. Thankfully, nothing untoward happened and I arrived home with every intention of getting an immediate start on my homework, but when I eased myself into the tired, old recliner, exhaustion took over and I was asleep in under a minute.

I woke up an hour later and, feeling refreshed, started on my homework. I finished the last of my algebra equations, marveling at the smell of a freshly sharpened pencil as the door to the apartment opened and my mom and Detective Sharply entered. The detective looked much the same as he did on our first meeting in the hospital, only this time his shirt looked as if it needed immediate attention from a dry-cleaner, such were the numerous wrinkles. Instead of a purple tie, today his choice was the color of pea soup. Another strange choice I thought.

"Hi, sweetie. How do you feel?"

"Totally worn out. I didn't think the recovery process would take such a toll. I'm exhausted."

"I had a feeling that might happen. Dr. Albermarle said your first week back might be rough," she said, heading toward the kitchen.

"Detective? Do you want something to drink? Coffee?"

"Thank you for asking, Mrs. Perault, but no. I can't stay long, or I'd say yes."

"Hey, detective. How's it going?" I asked.

"Oh, things are going OK. I stopped by to see how you're doing and give you an update on the investigation. You feel up to it?"

"Yeah, sure. Let's hear it."

"Well, unfortunately we don't know a whole lot. There was a surveillance camera across the street from where you were attacked, but the image was too fuzzy to get an idea who attacked you. We could see someone run up behind you and hit you on the side of the head. Looks like it might have been a baseball bat. After you went down, the individual gave you a few kicks to the ribs and took off."

"You couldn't see who it was?"

"No, like I said, the image was too fuzzy to make a positive ID, the weather didn't help either. It was a big dude though, that much we do know. Knowing how tall you are, we were able to determine that he's about the same height as your friend Mike Pigliani. We just don't have enough evidence to even come close to making an arrest. Mr. Pigliani's alibi checks out, at least on the surface. His father confirmed that Mike was home at the time you were attacked. We can't prove that he wasn't home, but we can't prove that he was either. And I don't trust his father as far as I could throw him. I'm convinced he's covering for his son; I just can't prove it."

"Huh. Well, that's not good news," I said, contemplating what I planned to say next. Toying with the idea of not telling Detective Sharply anything about my two most recent run-ins with Mike was gaining traction. My mind was a scrambled mess, conflicted over divulging Mike's veiled threats. If I talked to the detective, Mike was sure to find out one way or another. If I didn't talk to the detective, then what Mr. Lewis said might come true... Mike would eventually do something stupid, and people, maybe me, maybe not, would get hurt in the process.

"What's going on, Ashley? You've got worry written all over your face," Detective Sharply stated. When his detective radar was working, nothing escaped him. He saw right through me.

Evidently, my mom heard this as she returned from the kitchen with a look of concern etched on her face.

"Ashley, is something wrong?"

"I don't think I should tell you because it's only going to end badly. But I will."

I took a deep breath before continuing.

"When I went to the coffee shop yesterday with Koko, Mike and his dad walked in. Mike called me a half-breed and dared me to talk to the police again. He got right up in my face and asked me to say something to the cops. He did the same thing to me today at lunch in front of the entire cafeteria. He slapped me on the side of the head, called me half-breed, stole my apple, and yelled at Riley. He said the same things today that he said yesterday at the coffee shop. It's like he wants me to give him a reason to go after me."

"Why didn't you tell me about the coffee shop yesterday?" Mom asked.

"I don't know. I didn't want you to worry."

"Ashley, whether I worry is not up to you, it's not your decision or your responsibility. I'm your mother, I'm going to worry."

"Ugh, I shouldn't have said anything."

I lowered my head to the table.

"You did the right thing Ashley. I don't think Mike will do anything, but just to be sure, I'll have a little chat with him.

I'll see to it he understands that he'd be much better off leaving you alone."

"He's going to come after me, you know that right? I don't have a good feeling about this. There's something not right about him, he's unhinged. And his dad is even scarier than he is."

"Everything will be just fine. Trust me, OK Ashley?"

"Yeah, OK."

I said OK, but I didn't believe it for a second.

"Well, I must get going. I've got tons of criminals to arrest and no time to do it."

While I sat at the dining room table, resigned to my fate, Mom walked Detective Sharply out before she closed and locked the door. I didn't know for certain Mike would make good on his pseudo threats, but I wouldn't bet against it.

"Mom, do you mind if I go and hang out with Koko for a while?"

"No, that's fine. If you did your homework."

"Yeah, I just finished it."

That she didn't insist we sit down at the table and discuss the finer points of sharing information left me a bit puzzled. She wasn't happy that I hadn't mentioned yesterday's confrontation with Mike.

"Great. Hold on a minute, before you go, I've got something for you."

She walked to the back of the apartment, returning half a minute later with a small rectangular box neatly wrapped in bright red paper.

"I was going to wait until Christmas to give this to you but in light of what happened, I think now is a perfect time," she offered, handing me the small present.

"What is this? It's heavy."

I moved the small box up and down in my hand several times, getting a feel for the weight while my mind ran through the innumerable possibilities of what might be inside.

"Oh, I can't stand it anymore, just open it."

Her excitement was palpable, which only served to confuse me even more.

Not wanting to prolong her agony, I tore into the carefully wrapped box with enthusiasm. In a flash of flying paper, the removal revealed the unmistakable outline of a box holding the latest offering from the Apple Corporation, a brand-new iPhone.

I could not have been more stunned as my mouth dropped open and I turned to stare at her in stunned silence.

"Are you kidding? Is this real? An actual iPhone?"

"Yeah, it's the real deal."

"How?"

My question, even though it was none of my business, was a legitimate one. I was the only person I knew that didn't have a smart phone. Money was always so tight that I never even bothered to ask for one. While it was something I wanted, I knew better than to even mention it. To me, the subject was a nonstarter.

"A bunch of people from work chipped in to get it. I had talked about getting you one on several occasions, and after you were attacked, they all got together and talked about it. It's much safer to have one than not they figured."

"I'm stunned."

"I can tell."

I don't think I've ever seen her smile so wide in my life.

"Are you still going to go see Koko?" she asked.

"Huh? Oh, yeah. I completely forgot. Yeah, I think I will. I mean I could stay here and pour over my new phone, but if I did that, I'd be up all night. I'm not saying I'm not excited about it, because I'm over the moon. I just need to ask Koko about some stuff."

"That's fine with me. No problem, your phone will be here when you get back."

Leaving the apartment, I also wondered how Koko would react to me showing up at his place unannounced.

On my way to his apartment, I couldn't help but be repulsed, yet again, by the horrid color on the walls. It struck me as odd that the color sometimes made my stomach turn, other times I didn't mind it at all, and I deduced that it largely depended on my mood. When I was in a bad or depressed mood, the color seemed to make me want to puke; if I were in a good mood, I often didn't notice the color at all. Right now, I was in a puking mood. Stopping at Koko's door, I knocked three times in rapid succession. The slow shuffle of feet across the living room floor and the hollow, muted sounds of four locks on the other side of the door being unlocked were welcome distractions. Koko opened the door and immediately Fred darted into the hallway with an excited meow. Stopping abruptly in the middle of the hallway, Fred looked around, not sure what to do next.

"I'll get him. Sorry about that."

I slowly approached the wide-eyed cat. Bending over to pick him up, I marveled at how solid and muscular he was.

"Thank you, Ashley. That is the first time Fred has ever done that. I am quite surprised."

I handed Fred over to him.

"The first time he's escaped into the hallway?"

"Yes. Well, there are two firsts. That is his first escape attempt and the first time he has allowed anyone other than me to pick him up."

"You're the only person that can pick him up?"

"Please come in." Koko gestured. "Yes, his behavior is highly unusual. He has never allowed anyone to pick him up, not ever. He likes you very much," he admitted as he closed and locked the door.

"Sorry to show up unannounced like this."

"It is OK. You are always welcome here, Ashley."

Smiling, he gently placed Fred onto the floor.

With the weight of the world on my shoulders, I let out a huge sigh and sunk into the comfortable folds of the couch. Fred wasted no time sauntering over to me, rubbing against my leg, his insistent purrs informing me that he craved attention. Despite my protesting ribs, I leaned down to scratch him between his ears.

"How are you Ashley, is everything OK?"

"I'm fine. Wait, no, I'm not. I'm not fine. I'm kind of terrible. I was sitting at lunch today, with Riley and one of her friends, when Mike showed up. He slapped me on the side of the head, took my apple, and then repeated what he said yesterday at the coffee shop. He wants me to talk to the police."

"I think talking to the police would be wise, Ashley. They need to know what is happening."

He sat in the recliner next to the couch.

"Well, that's the problem. I already did. Detective Sharply came by the apartment a little while ago to bring me up to speed on the investigation, and I told him what happened yesterday and today."

"What did he say?"

"He said that he'd talk to Mike and was pretty confident he would be able to convince him to leave me alone."

I straightened up, slowly leaning back onto the cushions of the couch.

"He also said that they got some surveillance video from a camera across the street from where I was attacked. They couldn't get a positive ID on my attacker because the video was too fuzzy or something. But he was pretty sure that whoever it was that attacked me was about the same size as Mike. It's not definitive, but there can't be too many people of Mike's size running around the city."

"Yes, that is true, not many people are equal in physical stature to Mike. Well, this is not good news. The news about the video I mean. I think it is good that you told the detective what happened recently."

"I wish I felt the same way. I told the detective just a little while ago that I didn't have a good feeling about this. I really think Mike is going to come after me."

"What did your mom say?"

"Well, surprisingly, not much. She wasn't happy about me not telling her about what happened in the coffee shop yesterday. I'm not sure why she didn't blow up on me."

"It is difficult to say. She has been through a lot too and may need some time to process things. I think when she is ready to talk, she will."

"Yeah, I guess so."

Fred jumped up onto the couch to sit on my lap.

"Koko, I don't know what to do. There's a very good chance, I think, that Mike is going to do something stupid. I know we've talked about warriors and fear and all that, but what do you do when the thing you fear the most is your enemy?"

"It is difficult to react to something you feel certain is coming while not knowing exactly what that something might be. You are on the defensive for an action you know nothing about. But there is something we can do about this."

He rose from the recliner.

"What's that? I'm listening."

"Have you ever heard of counting coup?"

"Nope. I have no idea what that means."

"I will be right back."

Koko exited the living room to one of the two bedrooms in the back of the apartment.

Fred looked at me and meowed, content as could be as I gazed around the room at the meticulously displayed artwork. Koko returned half a minute later carrying two strange looking sticks.

In his left hand, he held a stick about six feet long with one end curved into a 'U' shape. From the base of the stick to about five feet high, it was covered in what looked like some kind of tanned animal skin, light yellow in color. Along the upper part of the animal skin were five black and white feathers tied to the stick with thin leather straps. The last foot of the stick, where the 'U' shape was located, was covered with thick fur. The 'U' shape was festooned with red tassels affixed to it on which were strung red and white colored beads. The stick in Koko's right hand was much shorter, about thirty-six inches and weighted at one end with a spherical black rock that had been tied with thin strips of leather. The shaft of the stick was covered with an intricate braiding of red and yellow beads. The end opposite the rock had tied to it a tuft of hair that swayed rhythmically as Koko moved the stick through the air. I couldn't begin to fathom what he had in mind.

"These," he said, raising each stick into the air, "are called coup sticks."

"Never heard of a coup stick."

"That is OK. Most people have not. Plains Indians in the Pacific Northwest, the Dakotas, Montana, and Southwestern Canada used to take part in a practice called counting coup. Counting coup was a way for a warrior to prove his courage and bravery. There are many ways to count coup but generally it is done by striking or touching an enemy in battle. The most courageous and heroic way to count coup, however, is to sneak into the encampment of an enemy warrior and touch him with your hand or a coup stick, like one of these, and then escape unharmed."

"All you have to do is touch him with one of those?" I asked, pointing to the sticks he was holding.

"Yes, that is all. It sounds very easy of course, but is, in fact, very difficult. After a battle or operation into enemy territory, the members of the tribe would gather, most often around a fire, and recount their acts of bravery. This is where the term counting coup comes from, the recounting, through storytelling, of their courageous acts. Tribes had different ways of recording coups. Some put feathers on their coup sticks like this one for each counted coup."

He handed me the coup stick in his left hand. I took the stick, which was lighter than I had expected, and examined it closely. The craftsmanship was excellent. All the knots that were attached to the feathers were identical in size and shape and there wasn't a single red or white bead out of place.

"Is this real? I mean is it old?" I asked, looking over the long coup stick.

"No, it is a replica. It is what a real coup stick would have looked like though."

"What about that one?" I asked, pointing to the shorter stick.

"This one," Koko said, taking the long coup stick and handing me the shorter one, "is real. It is quite old, likely from the 1850s or 1860s."

Taking the shorter coup stick in my hand, I noticed the craftsmanship was completely different than the longer replica I had just inspected. At first glance, it appeared crude and rough. Looking closer though, I noticed how remarkably robust it was despite its age. The stone was firmly attached to make it a formidable weapon. The thin leather straps that attached the tuft of animal hair to the shaft were brittle with age. Accordingly, I handled the older stick with great care.

"You can tell it's old. The leather looks kind of brittle. Still, I wouldn't want to get hit with this end." I said, pointing to the end with the round, black stone.

"Yes, you are right. The leather is quite brittle. The coup stick is, ordinarily, not used as a weapon, but some tribes would fashion them into a kind of makeshift club."

Handing the older, shorter coup stick back to Koko, he carefully placed them both on the coffee table in front of me.

"As time passed, counting coup evolved into not just the practice of touching the enemy with a hand or coup stick, but going into the enemies' camp and taking something of value from them. Warriors would seek to take the personal weapons or horses of their enemy. Warriors would return to their tribe with their spoils to prove their bravery."

"So, a warrior would go into the enemies camp, look around for their horses and weapons, take them, and then return to their own tribe?"

"Yes, and to do so unharmed was the ultimate way of proving your courage and bravery, which, in turn, proved your value to the tribe as a whole."

"I don't get it. Why not just go into the enemy's camp and kill him? Wouldn't that solve the problem?"

"You must understand, Ashley, that to these native people, killing the enemy only proved that you could kill the enemy. Killing the enemy was not a major accomplishment as it did not establish your courage in the face of fear. Any First Nation individual that was reasonably skilled with a bow and arrow could kill the enemy from a great distance with ease. This might be easy to do, but it does not require the warrior to face his or her fears and to conquer them. Do you see?"

"I think so. I mean, that makes sense to a point."

Obviously, I wasn't quite understanding what Koko was getting at because he said,

"Think about it in a different way. If a warrior goes into the camp of his enemy and kills him or shoots him from a distance with a bow and arrow and kills him, what has he gained? He has learned nothing of himself, of how he will react when he truly faces his fears. And there is something else to consider: when a warrior no longer has an enemy, what then? What is the purpose of a warrior that has no enemy? A warrior with no purpose in life is a very sad thing. How can a warrior with no purpose learn to face his fears?"

"Okay, all of those points I understand. Well, they made sense then, in the past. But what about now? We don't live in times where people go on raiding parties or use bows and arrows to settle their differences."

I'm sure I sounded rather incredulous.

"You are right about all of that, Ashley, to a point. No, we no longer go on raiding parties, not in the conventional sense. We don't settle our innumerable differences with bows and arrows either. Obviously, killing people is wrong. Currently, you cannot just go into the house or business of your enemy and take something that is valuable to them to prove that you are courageous and can face your fears either. That is called stealing. Doing all these things is certainly against the law, and I encourage you to stay away from all of them."

"So, how does counting coup apply to this day and age. How does it apply to me?"

"Ah. That is the question I have been waiting to hear from you."

"It is?"

"Yes, because it tells me that you understand the principles that were used in the distant past can be applied to the problems we are facing today. You may not yet understand how you can apply ancient principles to your own world, but you will."

"Well, that's good to know. But I still don't see how it's possible."

"In time, it will all make perfect sense."

Seventeen

I hoped Koko was right. Counting coups sounded like a great idea hundreds of years ago. How counting coup could be applied to me in the here and now, I had no idea.

"I have a feeling you're going to tell me that people count coup even today."

"Yes, this is exactly what I am going to tell you. Everyone does it; they just don't call it counting coup. They may call it 'facing your fears,' or they may define it as 'information gathering.' Depending on your goal, counting coups can be very broadly defined. When you faced your fear of being rejected when you asked Riley to the Christmas dance, you were counting coup. Every time Mike calls you a half-breed, you correct him. Right?"

"Well, almost every time. All I do is tell him that my name is Ashley."

"Yes, precisely. That is evidence of you facing your fears. That is counting coup. We no longer live in a world where a warrior can just take whatever he wants from his enemy to prove he has courage. Counting coup is much more subtle now, but it can still be just as effective."

"How else can I count coup when it comes to Mike?"

"A great place to start is by trying to understand him, learn what makes him tick. Every piece of information is valuable, no matter how small. When you understand your enemy, you will better understand how to defeat him. Businesses do this all the time."

"Businesses count coup?"

"In a manner of speaking, but they call it by different names. Obviously, a business is not a person. Sometimes this can be defined as corporate espionage, which is illegal of course. Other times, businesses study the products of their competitors, to see how they themselves can be better. Some companies study how their competition operates, how they attract customers. Now, do these companies do these things to prove their courage and to face their fears? No, of course not. But they are attempting to understand the competition just the same. They are learning to face the enemy, which, in this case, happens to be another company."

"Yeah, OK. But I'm not a company. I'm just a kid in high school."

"Yes, of course you are. But like I said, you have already been counting coup. You did this with your interactions with Riley and Mike. Whether you are learning more about your enemy, or you are facing your fears of rejection, you are counting coup. It is all about perspective Ashley, because counting coup can take many forms."

"So, if I'm facing my fears of dealing with Mike or I'm trying to get over my fears of talking to Riley without sounding like an idiot, those can be considered counting coup?"

"Yes"

"Huh. Okay, that doesn't sound too hard."

"Instead of thinking about it being easy or hard, frame it differently, perhaps as more of a challenge to be met and then overcome."

"Why is that?"

"Again, this is all about perspective. By instinctively defining a hurdle, no matter what it may be, as being hard or easy, you automatically place a limit on your ability to achieve it. By redefining an obstacle as merely a challenge to be met or overcome, you change your whole mindset. It now seems possible instead of impossible."

"This is a lot to take in all at once. I mean, I think I get it. And, on the surface, it sounds easy. But if it sounds easy, that means it probably isn't."

"This is true, it does sound easy. But conquering one's fears is a lifelong process, so it is not easy or hard. It is just something that must be done. Most people do not undertake such a process. For them, the process itself is too frightening. These people are not truly living, they are existing."

"This is starting to make my head spin."

"We shall leave it here then. I want you to think about what it means to count coup. Try it for yourself. Everything that instills fear can be used to count coup. The best way to count coup is to start small, being careful not to overwhelm yourself in the beginning. But the key is to start."

Leaving Koko's place with much to think about, I figured that counting coup by starting small was a pretty good idea. But from a practical standpoint, I had no idea how I would begin this process.

Eighteen

My first conscious opportunity to count coup arrived several days later in a way I hadn't anticipated. After lunch, Riley, Niki, and I headed to the Yorktown High Auditorium where the entire student body assembled to hear a distinguished alumnus speak. Entering the auditorium, I motioned for Riley and Niki to take their seats first while I snuck in behind. We were sitting quietly, making small talk, when I peered to my left to see someone squeezing down the aisle with the likely intention of taking the only empty seat as far as the eye could see, right next to me. It was Mike Pigliani. Here I was, in a cavernous room filled with over a thousand people, and Neanderthal Mike had to be right there. What were the odds?

"Great, what's next?" I said under my breath as Mike inched his way down the aisle.

"What's wrong?" Riley asked.

"Guess who's here? On my left."

Mike squeezed his way into the seat next to me in what I could only describe as a distinct lack of grace and absolutely no subtlety. Leaning forward to look past me, Riley's eyes grew wide as she recognized Mike.

"Not good."

"What's wrong?" Niki asked as she leaned forward, too. "Oh." She had answered her own question. "Yeah, that's not good."

After settling into his seat, Mike turned his massive head to the right, looking directly into my eyes. He didn't even smile.

Without saying a word, he simply turned his head front and center as if I didn't exist.

In that singular moment, I learned that the only thing more frightening than knowing what to expect from your enemy was not knowing. Being caught completely off guard by behavior that ran against the grain of everything you thought might happen was tortuous. Further throwing me off was that he didn't smell of body odor and cigarettes. He didn't smell of anything.

I was starting to sweat as my heart rate increased. As the fear inside me grew, I briefly entertained the notion of counting coup, but I didn't know where to start. I absolutely did not want to start a conversation with Mike. With no clue what he might do, I wouldn't have been surprised if he threw an elbow straight to my head. But nothing happened. Riley appeared both terrified and shocked as she stared straight ahead. We sat there, the four of us, not saying a word as the distinguished speaker walked across the stage and talked for almost an hour. Thankfully, we were told not to expect a pop quiz on the presentation because I had no idea what she said or why she was even there. Additionally, while I thought of counting coup in the presence of Mike, the idea was quickly forgotten. When the speaker's presentation ended, Mike got up from his seat and left the auditorium. He didn't say a single word, didn't even look at me. Maybe Detective Sharply had talked to Mike and gotten through to him, but I had my doubts.

"Well, that was weird." Riley said as we stood up to leave.

"Yeah, not what I was expecting," I replied.

"I really don't like that guy," Niki added.

I had to concur. Mike's behavior was inexplicable, completely out of character for him. The more I thought about it, the more concerned I became. I was certain Detective Sharply had talked to him and that was probably why he had acted in the way that he did. What I couldn't discern was whether Mike had decided to leave me alone. My intuition told me that things were going to get worse before they got better.

Nineteen

The next few days were as normal as I could have expected, given the circumstances. I got caught up with my schoolwork. Riley, Niki and I hung out at lunch every single day, which was nice, and I neither saw, nor heard, from Mike. It was as if nothing had happened. The bruising on my ribs and face changed from deep reds and purples to the more muted colors of yellow and brown. It was especially pleasing to see the swelling on my face reduced considerably.

I was beginning to feel somewhat normal again until one day, after lunch as Riley, Niki, and I had stopped by my locker so I could drop off a textbook, things escalated yet again as I had feared they might. The three of us were about to head our separate ways when I was cornered by three of Mike's friends as they forced their way between Riley and Niki, and me, effectively isolating me from them.

"Yo' where're you going, dipshit?" the lead bully asked, pushing me back into the row of lockers behind me.

I didn't know his name, but I recognized him. His voice was a dead ringer for the person who had encouraged Mike to throw the snowball at me several weeks ago. He was skinny with long, lazy, unkempt blonde hair that frequently fell over his eyes. He rarely moved his hair back with his hand, instead preferring to throw his head back whiplashing the hair backward over his skull. It was more of a statement, one announcing his confidence and bravado, both of which appeared forced and false. Wearing jeans at least two sizes larger than they needed to be, a once white T-shirt two sizes too small, and basketball shoes with the laces untied, everything about him was a poorly maintained façade. Slightly shorter than I was, he leaned forward on his toes to appear taller.

"I was just headed to the store, figured you needed some deodorant. Maybe some toothpaste for your friends. You gotta start them early, you know?" I replied, pointing to the two standing just behind shorty.

I was instantly angry by the confrontation, but I wasn't the slightest bit intimidated. More than anything I was nervous about an altercation, especially in front of Riley, Niki, and a hallway full of people. Being the center of attention, for any reason, was a detestable experience.

"Don't let him talk to you like that, Wayne. Beat his ass!" the similarly attired goon to the left and behind Wayne offered.

His name is Wayne, that figures. Waynes the world over always seems to end up in trouble. Science has yet to understand why.

"Yeah, beat his ass, Wayne!" the third goon added. This goon was hanging back a bit, evidently not wanting to get too close. He seemed the type that hadn't had an original thought pass between his ears in a painfully long period of time.

All movement and conversation in the wide hallway had completely stopped. For five long and very awkward seconds, no one spoke or moved a muscle. Wayne stared at me, not blinking, weighing the options in his head when the decision was made for him.

"Yeah Wayne, try something."

The voice was deep, almost cavernous and deadly serious. From behind Wayne, the gathering of students parted as four of the most popular students at Yorktown High approached. The cavernous voice belonged to Murphy McDaniel, senior defensive end for the Yorktown High football team and one who was being actively recruited by every major college football program in the country. He was one of the few people in school who was bigger than Mike Pigliani. He wore blue jeans, his varsity letter jacket festooned with patches of the many school records he had shattered and Chuck Taylor sneakers approximately 27 sizes larger than mine. I recognized the other three individuals but didn't know their names. They were also football players and very physically imposing in their letter jackets.

Wayne turned his head to the left, but I could still see how large his eyes became upon seeing Murphy pull up directly behind him.

"This ain't none of your business Murphy," Wayne offered, the conviction and false confidence in him disappearing as his voice sounded an octave higher than only moments before.

"Yeah, Murphy, it ain't none of your business," the third goon said as his head panned rapidly from side to side, looking for a sympathetic face in the crowd but finding none.

One of Murphy's teammates walked right up to goon number three, intentionally invading his personal space, remaining silent, daring him to utter another word. They stood nose to nose for a moment before the goon came to his senses.

"I'm gonna be late for class," he uttered, looking to his left wrist at his nonexistent watch. He turned and disappeared into the crowd leaving Wayne with only one soldier to back him up.

Simultaneously and without a word or signal, every person in the hallway walked forward until they were shoulder to shoulder, leaving Wayne and his cohort with no means of escape.

"Your move, Wayne," someone commanded from within the crowd.

"That's right Wayne. Time to man up and decide," Murphy added, stepping forward into Wayne's personal space. Murphy never broke eye contact, showing no sign of emotion, his intentions were still crystal clear.

"You … you ain't a part of this Murphy," Wayne replied. His nervous eyes darted left and right as he looked for support among the crowd.

"Stop looking around. You think they're going to help you? They won't. You got yourself into this situation; it's up to you to get out of it."

Knowing he'd been beaten; Wayne did the only thing he knew how to do and backed down. Turning away from me, he attempted to slide through the crowd, but Murphy sidestepped left and blocked his path.

"You're not done yet. You owe Ashley and everyone in this hallway an apology," Murphy demanded.

Wayne's level of discomfort increased dramatically as he realized the situation he was in. He turned his attention away from Murphy to face me.

"I'm sorry." he said, avoiding eye contact.

I nodded.

He turned to face the students crowding the hallway.

"I'm sorry."

He made his announcement while looking above the heads of those before him.

"Now take your little understudy here and go away," Murphy ordered.

Wayne and his friend melted into the crowd without another word.

As soon as they were gone, I felt the tension in my shoulders melt away. A moment later, the gathered crowd dissipated as everyone hustled to beat the tardy bell.

I stepped forward, extending my right hand to Murphy.

"Thanks, Murphy. You didn't have to do that, but I'm glad you did," I offered, shaking his hand.

"But I did. I did have to do it, Ashley. The world doesn't have to be the way it has always been. We can change it, in real time, if we just have the courage to step forward," he replied.

"Yeah, you're right. I just wish more people understood that."

"Maybe they do. You saw it yourself. Every person in this hallway stopped, and not to wait and see what would happen. They stopped to back you up if you needed it. That was spontaneous, unplanned … organic, you might say."

"So, there might be hope after all."

"There's always hope. Always. I've got to run; I don't want to be late for class. I'll catch up with you later, OK?"

"Yeah, OK. Thanks again, Murphy."

He turned and disappeared down the hallway.

This was the moment I came to the profound realization that I wasn't alone in my struggles at Yorktown High. This became clearer the next day as Murphy and several of his teammates joined Riley, Niki, and I at lunch. We all spent the rest of the school year together at lunch, which felt terrific.

Twenty

Several days later, having spent a few hours after school working on a group project, I started for home as light snow danced and reflected in the streetlights dotting the sidewalk. The utter silence of falling snow mesmerized me. How could so much movement create almost no sound?

Trundling down the sidewalk, what sounded like a trashcan lid being dropped onto concrete broke the peaceful silence as the tinny crash reverberated off concrete and brick. Approaching the source of the sound, I slowed when a form appeared from a narrow alleyway on my right. Through the gently falling snow there was just enough dim streetlight for me to be certain that the silhouette standing in front of me could belong to only Mike Pigliani. His mass, form, and cocky body language were unmistakable. I stopped in my tracks, frozen not from the biting cold, but from fear.

He approached slowly, sneakers pulverizing the crust of snow beneath him. My mind imagined bones snapping under his feet with every step, a Terminator pulverizing the skulls of his enemies beneath his skeletal, metal feet.

He smiled, and even in the muted light of the streetlamps, I could discern the yellow crooked teeth behind his evil sneer. Turning to my right to find an escape option, I spotted another large individual advancing toward me from the direction opposite Mike. Squinting in the darkness, trying to determine the identity of the new form, it took a few seconds to realize that it was the silhouette belonging to Mike's father, his paunch easily visible as he waddled his way forward.

Turning my attention back to Mike revealed his accelerating pace as his father closed the gap. I was trapped. I glanced to my right, looking for a door to open and dart through, only to find a blank, unconcerned brick wall staring back at me. Stepping to my left, I determined to run into the street to make my escape. Taking my chances with traffic on the slick, snow covered streets was a more favorable alternative than standing my ground and letting the Piglianis envelop me.

At that moment I remembered I had a secret weapon, my new cell phone. I could dial 911 in a matter of seconds. I retrieved the phone from my pocket but in my haste couldn't remember how to bypass the security screen. I tried to input my numbered pass code, but the phone wouldn't accept any input from my gloved hands.

"Run, half-breed. Ha, ha."

Mike sneered, the crunching snow under his feet assaulting my ears as the sound reverberated around me, getting closer.

Taking Mike's last statement as sound advice, I turned left, taking two quick steps toward the street when my vision became a blend of colors as the back of my neck exploded in pain. It felt like two white-hot pokers had been jammed into my neck just below the base of my skull. Streaks of black and gray interspersed with the bright lights of streetlamps and the sparkling of falling snow.

With the massive jolt of intense pain coursing throughout my entire body, my legs gave out underneath me, no longer up to the task of carrying me away from danger, no longer able to do what I asked of them. I crumbled to the sidewalk in a heap, my chin striking the concrete with a sickening thud. Confusion overwhelmed me as I lay on the sidewalk, the left side of my face buried in the snow. I tried to stand, willing noncompliant legs to carry my weight so I could run away. To keep Mike and his father from advancing, I swung my arms, but they didn't respond to any command my brain tried to send them. Through blurry vision, the bodies of my assaulters hovered over me, seeming far away and at the same time so huge.

My face sunk deeper into the snow as my muscles relaxed and from my tilted vantage point I spotted my brand-new iPhone sitting just beyond the reach of my right hand, itself half buried. I slowly extended my arm to grab it only to witness a large black boot crash down upon it, shattering the screen and my hopes of calling for help. Watching my phone being pulverized under the boot of a Pigliani was soul crushing. There was nothing sacred left in the world, no matter how small.

"See. Now wasn't that easy?" Mike's dad asked.

"Yeah, piece of cake. It surprises me every time they don't run," Mike replied, kicking me hard in the ribs.

"Uhhnnnggg!"

"Oh, did that hurt?" Mike asked in a mocking tone.

"Help! Help me!" I screamed.

Only it wasn't a scream. What came out of my mouth was a groaning, scratchy whimper. Commanding my voice to scream with as much intensity of feeling as I could possibly muster, my mind shrieked, shouting with unrelenting ferocity; my voice, however, was barely a whisper.

"Go ahead and shout... worthless maggot," Mike's dad said.

He stepped over me, leaning in to place his face directly in front of mine.

With my faculties slowly beginning to return, I detected alcohol and cigarettes. I wretched as the horrifying combination of smells assaulted me. Then, he spit in my face.

"Did you just spit in his face?" Mike asked.

"Yeah. Shouldn't have though. Total waste of spit."

"Ha, no kidding."

"Come on, let's get him loaded into the van," Mike's dad said as he leaned over to touch the back of my neck, causing sharp stabbing pains to erupt. His hand was thick, calloused, displaying a roughness born from a lack of compassion, closely mirroring his very soul.

They bent down and picked me up, holding me from under my armpits, Mike on the left, his dad on the right, dragging me half a block up the street to a beat-up black van that had been sitting patiently on the side of the street.

"Let go of me."

"Oh, OK. Yeah, that sounds reasonable. We'll just let you go and pray you don't mention this to anyone. Shut your mouth," Mike commanded.

Propping me up against the passenger door of the van, Mike's dad unlocked and opened the large sliding door while Mike leaned heavily with his right hand on my chest, both holding me upright and ensuring I didn't make a run for it.

The two grabbed me under the arms again, physically pitching me through the large open door with enough force that I collided with the left side of the van and fell to the bare metal floor in a heap. Piling in behind me, Mike sat down while his dad slammed the door shut and walked around to the driver's side and got in. Laying on the floor in a fetal position, I smelled dirt, oil and the distinct odor of urine. The combination of smells forced me to cough involuntarily, causing my now re-injured ribs to scream in pain. Why, I wondered, would anyone use the inside of a van to take a leak? It dawned on me that I might not be the first person subjected to this kind of inhumane treatment at the hands of Mike and his father. I was in very serious trouble, and I knew it.

"Give me the keys," Mr. Pigliani demanded of Mike as he turned to face us.

"I don't have them."

"Mike, I swear …" He hesitated. "You do this every time. I hand you the keys, then you lose them."

"Wrong. You never hand me the keys. You lose them and then blame me for it. You know, 'cause you're never wrong," Mike shot back. "Maybe if you stopped for a second and thought about what you did with them instead of blaming me, you'd realize that you left them in the ignition. Again."

"Wiseass," Mr. Pigliani muttered under his breath as he cupped the keys in his hand before turning the key to start the van. The motor turned over, wheezed, popped and then died. A second and third attempt achieved the same result.

"Mike, get out and push. Maybe we can bump start it."

"That'd be a great idea if this van wasn't, you know, an automatic." Mike answered, clearly mocking his father.

"Keep it up, Mike. Remember what happened last time?"

On the fourth attempt, the van started with a sputtering cough, allowing Mr. Pigliani to pull into traffic. Though I could barely see him, I sensed a palpable degree of tension wash off Mike as the van wheezed into life.

Bouncing along the pothole-strewn streets of the city, each jarring jolt sent waves of searing pain coursing through my ribs, and I couldn't help but wonder what my future held. The pain in my chin was tremendous, so I reached up looking for the source with my left hand. The back of the van was dark so I couldn't see the smear of blood, but I knew it was there. The fall to the pavement had split my chin open and I could only hope that enough blood had oozed out onto the snow to mark the scene of the crime. I realized that even if it had, the falling snow would soon cover it and all traces that I had been there at all.

A second wave of panic began to flood over me as I became more aware of the peril, I was in. I knew I had to pull it together if I was going to survive this ordeal. As I turned over to sit up, I felt the red marble bear in my left jeans pocket press into my thigh. I thought of the bear and what it represented; my courage and strength. Koko said the bear was to remind me to face my fears even, and perhaps especially, when the odds were stacked against me.

Being assaulted and thrown into a van against my will certainly qualified, I thought.

I didn't dare reach into my pocket to retrieve the small talisman. Dark though it may have been in the van, Mike and his dad would most assuredly discover what I was holding. I couldn't risk it. Instead, I decided to partake in another tactic Koko, and I had discussed, counting coup. I would face my fears (Mike and his dad in this case) and count coup, gathering all the information I could.

"What did you hit me with?"

I struggled to sit up in the dark and smelly van.

"Oh. Ha, ha. Dad's an expert with a stun gun. Hit you right in the back of the neck. Hurt, didn't it?"

"Why? Why are you doing this?"

"You know why. Now shut up."

His voice held a measure of calm I didn't share.

"Go ahead and tell him, Mike. It don't matter anyways."

Mike let out a large sigh as if complying with his father was a massive inconvenience.

"You talked to the police again, simple as that. I was kidding around when I asked you to talk to them. I didn't think you'd do it. You're not too bright, are you?"

I briefly considered asking Mike who, between the two of us, got better grades, but decided against it as I didn't want to risk angering him further.

"What? You started this whole thing. Why couldn't you just leave me alone?"

"Hey pops, turn on the interior light, would you?"

B nvThe light flicked on, illuminating the cavernous interior of the van. I turned my head toward the center to see Mike's enormous mass spin on his butt, legs bent inward at a forty-five-degree angle. He stopped his spin to face me, smiled, and kicked me in the face. A bright flash of light flooded my vision as I heard the bones in my nose flatten with a sickening crunch. I smelled and tasted blood as I fell over and mercifully passed out.

Twenty-One

Consciousness returned, but slowly. The entirety of my face was a conglomeration of pain except for my nose, which felt oddly numb, and I had a headache that far surpassed the ones I experienced after my recent attack and hospital stay.

Pushing up with my arms and locking my elbows, I threw up, mostly blood judging by the sickening taste of it in my mouth. Sitting up and leaning against the side of the van slightly eased the pain in my head. Breathing through my nose proved impossible. This was unsurprising, considering it had been completely rearranged by Mike's vicious kick. With the side of the van for support, I reached up, gently touching my face. Unable to feel my nose, my fingers told me there was a rather severe gash running across the top, just below eye level. Also evident was the already considerable swelling. How long I had been unconscious was not. I had been out long enough for the bleeding to stop and the swelling to be very well developed. Gazing forward from the back of the windowless van toward the windshield, the faintest slivers of sunlight penetrated the inky blackness ahead of us. If I could see the first rays of sunlight of the breaking dawn, it meant we were headed in an Easterly direction.

With no idea where we were, it was easy to surmise that we were no longer in the city. The understated and ever-present din of city life was noticeably absent. No rush of traffic, no honking of horns as the cabbies jockeyed for position between lights. Wherever we were was eerily silent, the only sounds coming from the squeaks, rattles and chirps of the van as it rocked back and forth on a chassis that was obviously well past its prime.

"Hey, turn on the light again, I think small fry just threw up." Mike commanded.

As the light flickered on, I instinctively threw my arms against my face, bracing for another kick. The soft glow from the interior light contradicted the terror I felt as I cowered from the violence I felt certain was coming.

"God, you're such a coward. Relax, I'm not going to kick you. Well, not right now anyway. Put your arms down, you wimp."

Slowly lowering my arms to my sides, I sat up as straight as my injured ribs would comfortably allow. Mike had moved to the other side of the van, leaning against the closed sliding door. I wondered why he wasn't sitting in the passenger seat next to his dad. My guess was he was back here with me to make sure I didn't try anything. As he leaned his considerable mass against the large sliding door, the image of it sliding open and him falling out backward to the pavement popped into my head. To my disappointment, it didn't happen, in fact nothing happened.

"So, did the little maggot throw up?"

"Yeah, a little bit. Mostly blood. It stinks."

"It don't matter. We're going to ditch the van in the woods and burn it anyway."

Mr. Pigliani's comment filled me with a sense of dread as it gave me a small hint of what was to come. We were headed into the woods, that much I knew. What woods and where they were, I had no idea. Instinctively, I placed my left hand over the area where the small marble bear Koko had gifted me sat warmly in my pocket. I had to be strong. I had to be the bear, knowing that to survive, I had to find a way to even the odds. Right now, I was hopelessly outmatched. It was time, again, to start counting coup.

"Where are you taking me?"

I opted for the direct route in my quest for information. Neither of them answered. I decided to leave it at that, not wanting to be subjected to another boot to the face.

Driving for what seemed like forever, no one spoke. As the sun slowly rose, I used its light to examine the inside of the van, searching for anything I might be able to use to my advantage. Sharing the back of the van with Neanderthal Mike and I were two large tires. Far too large for the van, they appeared to be off an eighteen-wheeler or moving van. Neither had rims. Sitting just in front of the tires in a loose pile were at least half a dozen license plates; a few were shiny and new, the rest, dented and old. None of them matched and some appeared to be from various surrounding states. I was certain they had been stolen and had every reason to believe the van was stolen as well.

My view from the back of the van forward was limited as I searched for something, anything, I could use to glean even the slightest hint of information. From my vantage point, I could see, in the center of the van's dashboard, a small circular clock. Glancing briefly at Mike before leaning painfully forward and up slightly to get a better view, revealed it read 9:15. If the clock was still operating, then I had just gathered my first tiny bit of valuable information.

I knew I had been attacked and kidnapped sometime between 5:30 and 6:00 p.m. the night before. With no idea how long it had taken us to get out of the city, it was now past dawn, so I could easily determine that we had traveled many hundreds of miles. Mentally calculating the possible miles we had driven, I looked again at the clock on the dashboard. It hadn't moved. My heart sank. Beyond the fact of knowing it was early morning, I had no idea what time it was. I let out a quiet, gentle sigh, not wanting to attract the attention of my kidnappers. Contemplating my failure at counting coup, I realized that I had not actually failed. Having tried, I just didn't get the result that I had expected or wanted. But at least I had tried. Just like asking Riley out to the Christmas Dance, which she had ever so politely declined, I had at the very least, tried. Without even realizing it, I had just boosted my own spirits.

Looking to the windshield again, a large green highway sign flashed into view as we passed underneath it. The combination of bad angle, the van's speed and the rising sun made reading the sign impossible. I had to keep working.

"Dad, you just missed the exit."

"No, I didn't. We're not even close to the exit. Moron."

How Mike could determine that his dad had missed the exit from his vantage point in the back of the van escaped me. I wanted to blurt out, "Yeah, you moron! Get your head in the game!" That would only earn me another beating, so I kept quiet.

Another half hour or so passed before Mike's dad began shifting uncomfortably in his seat. I considered he might be stiff and sore from sitting and driving for so long, but as time and miles flew underneath the van's protesting chassis, he became more and more agitated. He was losing patience.

The elder Pigliani shifted and turned in his seat, his head swiveling on his gargantuan neck. He began muttering under his breath, vocalizations that were, for the most part, unintelligible, but I did catch the odd four-letter word every now and again. It became increasingly clear that we were lost.

Evidently, Mike had been right; we had missed an exit. Mike had fallen asleep and was propped up in the corner formed from the back of the passenger seat and the side of the van. He was out cold, having no knowledge of the situation he had correctly predicted.

"Goddamnit!" Mike's dad yelled, pounding a sledgehammer sized fist against the steering wheel. The blow caused the van to slew wildly to the left as the ancient vehicle leaned heavily on worn out springs, threatening to roll over. I was thrown sideways, landing in a heap on top of Mike who awoke with a start.

"What the hell! Get off me, half-breed."

He grabbed to push me off him as his dad yanked the wheel to the right to correct the dangerous skid. Flying, this time toward the left side of the van, I landed halfway up the side before falling to the floor with a loud thump. My ribs and head renewed their attack on my senses, the pain so severe, I was on the verge of passing out.

"Mike. Get up here." Mike's dad commanded as he fought to bring the van under control.

"I'm coming! Calm down!" Mike yelled back, squeezing his mass into the front seat.

"Help me figure out where we are."

"Yeah, yeah. You don't have to yell."

For the next minute, neither Pigliani spoke as they scanned the road ahead and to the sides looking for recognizable landmarks.

"I have no idea where we are," Mike offered.

"Gee, no kidding? Thanks, Sherlock. You are worthless."

"I'm worthless? You're the one driving! I told you we missed the exit. I told you!"

Mr. Pigliani erupted with instantaneous speed and aggression. Whipping his head right to look at his son, his right arm shot out with alarming ferocity, striking Mike in the mouth with the back of his open hand. Mike recoiled from the blow, hitting the back of his head against the closed passenger window. The dull thump of Mike's head striking glass contradicted the sharp crack of his father's strike.

"Not another word!" Mike's dad screamed.

Sniffing loudly and wiping his split and bleeding lip, a single tear escaped the edge of Mike's left eye as he rubbed the back of his head.

Quickly averting my gaze to not fall victim, once again, to Mike's wrath, proved to be a wise decision as he turned to look at me.

The van groaned and creaked its way eastward, and I came to the realization that Mike and his dad had a very strange relationship. For Mike, aggression and violence were a daily occurrence. Counting coup. I understood, to some degree at least, where his violent tendencies were rooted. Counting coup. If Mike was raised by a father with the aggression issues Mr. Pigliani clearly had, it was no surprise he had issues as well. In an instant, I felt sorry for him. Quite often I felt lost and alone growing up without my father, but I knew it was better than growing up under the circumstances Mike was enduring daily. Somehow, I had to use this information to my advantage. Suddenly, I had the beginnings of a plan.

"I'm going to pull over. We need to get gas anyway."

Slowing, we left the highway at the next available exit as the van leaned on its old, worn-out springs. Coming to a stop as the exit ramp leveled off at the nearest intersection, we turned right toward what I could only guess was a gas station. Mike sat, pouting in the passenger seat, sulking and nursing his swollen, split lip. The van slowed again and turned right, bouncing up and down on the lip of the gas station's driveway. Mr. Pigliani pulled up to an unoccupied pump and stopped, shutting off the van while blowing out a long, wheezing sigh. The bright overhead lights of the gas station illuminated all but the very back of the inside of the van. Briefly looking around the space confirmed what I already suspected... aside from the old truck tires and the small stack of license plates, there was nothing else of value. Nothing to aid me in my predicament.

"If he tries anything," Mike's dad said, looking at his son and gesturing toward the back of the van with his right thumb, "rip his tongue out and feed it to him."

Mike sat dutifully on the other side of the van, nodding. A wave of frigid air flooded the inside of the van as Mr. Pigliani opened the driver's side door and exited, slamming it behind him. It was Mike this time that let out an exasperated sigh after the door had closed.

"Man, I really hate him sometimes."

"Why do you let him treat him you like that?"

I was unable to keep my fraying nerves from making my voice crack.

He turned in his seat to face me.

"Half-breed, what am I going to do? He's my old man. What would you do if your old man smacked you around all the time?"

"I have no idea. My dad died before I was born," I replied, much preferring the use of 'dad' to Mike's less respectful 'old man' honorific.

"Huh, that sucks. What happened?"

Why he cared enough to ask was beyond me.

"He was shot and beaten to death by a gang out in California."

"So, he couldn't stand up for himself. Big wimp just like you huh?"

"Always judging, aren't you? No, he was a Navy SEAL. About as far from a big wimp as a person could get."

"Damn. No kidding. Your old man was a Navy SEAL?"

"Yeah. For about ten years or so."

"A gang huh? They catch the morons that did it?"

"Yeah. There were eight of them, I think. They were all convicted and given life sentences from what my mom told me."

I was surprised that he and I were having a civil conversation.

"They should have gotten the death penalty. A life sentence is too easy."

"They got what they got. I don't know whether it's right or wrong."

"Oh, come on half-breed. They deserved to die. Do to them, what they did to your old man is what I'm saying."

His voice was full of conviction and rightness.

"There may be tyrants and murderers, and for a time, they can seem invincible, but in the end, they always fall. Think of it: always," I countered.

"What? What on earth does that mean? Sounds like some kind of movie quote."

"It is a movie quote. It's also a real quote by a real man named Gandhi, played by Ben Kingsley in the movie, Gandhi."

"Gandhi? Never saw it. Wasn't he from Pakistan or Israel or something?"

"No, India."

"Yeah, same thing."

An expert in geography, Mike was not.

"What about you, Mike? You like movies?" I asked, trying to steer the conversation away from his geographical ignorance and further confrontation.

"Yeah, I'm a total movie buff. Action movies mostly, you know, Dirty Harry, the Die-Hard movies, stuff like that."

That Mike and I had anything in common, I found astonishing.

"Yeah, those are all good. Of all the Die-Hard movies, the first one is my favorite."

"Yeah, same here. So, what about this Gandhi dude? What's his story?"

"He was largely responsible for freeing India from British rule in the late 1940s through the practice of nonviolence. He believed nonviolence as a form of protest was more effective than anything else."

"Nonviolence? That's crazy."

"Yeah, at first it does sound crazy. But you know? It worked. Over 300 million people were granted independence from British rule. Gandhi was so far ahead of his time. He proved that violence only creates more violence until it eventually spirals out of control."

"My old man would never go for that. All he understands is violence."

"That's sad. At some point the cycle of violence must stop."

"Yeah, it is sad. But it's worked so far."

I didn't have the energy to argue with him. Clearly, the way he and his dad were living their lives wasn't working. Mike would certainly take offense if I disagreed with him. He would likely argue that I believed my way of life was far superior to his. Seeing no point in incurring his wrath again, I kept my opinions to myself.

"Well, it's a good movie. You should look it up."

"Yeah, maybe I will. But only when The Tyrant isn't around." Mike replied, indicating with an extended thumb his father pumping gas outside.

"Yeah, good idea."

"What the hell are you looking at?" Mike's dad shouted.

Mike and I looked at each other as if to confirm we heard the same thing.

"Great, what now?" Mike asked, shifting his weight to look outside.

Mr. Pigliani's tirade continued, growing exponentially louder with every passing second and as those seconds passed, his obscenities became more and more filled with rage.

Making sense of what the confrontation was about was impossible, but I knew that if it didn't resolve itself soon, the situation would get much worse. Shifting in his seat, Mike leaned forward to peer out of the left side of the van to get a better look at what was going on. The shouting abruptly stopped, followed a moment later by the sound of glass shattering. The tinkling sound of broken glass bouncing on pavement forced Mike out of his indecision as he opened the passenger door and began to step out into the cold when his father ran back to the van, opened the driver's side door, and jumped in.

"Get back in the van, moron. What were you going to do? Leave him in here by himself?"

"What happened?"

"Some slant-eyed gook kept staring at me. He should have minded his own business."

The elder Pigliani started the van and put it into motion.

"What'd you do to him?"

"Punched him in the face right through the window. I've always wanted to do that. You should have seen it … knocked him out cold."

"Your hand is bleeding."

Mr. Pigliani looked down at his right hand as he steered the ancient van onto the side streets.

"Huh. Yeah, I guess it is. Whoa, that really hurts. I didn't feel a thing at first."

"Why was he staring at you?"

"Hell, I have no idea. Who really cares? He got what was coming to him, I can tell you that. We have to get out of here. No need to get the cops on our tail."

"Yeah, this place is going to be crawling with them in nothing flat. Let's get out of here."

"Shut up and get in the back. I don't want maggot getting frisky and trying to jump out the side door."

Heading to the on ramp and accelerating onto the highway, Mike's dad kept his foot down, pushing the derelict van well beyond the speed limit to put as much distance between us and the gas station as possible.

A mile or two down the road, the high-pitched wail of sirens echoed in the distance. My heart sank, realizing that by the time the police arrived, we would be so far away it wouldn't make a difference. My only hope was that someone got the van's license plate number, or the gas station had an operable security camera that might make identification possible. My time was running out.

Twenty-Two

Driving onward for another hour or so, Mike and his dad alternated between yelling at each other with alarming aggression and total silence, all to figure out where the wrong turn had been made. The yelling was nearly unbearable as both Piglianis were so filled with rage; it was hard for me to fathom.

The silence was nearly as bad. It gave me time to simmer in my own dreadful thoughts, thoughts of what hideous occurrences my immediate future might hold. These periods of silence drove me closer and closer to panic. Placing a hand over my jeans to the spot where my marble bear was hiding offered little comfort. Pulling the bear out of my pocket simply wasn't an option. Mike would see it and that would be the end of it. As hard as I tried, I couldn't seem to recall the many helpful things Koko and I had talked about. The enlightening conversations I had with Greg were similarly lost. I was able to remember the fun times I had with Riley and Niki at lunch, but that only recalled the confrontation I had with Mike in the cafeteria. I tried thinking about my mom. Surely, she had alerted the police already? Had word gotten out that I was missing? As I contemplated these thoughts my left hand moved over something hard and small on the floor of the van. It was too dark to see what it was, but it felt distinctly like a short, metal screw. Soon, an idea formed, one that might offer anyone looking for me at least some idea of where I had been. Placing the screw in my right hand, away from Mike, I began scratching, as quietly as I dared, the first three letters of my first name, Ash, on the van's floor. I did this without looking, not wanting to alert Mike to what I was doing. Fortunately, the creaks and rattles of the worn-out van muffled most of the sound the scratching made. With the first three letters complete, I added the first letter of my last name, P. It was a long shot, but if there was even a sliver of a chance that it might help someone find me, I was going to take it.

"Too many quatrains. Too many. Can't find an ... explanation. Not enough? Not enough quatrains," Mr. Pigliani muttered.

Mike ignored his father, opting to scan the road ahead.

"Quatrain forty-two. That's the one. No one knows, only me. Only I know the answer," he continued.

I had no idea what he was going on about and Mike didn't seem to notice. Or he chose not to.

"At the bottom of the lake. That's where they'll find it. The car. At the bottom. But I don't know anything about that. I told them so," Mr. Pigliani continued.

I was beginning to wonder if the stress we all were experiencing was influencing his well-being.

Mike stole a sidelong glance at his father but said nothing before slowly turning his head back toward the road.

"There it is, I knew I'd find it," Mike's dad offered, never admitting he had made a mistake. Mike rolled his eyes and shot a middle finger in the direction of his father. Apparently, he knew better than to tell his dad, 'I told you so,' twice in one day and remained silent.

Mr. Pigliani took the next available exit to merge with the correct highway. Lumbering onward into my uncertain future, Mr. Pigliani continued driving for another half hour before angling the van toward an off ramp. My heart started to beat faster knowing that whatever was going to happen was likely to happen soon. I had to develop a plan, something to buy myself a little time.

Steering the van along secondary streets, the elder Pigliani dutifully stopped at traffic lights and stop signs, enabling me to detect the faint smells of fast-food restaurants. Had my nose not been broken, I likely would have smelled them with ease. The smells forced upon me just how hungry I had become, having not eaten in almost 24 hours.

"Hey, you think we could stop and get a bite to eat? I'm starving. And I need to go to the bathroom."

"Shut your pie hole. Stupid half-breed maggot. We're not stopping for food, and if you have to go, then just go. Piss in your pants for all I care," Mr. Pigliani answered.

Surprisingly, he didn't yell. Mike had nodded off, thankfully adding nothing to the conversation. Both Piglianis looked extremely tired as Mike's dad hadn't slept since this whole ordeal started yesterday evening. Mike hadn't slept much either. Somehow, I had to use this information to my advantage, but I, too, was nearing exhaustion. My ribs ached, and my entire face hurt, but I knew I couldn't give up now and nod off. I had to stay as mentally sharp as possible.

Mr. Pigliani turned in his seat to look at Mike, asleep in the back of the van.

"Mike. You're so pathetic. Wake up!"

"You don't have to scream!" Mike shouted as he opened his eyes and sat up straight. The stress and strain were taking a toll on both, and they, the Piglianis, were taking a toll on me.

The journey continued, eventually turning left onto what felt like a narrow, two-lane, serpentine, and undulating road that had the van's back-end fishtailing around the bends. After a painfully long period of time, we made a right turn onto a road so bumpy and uneven, it could only have been dirt. Looking forward through the cracked windshield, snow had begun to fall. Combined with the falling snow and the unplowed dirt road, the van was having a hard time plowing forward, struggling to make it to the top of the uphill slopes.

"Come on, get moving." Mike's dad urged through gritted yellow teeth as the van labored to inch forward at the bottom of a particularly steep hill.

"We're going to get stuck. I hope you know that" Mike calmly stated.

"Shut up Mike. Now is not the time."

Mr. Pigliani struck the steering wheel with his right hand, a blow hard enough to encourage the van into a slow speed drift, veering, in slow motion, toward the right-hand shoulder. He tried every trick in the book to arrest the slide, but to no avail. The right front tire fell over the edge of the road, dipping the front end of the van into the ditch at the bottom of the hill. The van slowly spun, the back end swinging in a wide arc allowing the left front tire to catch the edge of the road and sink further into the ditch. When we came to a stop, I was looking through the windshield at the snow-covered ground.

"You never listen to me, do you?" Mike asked.

"No, I don't, because you never have anything of value to say."

Mr. Pigliani's tone was low and even, almost calm. Every time the man erupted in a screaming fit of rage, it filled me with fear, but hearing him chastise Mike in a calm and almost whispering manner left me terrified.

Slotting the transmission into reverse to back out, he pressed down on the accelerator, spinning the back wheels, but the van didn't budge.

"Hold on a minute. Let me get out and see what it looks like," Mike offered.

Unlocking and opening the passenger door, Mike and the cold air outside switched places, with the frigid air rushing in, trapping an untold number of stray snowflakes in the van as he slammed the door shut. Returning less than 30 seconds later, he opened the door and climbed in, shaking his massive head.

"We're not going anywhere. Both back tires are high and dry, not even touching the pavement."

"Get out and push from the front."

"How's that going to help if you can't get any traction from the back tires?"

It seemed like a reasonable question.

Mr. Pigliani clenched his teeth and gripped the steering wheel with such force his knuckles turned white.

"Just get out and do it before I pound you into the snow and leave you there."

Mike let out a huge sigh and exited, stepping through the deep snow to the front of the van. With his breath visible in the freezing air, he placed two massive hands on the hood and looked to his father, nodding, an indication he was ready to start pushing. Mr. Pigliani gunned the engine as Mike strained to push the front end of the massive van out of the ditch. Nothing happened. Mike stopped pushing and a second later, his dad eased off the accelerator.

"There's no way this is going to work. We're stuck for good!" Mike shouted.

Without a word, Mr. Pigliani waved to Mike to come back, so he forced his way through the deep snow around the front of the van and climbed in.

"So. What now?"

"I don't know. Let me think a minute."

We sat in silence for a length of time that grew more awkward, and stress filled with every passing second.

"Okay. We'll walk the rest of the way. Get out," Mike's dad stated.

With that, he and Mike simultaneously opened their doors and got out. A second later, Mike attempted to open the large sliding door to let me out but found the door locked from the inside.

"Unlock the door half-breed!" Mike shouted.

Without wasting a second, I sprang into action, crawling between the front seats to lock the passenger and driver's side door, effectively locking myself in and the Pigliani's out. Of course, I had no idea what I was going to do next, but at least I had acted. Counting coup, I figured.

"Oh, come on. Unlock the doors! Dad, he locked us out."

Mr. Pigliani high-stepped his way through the deep snow to stand at Mike's side.

"Open the door, maggot!"

He pounded on the side of the van with his fist, the sound reverberating inside the cavernous space.

"You've got the keys right? Just unlock it." Mike asked.

From my vantage point, I watched Mr. Pigliani search the pockets of his jeans and jacket. Swinging my head left, the shiny glint of keys bouncing light across the dash as they hung snuggly in the ignition explained everything.

"Nope, still in the ignition." Mike's dad replied, peering into the passenger window.

"Great. What now?"

Mike blew into his hands to warm them from the frigid air.

"Look around for a rock or a stick or something. If he won't unlock the door, we can just as easily break a window."

Their relative civility toward each other was surprising. I had expected them to spew forth a deluge of obscenities toward me, as well as each other. What scared me at that moment was how completely unpredictable the Piglianis could be. One moment they were unspeakably violent, and the next, as I witnessed with Mike, they would engage you peacefully in conversation. There was no way to determine what might set them into a rage. I felt like I was juggling dynamite.

The pair began digging through the snow, looking for something to smash the window. It didn't take long. Without alerting his dad, Mike returned with a large black rock, hurling it at the closed passenger window. As the rock struck home, I instinctively fell backward into the gap between the two front seats. The back of my head struck the steering wheel at the same moment the rock crashed through the window. My head flew forward as my chin struck my chest and I was showered with broken glass. The rock landed on my chest as I crumpled into a ball on the floor, legs splayed skyward. The knock on my head was minor compared to the pain coursing through my entire face. Bright stars flooded my vision as thick rivulets of blood coursed down my chin from my broken nose.

In my confused state, Mr. Pigliani was on me in nothing flat. Leaning into the gap between the seats and grabbing two handfuls of my jacket just below my shoulders, in one fluid motion he effortlessly picked me up, swung a full 180° and pulled me through the open passenger door and heaved.

Flying through space, momentarily weightless, my vision was full of gray sky and snowflakes peacefully falling toward terra firma. I landed in the ditch on my back a full ten feet from the van, the deep snow mercifully breaking my fall. My head ached as I spat blood into the snow while Mike and his dad stood over me laughing, their twin yellow smiles contradicting the hate in their eyes.

"Either of you guys ever heard of a toothbrush?" I asked, laying face up in the snow.

There was no delay between thinking the words and saying them. My mind was simply growing tired of the mistreatment and lashed out, damn the consequences. While the outburst surprised me, I had to admit, at least for a moment, it felt pretty good. Also to my surprise was the laughter that my insult elicited as both Pigliani men simply looked down at me and chuckled.

"Well, he finally got a little spitfire in him" Mike's dad said to no one in particular.

"It's about damn time. Get up, we have to get moving," Mike commanded.

Rolling over onto my stomach and pushing myself up was enough exertion to cause my head to throb to the point I was sure it would explode. Again, I spat blood from my mouth that had run down from my damaged nose. I stood, nearly falling over in the process on the uneven snow before climbing, hand over hand, out of the ditch, with neither Pigliani offering a helping hand.

"Alright, let's go., Mike's dad ordered.

Stepping onto the snow-covered road, I stared at Mike and his dad. There were so many questions I wanted answers to, and I figured now would be as good a time as any to try and find them.

"Why do you guys think you can treat me like this? I never did anything to hurt you."

Mr. Pigliani rolled his eyes as if bored.

"Shut up and walk."

"No. What gives you the right to mistreat everyone you come into contact with?"

"It's not about rights. It's about doing whatever the hell we want. Who's gonna stop us?" Mike answered.

"Um, the police perhaps?"

Mike threw his head back and laughed.

"They've got nothin' on us. What are they going to do, ask us a bunch of stupid questions? They've tried that before and nothing stuck. They can't touch us."

His arrogance was astonishing. The pair had already made so many mistakes I could hardly keep track of them. They would almost certainly be the first people the authorities would want to talk to considering my disappearance. The police were probably looking for them already anyway. With the van hopelessly stuck in the ditch were they going to just march to wherever we were going to do whatever they had planned and then march back? Were they going to burn the van like Mike's dad mentioned?

How would they get home? Wouldn't someone notice the smoke from the burning van and investigate? Of course, the police were going to ask questions, but I didn't see either one of them giving even remotely adequate answers. I kept these observations to myself as I felt no need to assist them in their treachery. Whatever happened to me, they were going to get caught one way or another.

"Get going, maggot. Mike, you walk in front of him."

Mike took his position in front of me and began walking while his father pushed me from behind to make sure I moved. Following Mike as I had been instructed, I knew my time was running short. I needed to act, and I had to do it soon.

We walked, plowing our way through the snow, up and down hills and around bends of varying degrees, for a considerable length of time. The snow fell with greater intensity, obscuring the road ahead. The wind picked up, causing the naked tree branches to audibly clack against one another. The effect was an eerie combination of muted clacking and dull echo as the sound bounced around the forest. It was devilishly cold, forcing me to put my gloves on and shove my hands into my jacket pockets. Neither Pigliani had gloves and both had their hands in their jacket pockets as well.

"Nothing to see here. Ask the roadrunner where the car is. Not in the quatrain. I've said it before, but you're not listening," Mike's dad said to no one.

The seemingly endless slog on the unplowed road was taking its toll on all three of us. My feet, specifically my toes, were freezing cold as clumps of snow had affixed themselves to the jeans around my ankles, adding unwanted weight to my legs. The silence of our march was deafening, fraying my already mangled nerves. I decided to speak up.

"Hey, are you guys' members of the KKK?"

Mike turned his head to answer me but continued walking forward.

"No. Most of those guys are cowards. And they have too many rules and regulations. You have to wear this and say that and think what they tell you to think. It's ridiculous."

"Shut up, Mike. And one more peep out of you half-breed and you get another beating."

I kept my mouth shut.

Twenty-Three

Mr. Pigliani's labored breathing grew more pronounced as we trudged through the increasingly deeper snow. He occasionally grumbled about something, most of it unintelligible, under his breath. Having such a dangerous hulk walking so close behind was unnerving to the extreme since I had no idea what he was capable of.

While contemplating this threat, a snowball, careening in a lazy arc over my head, struck Mike on the back of his, splattering snow through his unkempt hair. With dinner plate eyes, Mike spun to confront me, his face flushed with immediate and uncontrollable rage. He afforded me little time to react as he bull-rushed me. Despite the ever-deepening snow, he struck me full force with his body, leading with his left shoulder, forcing the air from my lungs. Flying backward, I found myself caught in the middle of a Pigliani sandwich with the huge wall of Mike's pot-bellied father stopping my backward motion as Mike's progress squashed me from the other side.

My ribs instantly responded with an explosion of pain as I landed face first in the snow, unable to breathe. Instinctively curling into a ball, covering my head with my arms, I prepared for the onslaught of blows I knew was coming. Mr. Pigliani's muffled laugh carried through the snow that had filled my ears. Slowly lifting my head, I looked cautiously at Mike, who, inexplicably, was still standing only a few feet in front of me, his ungloved and clinched fists rhythmically rising and falling with his own labored breathing.

"Oh, for the love of Pete, that was hilarious! Funniest thing I've seen in years!" Mike's dad roared, his belly wobbling in protest.

Mike turned to look at his father.

"What's so funny?"

"Whew! You didn't even hesitate. Great hit, led with the shoulder, excellent form. But the little maggot was asking for it."

"Me? I didn't do it. Why would I do that?"

Mr. Pigliani looked at me, furious.

"Seems like you're calling me a liar, maggot. I wouldn't do that if I were you."

"No. Not calling you a liar. I'm just saying I didn't do it, there's a big difference."

Mike looked at me, then at his father, trying to make sense of what had happened.

"Half-breed?"

"Seriously, Mike? Look at me. My ribs hurt so much I couldn't bend over to make a snowball much less throw one."

Turning to look up at Mike's dad, his smile and laughing now gone, I pointed to his hands.

"Plus, look at his hands, they still have snow on them. His hands are still wet."

This was a mistake. Mr. Pigliani instinctively looked down at his wet, cold hands, and without taking the time to consider what he was doing, wiped the evidence on his jeans.

Mike watched his father's attempt to hide the evidence while his own understanding of what happened changed in an instant.

"Why do you have to be like this all the time? For once in your life, can you stop making everyone around you so miserable? What's wrong with you?"

Exactly as Mike had gone from placid, into an instant rage when hit with the snowball, his father reacted in much the same manner, laughter one second, uncontrollable rage, the next.

Marching toward Mike, the bull-headed man kicked my right arm on the way by, the strike landing just above my elbow, hyper-extending it. My scream fell on deaf ears as Mike's dad shortened the distance between himself and his son. Cradling my right arm, I looked up just as Mr. Pigliani's massive right hand swung upward from his hip, landing a crushing uppercut to the underside of Mike's exposed chin. The blow lifted him clear of the snow, dumping him unceremoniously on his back with a snow muted whump. Standing over him, shoulders rising and falling with each labored breath, without saying a word, Mr. Pigliani dared him to say something.

Eventually, Mr. Pigliani shouted, "There's nothing wrong with me! The real problem is you, because you never learned to keep that stupid mouth shut! You're soft! Too much like your mother!"

Mr. Pigliani's screaming admonishment echoed off trees and rocks before being absorbed in silence by the snow.

The Tyrant, giving his son no more thought, spun in place before marching toward me, his wide, unblinking stare fixated on mine. Following his eyes with mine, I didn't allow my gaze to waiver, not wanting to show him any glimpse of fear or weakness. It was my way of counting coup, because I was terrified.

As I clutched my right arm with my left, the hulking man stopped in front of me. I looked up to his massive silhouette framed by the falling snow behind as he crouched down beside me, knees audibly cracking. When he had stopped, his face was inches from mine, his yellow teeth hiding behind dried, chapped lips.

"You know Big Mike over there is fond of movie quotes?" he asked, looking back at the unmoving form of his son lying in the snow.

Without saying a word, I nodded.

"Well, I could care less for movies. Or quotes. But I'll let you in on a little secret."

He looked to the right, then left, I assumed just in case anyone might be close enough to hear him, out here in the middle of nowhere.

"I have a favorite movie quote myself. Would you like to hear it?"

His voice was a faint whisper, but he was so close now, I had no trouble hearing him. In silence I shook my head. Smiling, he let out a little chuckle.

"I didn't think so. Doesn't matter, I'm gonna tell you anyway. You like those stupid Batman movies? I mean the new ones, not those older cheesy ones."

"Yeah, they're pretty good."

My voice was also just a whisper.

Every time he spoke, my level of terror clicked up a notch like the rotating cogs of a medieval torture device.

"I don't remember who said it, some old English guy, I think. Whatever. Anyway, here it is...."

And with that, he hesitated and leaned forward, closing the distance between us.

"'Some men just want to watch the world burn.' That's it. Short and to the point, I like it. 'Some men just want to watch the world burn.' Well, guess what, half-breed? I'm one of those men. Nothing would make me happier than to watch the world burn, with you and everyone like you, at the center of it. And guess what? I'm the man that's going to light the match."

I had no idea what to think anymore, with no understanding or comprehension of people like Mr. Pigliani and no frame of reference in which to draw from. His world was one full of hate, and from what I could tell, he pretty much hated everyone and everything. The man before me was a destroyer who would, and apparently did, annihilate everything good and decent that surrounded him.

"You know that quote?"

I nodded.

"Alfred Pennyworth said it to Bruce Wayne in The Dark Knight."

"Alfred Pennyworth? What a dumb name. Why do you waste your time memorizing stuff like that? God, you're an idiot."

I didn't offer a response. He took a deep breath and looked up, lost in thought.

"You know, I just had a brilliant idea. When I'm done cleaning up this mess you've created, I'm going to go on a treasure hunt. Ooh, goody … a treasure hunt." He clapped his hands like a child. "Want to hear about it?"

I shook my head.

"I'm going to find out where your mom lives and take care of her, too. It'll be so easy. My old lady, she's useless, but I bet she can find out where you live easy enough, you know since they work together."

"That would be a mistake," I replied.

"Maybe so. But who cares? She has to pay for her crimes, too, just like you will. She's not blameless in all of this. Oh, the horrors I will unleash upon her."

He uncoiled his massive frame and backed away.

I remained silent to his threats and badgering. Trying to reason with this man was an endeavor I wanted no part of.

With great difficulty, I struggled to my feet as the muffled sound of shuffling snow broke the stillness. Looking past Mr. Pigliani in the direction of the sound was Mike, charging forward as fast as the snow would allow, rapidly closing the distance to his father. The junior Pigliani, his face bright red from the freezing weather and his boiling anger, with a stream of blood flowing from his chin where his father had struck him, was in another place: a place born of anger, rage and resentment. I said nothing as Mike quickly advanced toward his unsuspecting father, gaining speed while closing the distance.

When his son was close to within a few feet, Mr. Pigliani's awareness kicked in and he began to turn around. Whether his lethargic reaction was caused by the stinging cold or simply from letting his guard down, it was too late.

Lowering his head, Mike hit his father in the lower back, wrapping massive tree trunk arms around his midsection as he drove forward. Mr. Pigliani let out a muted shout, one significantly dampened by air being forced from his lungs. The dull, unintelligible shout found no sympathetic ears. I instinctively ducked as Mike lifted his father clear of the ground and over my head. Landing with a thud, the Pigliani men rolled in a massive tangle of arms and legs and flying snow.

Twenty-Four

Both Piglianis, covered from head to toe in snow and swinging wildly, became enveloped in rage, completely oblivious to their surroundings, while I sat in the snow, utterly dumbfounded by the scene unfolding before me.

Shaking my head from side to side, I finally came to my senses and realized that my chance to escape had arrived. I stood up and looked to my right, inwardly cursing my cold addled senses for not having moved sooner and noticed a small dip in the landscape, falling away from the road before rising sharply in a craggy vertical expanse of black, unforgiving rock. Turning to my left revealed a steep, but not insurmountable, rise. Without looking back at the increasingly noisy conflagration behind me, I took my first steps toward freedom, stepping off the road and up the embankment. Slipping up the snow-covered hill, which now appeared twice as high as when I started, drove me to levels of panic I never would have thought possible.

"Seven, eight, uh… ten, eleven. Seventeen, twenty-two, twenty-three." I huffed my way up hill, counting stairs that didn't exist as my mind attempted to force a sense of order in a maelstrom of chaos.

Hearing the fight below me continuing unabated, my mind still convinced me that one of the Piglianis would crush my ankle in an iron grip and drag me back into the turmoil.

Having reached the top of the hill some forty to fifty feet above my kidnappers, I turned to see Mr. Pigliani straddling Mike, sitting on his chest, raining down heavy blows on his face and head. His face covered in blood and his father cursing at the top of his lungs, Mike was giving nearly as well as he was receiving, wriggling and swinging to defend and free himself. Turning my back on the chasm of blood and violence below me, I began running, allowing the forest to swallow me whole, away from the madness.

Moments after entering the forest, my world became uncomfortably still as the Piglianis realized what I had done.

"Where'd he go?"

Echoing through the forest, the muffled, questioning tone of Mike's father sounded almost comfortably distant.

"How the hell should I know? This is all your fault."

"How can it be my fault? You started it!" Mr. Pigliani shouted, sounding the clarion call known to schoolyard bullies the world over. Nothing bad could ever be their fault.

"That way, up there." Mike said as I pictured him in my mind, pointing his gigantic snow-covered arm to the trail of blood I left in the snow, leading up the hill.

"Let's go. If he gets away, we're both screwed," Mr. Pigliani commanded.

The grunts and groans of my pursuers, huffing and puffing their way up the hill, assaulted my senses. No longer caring what they said to each other, and perhaps only a half a minute ahead of them, I didn't have the luxury of wasting time. Plowing my way through the snow, over large boulders and fallen trees, I became keenly aware of the light beginning to fade. Whether from the cover of the forest or the sun falling lower in the sky, I couldn't tell.

Not knowing the fitness level of either Pigliani, I surmised that Mike's father hadn't seen the inside of a gym in ages. Of Mike and his fitness, I was less certain. Despite my own admittedly questionable level of physical fitness, I soldiered on, silently badgering myself for not having taken my physical education classes more seriously. With my pace slowing, I needed to find my second wind, but stopping was not an option, no matter how badly my lungs burned, or my head pounded. The combined effects of the cold, a broken nose, concussion, and a lack of oxygen were taking their toll. The shadows of unconsciousness were closing in as the perimeter of my field of vision grew dark. It was decision-making time. Stop now and risk getting caught, or continue and risk blacking out, in which case I would certainly get caught.

My decision was made for me seconds later when Mr. Pigliani's raspy, out-of-breath voice called out.

"There he is!"

Following Mr. Pigliani's declaration was a sound that stopped me in my tracks, the unmistakable bark of gunfire. Whizzing past my head at what I could only guess was mere inches away, a bullet imbedded itself in a tree to my right, just a few feet in front of me. Ducking immediately behind the nearest tree on my left, I ruminated not on being shot at, but the surprise I felt when realizing that, if a bullet flies close enough to one's head, it can be heard.

"Did you get him?" Mike asked.

"Nah, I don't think so."

"Do you see him?"

"No. Whew, hold on, I need to take a breather," Mike's dad replied.

Looking down into the snow, I noticed a small pool of blood and realized that even if the Pigliani's couldn't see me, they could track me. I had to keep moving. Without looking back, I quickly walked a straight line away from the tree, not straying right or left, to keep the tree between me and my pursuers. Having moved perhaps twenty yards, I encountered my first obstacle, another tree. As rapidly as I dared, I darted around its left side and continued my straight line. Not moving as fast as before gave me a chance to catch my breath, allowing my vision to clear considerably and giving me the confidence that I would remain conscious.

"Come on, we have to keep going. You can catch your breath later."

"Shut your mouth. We'll go when I say and not a moment sooner."

"He is going to get away!" Mike said, annunciating every syllable.

Skirting around another tree, a second shot rang out, the crack of the gun reverberating around the forest, bouncing off trees, snow and rocks. Mr. Pigliani's aim wasn't as true as his first shot as I didn't hear the bullet whiz by my ear, nor did I see or hear an impact beyond me. Again, I stopped to lean against a tree to catch my breath.

"What are you doing? You can't even see him. You're wasting bullets and making a lot of noise."

"You're not helping, Mike. Just keep your stupid pie-hole shut from now on. You're worthless anyway!"

"If I'm worthless and you're my father, then what does that make you?"

It was a savage comeback, one I didn't expect Mike to be capable of, but he paid for it. The only reply from the senior Pigliani came in the form of what sounded like a solid punch to Mike's gut, a great whooshing sound escaping from him as he absorbed the blow.

Turning around and leaning ever so cautiously to my left, I peeked around the tree to get a better look at what was happening. Mike was down in the snow on all fours, gasping for breath, his father standing over him like a dictator.

"Look at you, you can't even stand up straight. Absolutely pathetic, just like your worthless mother."

He laughed, a wet and raspy guffaw that spoke of decades of nicotine addiction.

"At least she can hold down a job for more than six weeks at a time."

He didn't risk looking at his father when he said it.

Instant rage. Mr. Pigliani kicked his son in the ribs with ferocious anger. Rolling sideways, Mike came to a stop against a fallen tree. The need to put as much distance between the Piglianis and myself was momentarily forgotten as I was watched a train wreck happening in real time. I couldn't turn away no matter how hard I tried. I should have turned around and not looked back, but something inside of me wouldn't allow it.

"I dare you to say that again. Go on, you worthless excuse for a son, say it again!"

The only response from Mike was to lie in the snow, trying to force air into his lungs.

"You couldn't pour water out of a boot with the instructions taped to the heel!"

An awkward silence filled the air as Mr. Pigliani stood over his son, basking in the false glory of Mike's humiliation. But the tyrant had lit the fuse to a powder keg of his own making, a fuse he had no hope of extinguishing. Mike's massive body tensed like a coiled spring suddenly put under great tension. He hesitated for a moment and then exploded, the spring suddenly released its massive, time worn burden.

In a single, fluid movement, Mike rose to his feet and swung an impossibly long right arm, his anvil-like fist grasping a piece of wood nearly half as long as Mike was tall. Mr. Pigliani, no doubt priding himself on never showing an outward sign of emotion or weakness, was unable to hide the terror now consuming his face. He saw the arcing motion of the timber, rigidly connected to the arm of his son, as it made its way toward his own head.

Standing behind the tree, I felt rooted to the ground, transfixed by the violence I was witnessing, all of it happening in slow motion. Mike's face was twisted, tangled with rage and emotional torment, eyes red and burning with anguish as a flimsy spiral of spittle clung to his back curled lips before the force of gravity tore it loose, allowing it to free fall to the frozen earth below. Years of bullying and ridicule at the hands of his father were unleashed in one titanic explosion of grief.

Mr. Pigliani began raising his left arm to ward off the oncoming blow, but it was too late. At the stick's apogee, time resumed its normal pace, and it came down, not in a thunderous crash, but a dull thud. Impacting the left side of his face and head, the stick splintered into hundreds of pieces as the big man immediately went limp, falling without sound into the snow.

Turning back to the tree, I took a short breath and threw up. Looking down into the snow, expecting to see a pile of vomit, the only thing visible was a small splattering of blood. It was the sound that did it, the sound of wood striking the elder man's head, a sickening, dull sound I will never be able to erase from my auditory memory. As repulsive a sound as I've encountered, it was also the sound of Mike freeing himself from a lifetime in his father's never-ending torment.

I leaned out from the tree again to see Mike kneeling beside his father, sobbing, mumbling incoherently and staring at the unmoving form before him. A part of me wanted to reach out to him, to see if he needed help, but I knew better. Had I been within arm's reach, he would have torn me limb from limb. Quickly and quietly, I turned around and, with the tree again as my shield, continued my escape.

"Damn you, half-breed!"

Mike's voice echoed through the forest. Knowing he had resumed the chase, this time fueled by an insatiable quest for revenge, I quickened my pace. Forcing his way through the snow, grunts and groans were occasionally interrupted by a breaking branch as anger and adrenaline drove him forward. Mike's blitz of speed and anger, fueled by rage and blood lust, would eventually run out, I just didn't know if my adrenaline would outlast his. Terror coursed through my system as I contemplated the consequences of being captured.

Twenty-Five

Mike's physical conditioning was far greater than I had anticipated because, though I moved as quickly as possible, his labored breathing edged closer with every passing second. Quickly running out of energy and with Mike gaining ground, I was in serious jeopardy, with no way out.

"If you stop running right now, I'm only going to beat you half to death!"

I took a chance and peeked back over my right shoulder, shocked to see him trailing me by only about ten feet. I decided right then and there that no matter how tired I became, I wasn't going to stop; I would keep running until he either caught me, or I dropped dead from exhaustion. Adding to the threats I faced, the rapidly fading light made traversing the hazards of the forest increasingly difficult as I bounced off a tree with my left shoulder as I ran. Spinning, I caught a glimpse of Mike behind me, much closer now, so close I could hear every single inhale and exhale as he labored to secure my capture. Starting down a steep embankment, I half ran, half slid down on my backside as standing upright would have sent me careening down the hill in a violent tumble.

"That's it half-breed. Now I'm really mad."

As he descended the hill after me, nearly within arm's reach, a strange, out of place sound interrupted the chase, the sound of Mike grunting followed by a loud crack and a soft thump. Immediately following the thump, the most horrifying sound I've ever heard emitted from a human being echoed throughout the forest. A blood-curdling scream so chilling in its immensity that I immediately stopped halfway down the hill and turned around to see Mike lying face down in the snow, a mere five feet behind me. Facing down the hill and bent at the waist, he held his lower right leg with both hands. Lifting his face from the snow, he looked at me and screamed again.

In a fleeting moment of self-preservation, I considered the possibility that he was faking an injury to lure me in and beat me to death. But, remembering the loud crack and scream that followed, a ruse seemed unlikely. Mike's contorted face confirmed my suspicion, and I knew in an instant, his pain was genuine.

My path to freedom had never been clearer than it was now, all I had to do was turn and simply walk away. A devious voice in my mind told me to turn around and put as much distance between Mike and myself as I could. He had tormented me, nearly beaten me to death, he and his father had kidnapped me. Didn't he deserve to die out here in the cold? But my conscience wouldn't hear of it. Regardless of how he had treated me, he still didn't deserve to freeze to death, all alone on the side of some nameless hill. I took a small, tentative step back in Mike's direction.

"Mike, what's wrong?"

With great caution, I inched closer.

He looked at me, his face contorted in pain, deep wrinkles creasing the skin around his eyes and mouth.

"Leg. Leg's broken."

He gritted his teeth before burying his face in the snow. Shifting my gaze from Mike's face to his right leg, the lower portion, roughly midway between the knee and ankle, was bent at a truly sickening angle.

Abandoning my thought of escape, I stepped up the hill and crouched down next to him to get a better look at the damage. Blood was already seeping through his jeans, spreading randomly down his leg, staining and soaking into his dirty sock.

"Mike, move your hands, I need to get a better look."

But his hands remained in place as he lifted his head clear of the snow to look at me again, his face twisted in agony, the chapped blue lips tightly curling back to reveal hidden yellow teeth I had learned to hate. I don't think he really saw me; the pain had taken him to a place unseen, a place of terrifying brutality. His breathing had already become shallow and rapid, and it wasn't hard to figure out he was going into shock.

"Mike! Move your hands out of the way!"

I've never been a fan of shouting, but I could tell I wasn't getting through to him.

"Huh? What?"

"You need to move your hands clear so I can see what's wrong."

"I already told you what's wrong. My leg's broken, you moron."

At least he didn't call me half-breed.

"Stop being so stubborn and move your hands."

An exasperated sigh escaped from my chest as I stood at the edge of panic.

Exhaling deeply, he slid gargantuan hands away from his leg. Leaning in to get a better look, I knew immediately the situation was dire. The stark white, jagged end of both of his lower leg bones protruded through a clean tear in his jeans as blood stained the newly fallen snow around his damaged leg.

"Oh, man. That's not good. Umm, shoot."

My heart was racing, and my hands were shaking as I more fully realized the seriousness of the situation. Close to panic, I consciously and silently told myself to breathe deeply and slowly. Panicking would do neither of us any good.

"Okay Mike, first things first. If I were you, I wouldn't look down at your leg. It's not pretty."

He immediately looked down and when his eyes locked onto the sharp bend in his lower leg and the white, protruding bones, his eyes rolled back into his head, and he passed out.

"I told you not to do that."

I closed my eyes, shook my head slowly, and wondered about the nature of the universe and my place in it. Tell someone not to do something and that will be the first thing their mind commands them to do. I surveyed the graying landscape, questioning whether I would have done the same thing. If my leg had been broken in such a graphic way, would I have looked at it after being told not to? Almost certainly. So, I had something else in common with Mike. Acknowledging the fact didn't make me feel any better about the current situation.

Getting the bleeding stopped was the first order of business, so I bent down again, taking a closer look at the misshapen leg. His right foot was still wedged into the hole he had stepped in, and it became clear that his forward momentum and weight were enough to snap the weak link in the chain, his lower leg. Brushing away the snow to expose the rocks surrounding his leg made removing them a straightforward affair, most were reasonably light and loose enough that they came free with little effort.

Lifting Mike's broken leg out of the hole without at least some help from him presented my next series of challenges and I had serious doubt it could be accomplished at all without causing more damage.

"Mike. Mike, wake up."

My voice was calm but stern. The only reaction I received was watching his chest rise and fall with each breath; he was an unmoving lump in the snow.

I tried shouting next.

"Mike!"

His incoherent response was little more than a soft moan.

"Mike, wake up!"

His eyelids fluttered open briefly before slamming shut.

Taking a couple of steps down the hill, I stood even with his head, bent down and slapped him hard across the face. Surprising me more than the action of slapping Mike was the fact that I didn't even think about it; it just happened. A moment later, he opened his eyes and stared at me.

"Did you just hit me?"

He looked around, perhaps wondering if anyone had witnessed the assault.

"Yeah, I had to. You passed out and I need you to help me lift your foot out of this hole."

I pointed my right hand up the hill to his still immobile foot.

"Oh, man it hurts." He attempted to roll over on his back.

"Wait, did you say I passed out? No way that happened. I'm Mike Pigliani. Pigliani men don't pass out. You're lying."

"I'm not lying. Listen, we really need to get your foot out of that hole as quickly as possible so we can stop the bleeding. Can you lift your leg up a little?"

He rolled over, bending up at the waist to get a better look, placing his right hand in the snow to hold himself up so he could survey the damage. As soon as his vision focused on the leg, his eyes fluttered while his arm wobbled underneath him.

"Mike! No, not again. If you pass out, I swear I'll tell everyone at school."

It was no idle threat. If it came to it, I'd use the school's PA system to announce it. That did the trick. He opened his eyes, locking his gaze on me.

"Come on, Mike. I can't do this without your help. Just lift your leg as high as you can, and I'll support the umm…"

I was at a loss for words, stuck in the freezing cold, worried about offending Mike's obviously tender sensibilities. The last thing either of us needed was for him to pass out again and I had no idea what might cause him to cross the line into unconsciousness.

"Your, umm… I mean… You know, the mangled, broken part."

He didn't seem to notice my tripping vocabulary and nodded. Walking over to his broken and bleeding leg, I kneeled on the frozen hillside, gently sliding my hands between the snow beneath and his leg above.

"Okay, I don't care how much it hurts because we only want to do this once. Are you ready?"

"Yeah."

He gritted his teeth.

"Yeah."

"Okay, on three. Ready? One. Two. Three."

He threw his head back, grunting loudly as he engaged his leg muscles, commanding them to move. I lifted with all the energy I could summon, shocked at just how heavy his leg was.

"Ahhhhhh!"

He gripped the snow, yelled and together, with considerable effort, we lifted his lower right leg out of the hole.

"Come on, we're almost there. Just a little higher. Okay, now swing it over to the right a little bit so we can get clear of the hole. Great. Now set it down, nice and easy. I'll support it as much as I can."

As he lowered his leg to the ground, I maintained support while stretching his lower leg out as much as possible to relieve the pressure on the area of the break.

Mike's scream faded as he collapsed into the snow, his chest rising and falling deeply with each taxing breath. I noticed a light sheen of sweat across his expansive forehead.

"Okay, great. The hard part is over. No problem."

Outwardly projecting a calm and focused demeanor, as much for my sake as well as Mike's, was a monumental task, because on the inside, I was freaking out. Time was critical, but still I gave Mike a moment to recover before asking more of him. After 30 seconds or so, he sat up, and despite the bone numbing cold, his forehead was now dripping with sweat. Recalling what I learned from my freshman year health class, I identified this as an ominous sign. If I didn't get him some help, and soon, he stood a very real chance of dying. The enormity of this realization terrified and confused me. Before me was a person who tormented me, both physically and mentally, and here I was, trying everything in my power to save his life. In an instant, that became the only thing that mattered.

"Okay, Mike. How are you feeling?"

"Terrible. How do you think I feel? Why are you even asking? Get the hell out of here. I'm tired of looking at your stupid face."

I rolled my eyes at his irrational admonishment, but he didn't notice.

"I can't leave. If I do, if I leave you here, you're going to die. It's guaranteed, no question about it. You'll die from blood loss, or you'll freeze to death. My guess is you'll freeze to death first. I'm not going to let that happen."

"What's wrong with you? Are you some kind of do-gooder? You could beat me to death with a rock and just walk away. So? Come on, do it, you coward."

His face was red with anger as he threw a handful of loose snow at me. This latest attempt at hurling snow was woefully inadequate, so much so that I wanted to mock his ability. But chastising him would only succeed in angering him further, and he needed to save all the energy he could if he was going to survive.

"That's just not who I am. That's not how I treat people."

"Because you're weak. If I were you, I'd bash my skull in with a rock and be done with it."

"Well, it's a good thing for you and me both that you're not. Why is violence your answer to everything?"

"Because it works."

"Does it? Look around Mike, look at this whole situation."

I held my arms wide, spinning them in an arc covering a wide swath of forest.

"Does this look like the picture of it working for you? You're such a dumb shit."

I dropped my arms to my side in frustration.

"Because I understand violence, I grew up with it. You've seen my father. That should answer your question."

"But violence never solves anything. Nothing good comes from it. Nothing."

"Come on, half-breed. Haven't you ever wanted to give someone a good beat down just for the fun of it?"

"What? For the fun of it? No, I haven't. What the hell is wrong with you? Can we please try to concentrate on the situation at hand, which is getting you back up the hill. Or down the hill, whichever is easier, I don't care."

I was so angry at this point I figured changing the subject might be a good idea.

"Fine. And how are we going to do that?"

"Can you stand?"

"No idea. Hold on."

He gently spun himself around on his butt, so his legs were pointed down the hill. Digging his hands into the snow, he tried to force himself into a standing position but was only able to elevate himself three or four inches clear of the ground before his arms gave out. Leaning into the snow on one elbow, he was already out of breath.

I considered offering to allow him to use my shoulder as a crutch, giving him a chance to hobble up the hill. Though considering how easily he could strangle me to death in such a situation horrified me.

"God, it hurts so bad. Umm, I think I might be able to scoot myself up the hill. It's a lot further to go down, so I think going up might work better."

"Yeah, good idea. You need any help?"

"No. I don't need your stinking help. Stop asking."

"Suit yourself."

I crossed my arms over my chest and waited.

Pulling his left leg in, he dug his foot into the snow to prepare a firm place with which to push off from. He then dug out the snow behind him, first on the right, then on the left, giving his hands a more stable platform to begin. Then, looking skyward, he took a series of rapid deep breaths and lifted with all the effort he could muster.

"Arrrgghhhh!"

Screaming, he managed to move himself a few inches up the hill. Taking a brief rest and repeating the entire process, digging out the snow, deep breaths, and then expending far more effort than it was worth for only having moved two or three inches, he collapsed into the snow, utterly defeated.

"So, how's that working out for ya'?"

My question was thick with sarcasm as I surveyed the surrounding forest, an eerie pallet of grays and whites.

"Shut up, goddamn shit-eating maggot. So, you're going to be a wise guy huh? You think just because I'm lying here with a broken leg you can say whatever you want?"

"Kind of seems that way, doesn't it?"

"Okay, fine, I need your help. Are you happy?"

"Not really. But let's get on with it."

Walking over to him, I bent down, gingerly sliding my left hand under his knee and my right just below the break.

"Okay, I'm ready. Just count me down and I'll lift when you lift. Okay?"

"Sure, fine, whatever. Okay, one … two … three."

At three, Mike grunted and groaned while I carefully lifted his broken leg clear of the snow. Shifting his weight up the hill, I followed, holding his leg aloft. Repeating the process two more times, Mike finally sat down on his butt, crying out in pain.

"Mike, give it a rest for a minute, catch your breath."

"No, we keep going. I'm fine."

Only he wasn't fine. Sweating profusely, his face was red from exertion. I was beginning to sweat as well, but he was determined to push on, and I saw no point in arguing with him. We continued the process as before and in five or six minutes, had made it to the top of the hill.

Leaning against a tree near the edge of the incline, Mike closed his eyes, tipped his head back, and just sat, catching his breath, no doubt trying to deal with the pain. Looking down the hill from where we had just been, I saw a trail of blood tracing itself to our current location. The crimson trail was a combination of his blood and my own, one indistinguishable from the other, the significance of which I fully understood, a significance I suspected was completely lost on someone such as Mike. Not that it mattered, the falling snow would quickly cover the evidence of our undeniable similarities, leaving only our glaring differences, the only thing Mike seemed willing to acknowledge.

"We made it. Now let's see if we can get the bleeding stopped."

"I made it. Enough with the 'we' crap. WE, are not a team."

He put a heavy emphasis on the 'we' part.

"You're welcome." I answered.

"So, what now, Dr. Phil?"

Even when injured, he still badgered me.

"I told you what was next, get the bleeding to stop."

I made no attempt to hide the frustration in my voice.

"Yeah. How're we going to do that?"

His eyes were still closed as he rested his head against the tree.

"Don't you mean you? How are you going to do that?"

Though I shouldn't have, I played Mike's childish game with a heavy emphasis on 'you.'

He opened his eyes to glare at me.

"What are you talking about?"

"We are not a team. Your words. So, I can take that to mean you certainly don't need my help."

"Okay, here we go. Don't even bother, I've had enough lectures from people like you to last me the rest of my life."

"People like me? Do you even hear yourself? Ugh, if I weren't such a nice guy, I'd kick you in your stupid broken leg."

"Go ahead, softy, kick away. Bend it like Beckham if you think you've got the stones for it. I dare you."

"Yeah, see I can't do that. You'll just pass out again. Oh, I'm sorry, Pigliani men don't pass out. Pardon me, my mistake. What should we call it? Oh, I've got it. You'll faint. I'm sure Pigliani men are well known throughout the land as fainters. And I don't need to bend it like Beckham, you jackass, it's already there."

"That's it, Half-Breed, you just earned yourself another beating. I'm going to one punch you into the next area code!"

"Go right ahead, Tyson, swing away. How's an uppercut sound?"

I defiantly stuck my chin out, making it an easy target.

"Wait, do you need my help to get up?"

I cocked my head to the right.

"All you need do is ask, Mike. I'm here for you buddy."

"Shut up."

"Nice comeback, been saving that one for a long time, I bet. Okay, I'll shut up. In the meantime, how about I just stand here and watch you bleed out?"

I crossed my arms over my chest, hoping he got the point and waited.

"Yes, I need your help. But remember one thing … without this broken leg," Mike answered, his voice unusually calm, nodding in the direction of his broken appendage, "you wouldn't have the guts to say any of the things you are now."

"You have a point. But if you behaved like a normal human being, I wouldn't need to," I countered, not caring whether he agreed with me or not.

"Can we stop going around in circles before I kick off, please?"

"Fine. You took health freshman year, right?"

"Yeah. Passed it too, got a D+."

"Great. So, you need to put pressure on your femoral artery. Start with that while I figure out what to do next."

"My what artery?"

"Femoral artery, it's the main artery in your leg. It's right here next to your groin. Look."

I showed him where the femoral artery was located by placing my right hand on the inside part of my right thigh, next to my groin.

"Looks a little weird to me."

"Then keep bleeding if you're so sensitive."

He applied pressure to his inner leg.

"Fine, how hard should I press?"

"Pretty hard. You'll know how you're doing by how much the bleeding slows down, so keep an eye on it. Just try not to pass out again."

"One more crack on passing out and I'm going to pound you again!"

"Really? We've been through this already. Pretty recently, remember?"

"Shut up."

"OK, I'll shut up. Idiot. You wouldn't have a knife, would you?"

"Yeah, why?"

He began digging into his left jeans pocket.

"Because I need it."

He handed over a large lock blade, brown in the middle and bronze on both ends. I opened the heavy blade, locking it in place with a solid, loud click. Crouching next to Mike's leg, I carefully began cutting fabric around the exposed bone protruding through his jeans.

"Hey! Don't go cutting on my jeans, you're going to ruin them."

"Your jeans are covered in blood, and they already have a hole in them, and you're worried that I'm going to ruin them?"

"Get on with it."

Cutting the lower part of his jeans into long strips, I tied them together, making a single long piece that I looped around his leg below the knee and above the area of the break. He winced as I made the makeshift tourniquet snug.

"Sorry about that. Too tight?"

"No, it's fine."

"Okay. We have to make sure the tourniquet isn't so tight that it shuts the blood supply off to the rest of your leg. So, if you feel your toes or your lower leg going numb say something immediately."

Mike nodded his understanding.

"You learned all this in health class?"

"Yeah."

"Huh. I don't remember any of that stuff."

"Yeah? I have the same problem with math. Numbers trip me up all the time."

"Math is the worst. What a totally useless subject."

While I was admittedly terrible at math, I hardly considered it a useless subject. I went the diplomatic route in any case.

"You won't hear me argue with that."

"Okay, so what now?"

With no idea what to do next, I wasn't sure how to answer him. Looking skyward, snow continued to fall as the light faded into a deeper transition, from a medium blue high in the sky to darker purples that invaded the treed horizon. Evidently, the universe kept moving despite the hardships and obstacles that Mike and I were now facing.

Before answering him, I briefly wondered what my mom was doing now. Probably worried sick about me was my guess. I thought about Koko and Fred, suspecting Koko of doing everything he could think of to ease my mom's mind. He probably offered her a mug of hot chocolate at least twice.

"I don't know about you, but I could really go for a huge steaming mug of chocolate right about now."

"Yeah, that'd do the trick. I don't remember the last time I had hot chocolate."

"I had some recently at my friend Koko's place. He loves the stuff, makes it all the time."

"Koko? You have a friend named Koko that loves hot chocolate? That's appropriate."

He laughed at his observation. A guy named Koko that loves to make hot chocolate? How had I missed that connection? It seemed impossible he could make astute mental connections ahead of me. Was I selling Mike short, like everyone seemed to do? Did he offer more to the world than he was letting on?

"Hmm, you're right. I never would have put that together."

Mike shifted his weight, leaning more to the left to ease the pressure on his right side.

"So, who's this Koko?"

"He's an older Native American guy, lives in the apartment above my mom and me. He was with me in the coffee shop that day you and your dad came in, you met him."

"Yeah, I remember him. Weird looking dude."

"He's not weird looking. He looks like a Native American Indian, which is what he is."

"Whatever, half-breed. He's probably as much a weak-kneed waste of space as you are."

"Do you always have to put people down? I mean, have you ever said anything nice about anyone in your life?"

"I can't stand being around people that are weak, which is most people. So, what if I put people down? They need to hear it. I'm doing them a favor because I'm being honest."

"You're being a bully is what you're being."

"Call it what you want. I'm just being me."

"No, you're being who your father taught you to be. Every opinion I've ever heard come out if your mouth is one I can hear your father saying. You might consider forming your own opinions about people and the world around you instead of repeating something you heard your father say."

I made no attempt to conceal my anger.

"You shut your mouth, my dad's a great man."

"Really? Is he? Is this the same man that knocked you out earlier today? The man that later gave you that bloody nose? The same man that you helped kidnap me? Is that the man you're talking about?"

My calm demeanor belied the anger boiling inside of me, but I remembered the advice of my mom, "When someone shows you hostility and anger, show them peace and serenity in return." Until now, I never fully understood exactly what she was talking about. While what I said to Mike was certainly provocative, the outer image I projected to him was not. Mike's facial expression changed from anger to confusion, as if saying to himself, "How could he say those things so calmly, so peacefully?"

"If my leg weren't broken, I'd pound you to a bloody pulp. You don't know what you're talking about."

I had gotten to him, hitting an emotional nerve that had been exposed sometime in the past. Looking at him, I could see the wheels turning in his mind, filtering through what I had said.

Twenty-Six

In that instant, knowing that I had inadvertently touched a deeply rooted emotional scar, I came to the profound realization that I was no longer afraid of Mike Pigliani. It had nothing to do with the fact that his leg was broken, rendering him physically unable to harm me and everything to do with the fact that I was seeing him, for the first time, for who he truly was.

Mike Pigliani was scared. Koko had, in no uncertain terms, told me that very thing, but I didn't really believe him. I did now. What Mike was afraid of, I could only guess. My intuition told me he was afraid of people that were in some way different from him, afraid someone might say or do something that would challenge those things in his mind he knew to be right and true. I pondered whether he might be afraid of his own feelings. Probably so. One thing of which I was certain, without question, he was afraid of his father.

"I don't know what I'm talking about? Listen to yourself, Mike! Why are you defending him? Why do you blindly believe everything he says? Maybe start forming your own opinions and stop adopting those of your dad."

Rising to my feet in complete disgust, I teetered on the edge of losing my composure, such was my desire to yell at him at the top of my lungs.

"Well, finally. You finally got a little bit of spitfire in you. Took long enough. You know, there's nothing wrong with getting boiling mad occasionally. It'll do you some good."

"Well, what am I supposed to do? Half the time you open your mouth, you say something so unbelievably ridiculous, it's a wonder your head doesn't explode!"

I was boiling mad now.

"There you go. See? Now doesn't that feel better? Let it out, allow the anger to flow. It's not healthy to keep it all bottled up inside you know."

We were both breathing deeply, trying to manage the pain, both physical and emotional.

"No! No, it doesn't feel better!"

I lied, not wanting to admit he was right, that venting my feelings, did, in fact, make me feel better.

"Well, now you're not being honest with yourself. Or me. Okay, suit yourself."

"Shut up, Mike! I'm tired of listening to you. What do you know anyway?"

It was a lame attempt at a comeback, and I knew it.

"I know a lot more than you give me credit for, that's for sure. You think I grew up with an old man like mine and didn't learn a thing or two about people?"

The frustration in his voice was obvious.

"Whatever."

"Yeah, whatever. Nice retort, Shakespeare. Jeez, you're not even trying. Look, I grew up under the thumb of a tyrant and it messed me up. I can see it just as clearly as anyone. You? You grew up without a father. So, genius, riddle me this … Which is better? Growing up with a father like mine or growing up without a father, like you?"

"Honestly? I have no idea."

I shrugged and shivered against the cold. I had hit a nerve with Mike just minutes before. Now, it was his turn.

"It's simple. The answer is neither. You and I are a lot more alike than you'd care to admit. Don't look so shocked; it's true."

Having him read my body language, since my eyes widened and jaw dropped open, was unnerving.

"Think about it, really roll it around in your head, commit to it. We both have trust issues. I don't trust anyone that looks at me twice. And what about you? What do you immediately think when someone gives you a compliment?"

I shifted my weight back and forth on my feet, surprised by a question I didn't think he was even remotely capable of asking. He had forced me into an uncomfortable position and made it look easy.

My carefully prepared mental case study of Mike Pigliani was crumbling before my eyes and via his own mind. I was furious with myself for being wrong about him.

"Umm, well. I guess I think they're lying to me. Not that it happens all that much."

I was completely unable to hide my discomfort.

"That's bullshit and you know it. That little girl you sit with at lunch, you think that's an accident? You think she and her friend are sitting with you because they feel sorry for you?"

"Well, yeah."

My answer was honest despite being completely dumbfounded by his insight.

"Yeah, that's bullshit, just like I said. You're lying to yourself and you're completely disregarding her feelings. She's giving you a compliment without saying a word. It's like she's saying, 'I enjoy your company,' so she eats lunch with you every single day. Only you're not buying it because you don't trust her. Go ahead, tell me I'm wrong."

But I couldn't. He was right about all of it, I had trust issues.

"You're an asshole."

"You just told me something I already know, but you didn't tell me I'm wrong. You're not very good at this are you?"

He had a point.

"I know what people think about me. 'Oh, here comes Big Mike....'" He raised his hands to make air quotes with his fingers. "'Doesn't have a brain in his head.' No, they don't say it, but they think it. I see what goes on. I listen. I notice."

"So why do you treat people the way you do? Why do you live up to that stereotype?"

"It's easier that way. If people saw the real me, they'd think I'm weak."

"No, they'd think you're a real human being. And pardon me for saying it, but that sounds exactly like something your dad drilled into your head."

"Huh, you're right."

He hung his head, perhaps realizing for the first time one of the truths about his relationship with his father.

Then, something in Mike abruptly changed as the light in his eyes faded, his head sunk lower, and he grew still.

"Mike, what's wrong?"

Streaming down his face, a face twisted with pure agony and from red, swollen eyes were tears that could only come from a place of abject despair.

"I killed my old man. I killed my dad!"

He cried out words of certainty. In a moment, I understood his agony was not one of physical pain; it was deeply emotional. Here was Mike Pigliani, one of the most callous, foul-tempered and uncaring humans I had ever encountered, openly weeping about the fate of his father, a man who, by all measures, was many degrees worse than Mike himself.

"Mike, you don't know that. You don't—"

"Shut up! You don't know! You didn't see him. There was so much blood. He wasn't breathing!"

Tears streamed down his face.

"Mike, I saw the whole thing. What you did was clearly self-defense. I mean, you had no choice. I'll say that to anyone who'll listen."

Mike looked at me, but said nothing, choosing only to shake his head and allow the tears to run down his face, undisturbed. I sat in the snow a few feet away, affording him the time he needed despite the seriousness of his injury and our current situation. His sobs grew infrequent as time passed and eventually, he fell silent. For a long time, neither of us spoke.

"Hey, a little while ago, and earlier in the van, your dad started talking about quatrains and a car in a lake. What was that about?" I was attempting to change the subject.

"Oh, yeah. He gets like that when he hasn't had enough sleep, or when he's under a lot of stress, or when he forgets to take his medication. Usually it's all three."

"Oh, OK."

"See, he's bipolar. Or something like that. Hell, I don't know. He's supposed to see a shrink every other month and take his medication. Problem is, he hates his shrink and doesn't believe in taking medication because he's convinced he doesn't have a problem."

"So, not a good combination."

"No. More like a terrible combination."

Twenty-Seven

"So, what's next?"

He didn't bother looking at me.

"I don't know. I've been trying to figure that out and I don't think I can stay here. We might sit under this tree for a week before anyone finds us. I don't think I can help you walk out of here either. I wish I could, but I'm just not big enough. Our best shot, I think, is for me to hike out and get some help."

I looked directly into his bloodshot eyes as he silently nodded, staring directly at me. Only he wasn't looking at me, he was looking through me, lost in a far-off memory he chose not to share.

"What do you think? I'm open to ideas."

Blinking half a dozen times, he shook his head, freeing himself of whatever memory had carried him off to parts unknown.

"What'd you say?"

"I asked you what you thought we should do next."

"You know, you might be the first person that has ever asked me for my opinion. No one ever asks me what I think. I guess they never cared enough to ask."

"Well, I do, so I'm asking. I certainly don't have all the answers. The problem is, I don't even know what questions to ask."

"I don't either. I'm not really thrilled with the idea of being left here, but I can't think of a better option."

"Yeah, same here. I'm not excited about hiking off into the woods. I don't even know where we are. I'd head back toward the van, but I have no idea what the right direction is to start with."

"If you hadn't run off, we wouldn't be in this mess."

He was obviously frustrated.

"Are you kidding me? If you and your dad hadn't kidnapped me, none of this would have happened in the first place. There's no point in arguing about it now anyway."

Casting my gaze toward the heavens, the snow had tapered off considerably as the light loosened its grip on the pewter sky. Before long, darkness would completely envelope the forest.

"I better get moving, the light's fading fast."

Standing and brushing snow off my pants, I waited for him to speak.

"Why are you so calm, so low key?"

His question caught me off guard. It was a question loaded with heaviness and depth, qualities I would never have associated with Mike Pigliani. Looking at him, I tried to figure out where his question had originated and what he was searching for in an answer.

"What do you mean?"

"I mean, does anything ever get under your skin? Do you even have a mean bone in your body?"

"Sure, lots of stuff gets under my skin. You, for instance, you get under my skin all the time. Also, I can't stand it when someone kicks the back of my seat when I'm at the movie theater. Why do you even care?"

"I don't care. I'm just trying to figure out what makes you tick. Like, why would you help me after all the shit I've put you through?"

"Because I wouldn't be able to live with myself if I just left you out here to die. I'm just not built like that. Yeah, you treat me like a doormat every time I turn around, but that doesn't mean I'm going to treat you like that in return."

He didn't say anything, opting to stare at the ever-darkening landscape.

"Why are you so violent?"

"It's all I know. I grew up with it."

His reply was chilling in how casually he said it.

"Well, I don't understand. So, you grew up with it. That doesn't mean you have to grow old with it as well. This cycle of violence you seem so consumed with? At some point it has to stop, and I've decided it stops with me. I'm not going to treat you in the same way that you've treated me. It's that simple."

"I just don't get it."

"Neither do I. At least we can agree on something."

Turning around to stare in the direction I planned to travel, I surveyed the landscape. Everything that had previously been stark white with snow, was now a dull, light gray in the rapidly fading light. When I turned around to look at Mike again, his expression had changed, bearing the unmistakable mark of fear.

"What's wrong, Mike?"

"I'm going to die out here, aren't I?"

His voice was just above that of a whisper.

"I will do everything in my power to see that that doesn't happen. I promise."

"I'm scared."

"Me too."

Reaching into my jeans pocket, I retrieved the red marble bear Koko had gifted me. It had an invisible warm glow to it. Thinking about it, and Koko, made me smile. Taking two steps toward Mike, I extended my hand, offering it to him.

He took the bear from my hand and turned it over in his, so tiny in his palm.

"What's this?"

"A bear that Koko gave me. It's a representation of and a reminder of the courage that we all have inside us. He gave it to me and told me to think about it whenever I was facing a difficult situation."

"Koko? The old Indian guy from the coffee shop? What am I supposed to do with it?"

"You just hold it, gain inner strength from it. That's what it's for. But it's only on loan, I want it back when you get out of here."

"This is stupid."

"It's not stupid."

My reply was rapid and forceful as I was losing patience with his foul attitude.

"Just hold on to it like I said. Oh, and whatever you do after I leave, don't fall asleep. You cannot allow yourself to doze off even for a second."

"I can't sleep? Why not?"

"Because if you do, there's a pretty good chance you won't wake up. I can't stress enough how important it is. I learned it in health class. Just don't do it OK?"

"Whatever. You're just being overly cautious. Don't sleep, that's ridiculous."

"I'm serious. If I find out you fell asleep out here, I'll tell everyone at school you pissed yourself and passed out."

Would I have carried out this threat? I doubt it, but he didn't know that.

"You're bluffing."

"Am I? Can you be certain I won't? I'll tell anyone that'll listen that you pissed all over yourself."

"Fine, I won't fall asleep. Are you happy now?"

He was clearly irritated.

"No, I'm not happy. I don't care what it takes, sing '99 Bottles of Beer on the Wall' if that's what it takes. Just stay awake."

"Alright, I got it. No sleeping!"

His shout reverberated through the forest.

"Okay. I'm out of here."

"Ashley?"

"Yeah?"

I turned to face him, silently shocked that he had, for the first time, called me by my real name.

"Don't let me die out here. Okay?"

A single tear ran down his right cheek.

Nodding, I turned around and began my solitary trek through the forest.

Twenty-Eight

Normally loathing the thought of being anywhere near Mike Pigliani, walking through the frozen forest, I still felt a profound sense of loneliness and isolation. The realization that his survival was very much in my hands was too much for me to process. Would I have to live the rest of my life knowing that Mike died because I failed to act? What did my immediate future look like? How long would I have to walk to find help? Would I survive? All were all open questions. Simply put, I was terrified.

The silence of the frigid, early evening was devastating in its completeness. Nothing stirred in the stillness. The howling wind and falling snow, now just memories. Not a single bird chirped.

Stopping at the edge of a clearing, I stared at the biggest, brightest, full moon I had ever seen, illuminating a field of undisturbed snow. The full moon gave the field a strange bluish-gray hue that seemed to glow in the dark. Sharing the sky were so many stars and twinkling celestial bodies, I briefly wondered if I were dreaming.

Standing in the cold, taking in the most beautiful sight I had ever witnessed, a thin streak of light flashed across the sky, moving rapidly from left to right, changing from a bright white to brilliant orange before changing yet again to red and finally to various shades of blue and purple before disappearing, leaving no trace it had been there at all. My first shooting star. Growing up in the city, I had never thought to look skyward, the stars were never visible, a product of significant light pollution. I had no idea or understanding shooting stars could be so brilliant, so colorful.

How far and for how long must it have traveled to be delivered to me at that exact moment? Likely millions of years and millions of miles. Probably billions. Having not traveled nearly that far or long, I still felt as isolated and alone as I ever had. Despite the beauty surrounding me, or perhaps because of it, I felt completely dislocated from time.

Knowing I had to keep moving, I lowered my eyes, putting one foot in front of the other, feeling somewhat guilty about ruining the peaceful smoothness of the snow-covered field with my tracks. Traversing the field took far longer than I had anticipated as the moonlit canvas made judging distances nearly impossible. Reaching the far edge of the wood, I looked back to see the deep black furrow of the trail I had left in the snow. The scene was remarkably depressing. Turning away from the field, I stepped forward, allowing the forest to swallow me once more.

Surrounded again by the naked trees and missing the dazzling radiance of the starry sky, I became mired with an overwhelming sense of doubt and dread. My preference was to just sit down in the snow and give up. My previous life, the one I had lived before Mike and his dad kidnapped me, flashed through my mind. That life was now gone, replaced by one I didn't recognize. Mom would always be there for me, but she could no longer protect me from the world, and I couldn't shake the thought that somehow, she would be sorely disappointed in how I was handling my current situation.

Thinking about Riley, my heart sank, as deep down I felt certain she wasn't really interested in me as a person but had merely been taking pity on me. It seemed impossible Mike had read the situation correctly. The card that she had presented me in the hospital, carefully signed by so many people, as well as her and Niki sitting with me at lunch every day at school, had been nothing more than a crystal-clear illusion. It was all smoke and mirrors, no more, no less. If I ever returned to Yorktown High, I would once again walk the crowded halls in abject and pitiful anonymity. Everything that had happened to me in the last few days had been my fault. The only person I had to blame was myself.

Leaning against a tree, I blew out a large sigh and slid, defeated, into the snow. No longer was there a point in continuing, in prolonging this misery. The easy way out would be to just sit here and freeze to death. Contemplating this, an image of Koko flooded my brain. At a time like this, I would have expected an image or thought of my mom. Both would be sorely disappointed seeing me give up like this, but Koko's visage wouldn't stop intruding into the recesses of my mind.

"When faced with a situation such as yours, would a true warrior give up? Would she or he slump, defeated, into the snow and refuse to rise?" I heard him ask.

The answer was perfectly clear, and I felt guilty immediately. No, a warrior would never give up, no matter the circumstances. Not allowing my head to hang for another second more, I picked myself up, brushed the snow off my jeans, and continued walking.

The hard, enduring cold, what I recently considered miserable and perhaps even dangerous, now entered the realm of life threatening. My fingers and toes had lost all feeling, and my jeans, despite temperatures well below freezing, were soaked through from the knee down. My head ached, the result of either being kicked in the face or dehydration. Probably both. Coming to a stop, I bent down and picked up some snow, studying it briefly before placing it in my mouth. It took longer for the snow to melt than I had expected. When it did, I forced it down, receiving the unwelcome sensation of instant brain freeze. My head pounded to such a degree; I feared I might pass out. Clinching my eyes shut, I waited for the storm of pain to pass.

Opening my eyes, I saw, directly in front of me, silhouetted against the full moon, something completely unexpected. Sitting on a branch roughly fifteen feet off the ground was a huge bright-eyed owl. Had the moon not been full, I wouldn't have seen the bird at all. He sat on his perch, tall and regal, seemingly all knowing, surveying everything in his vast kingdom. What must he think of me, I wondered. I considered that he might be a she. But how would I know?

"Whooo."

"Ashley."

"Whoo."

"I just told you."

The bird continued staring at me, unblinking.

"You wouldn't have any hot chocolate, would you?"

No reply.

"Yeah, I didn't think so. Thanks anyway."

Walking onward for several hours, my gait became one defined less by walking and more by stumbling and shuffling as I arrived at an abrupt rise in the landscape. At the bottom of the rise, the forest ceased to exist. The trees obviously couldn't be bothered with attaching themselves to such a steep incline, a notion making perfect sense in my delirious state. Looking left, then right, the forest continued along a line parallel with the steep incline which stretched for as far as I could see in the silver moonlight.

Slowly clambering my way up the steep slope, I reached the top and stood to see a sinuous ribbon of interstate, two lanes wide, shrinking to infinity as it reached the horizon. The far-left side of the roadway gave way to a wide expanse of snow-covered ground, beyond which lay two more lanes, no doubt for traveling in the opposite direction. The highway had not yet been plowed, though I noticed the unmistakable sign of traffic in two tire tracks running along the middle of the road. Reaching the highway, the first sign of civilization I'd seen in what seemed like ages and seeing evidence of life in the tire tracks, should have buoyed my spirits. It didn't, because I no longer cared. The combination of dehydration, lack of food, and the bone chilling temperature was taking a toll.

Turning to my right, I started walking, putting one foot in front of the other in the tire track on the right-hand side of the highway, the packed snow making the going just that little bit easier. Walking the tire track had not been a conscious decision, and I wondered how it had happened and how long I had been doing it.

Walking until I completely lost track of time, my mind wandered, conjuring forth images of my mom, Koko, Fred, and Riley. I thought about hot chocolate but couldn't remember what it tasted like. Oddly, I wondered what Mike was doing. Likely terrorizing a poor, hapless creature of the forest, despite his broken leg. Mike Pi— what was his last name? I should know this.

No longer picking up feet I was too tired to lift, I shuffled along the middle of the highway, barely able to keep my eyes open. Staring straight ahead, zombie-like, a brief twinkle of blue light flashed in front of me, there and gone so quickly, I realized I had seen another shooting star racing across the silent horizon.

Another shooting star, this one bright red and equally as fleeting as its blue companion, streaked across the sky. How lucky must I be to see two bright shooting stars in such quick succession? Struggling, stumbling forward, I saw more shooting stars, all bright blue and red. A meteor shower, I was witnessing a meteor shower! As if to celebrate my astronomical discovery, my friend the forest owl called out from what sounded like every direction possible.

"Whooooooo! Whoooooooo!"

"Please stop yelling, I have a headache."

As I pondered what my owl friend was scolding me about, the highway in front of me lit up as if someone had thrown a switch. One moment I was staring into the silver hued night sky and the next, it was daylight, as if, during a brilliant blue and red meteor shower, the owl felt the need to yell at me at the top of his lungs and suddenly turn on the sun.

Slowly turning around to determine the cause of the commotion, I was greeted by a pair of blinding headlights and the pulsating rhythm of blue and red emergency lights that could only belong to a police car or ambulance. The deafening sound of my owl friend came to a merciful stop, replaced by the dull thump of a car door being closed. Standing motionless in my bewildered state as an individual approached, I made no attempt to shield my eyes from the piercing headlight beams. The person, who I hoped was police officer, stopped a few feet in front of me.

"Wow, what happened to you?"

"Are you Detective Sharply?"

He closed the distance between us.

"No, I'm Officer Bentley. What's your name?"

Looking me up and down, I noticed concern in his eyes.

"Half-breed"

A niggling feeling in the back of my mind wondered whether my answer was correct, but I couldn't figure out why.

"No, I don't think so. Are you Ashley? Ashley Perrault?"

He had a thick accent; one I couldn't place. Nodding, I swayed back and forth, my balance and ability to remain upright becoming more precarious with each passing second.

"Whoa, there. Let's get you back to my patrol car, get you warmed up, OK?"

Officer Bentley reached out to grab my shoulders to steady me. Remaining silent, I slowly nodded as, with much deliberateness, he guided me back to the passenger side of his patrol car. As we walked, he spoke to his radio, the words and numbers sounding like another language entirely. Arriving at the patrol car, he opened the door and helped me get situated in the seat. Convinced I was comfortably in place, he closed the door, walked around the rear of the car, got in, and closed the door.

Immediately, the warmth of the car's interior enveloped me. Leaning my head back against the seat, I closed my eyes, wanting nothing more than to sleep for a few days straight.

"Nope. No way, Ashley. Keep those eyes open for me, OK?" He said, flipping on the interior light. "I know you're tired, but you need stay awake." he added.

I dutifully opened my eyes and lifted my head off the seat.

"That's better. You thirsty? You look parched."

"So thirsty."

My voice was scratchy, almost gravelly, not sounding like my own.

"I thought so."

He miraculously made a bottle of water appear from nowhere.

"Okay Ashley, you need listen to me, alright? I'm going to give you this bottle of water, but you must promise me that you're going to sip it very slowly. If you start to guzzle it all down at once, I'm going to take it away and not give it back. I'm not trying to be a hard ass, but if you drink it too quickly bad things could happen. Okay?"

"Promise."

Watching intently, he handed me the bottle and I took the first tentative sips of water I'd had in days. It took all the effort I could muster to not empty the entire bottle. My body cried out for every precious molecule of water it could get.

"Okay, that's good. Take a break for now OK, let your body adjust. You're severely dehydrated. We want your body to take it in slowly."

I did as he asked, lowering my arm and allowing it and the bottle of water to rest gently in my lap.

With my mind struggling to stay awake in the warm, dry confines of the patrol car, I remembered Mike and his gruesome injury. Sitting bolt upright in the seat, I looked at Officer Bentley, my mind striving to force the words from my mouth. Knowing what I wanted to say, my mouth refused to cooperate.

"What's wrong Ashley?"

"Uh ..."

My mind raced as I tried to formulate the correct combination of words.

"Neanderthal. We need help him! He's broken. Bleed to death. You have to help!"

"What? I don't know what you're talking about Ashley. Slow down."

His calm demeanor irritated me.

"Follow my tracks in the snow, you'll find him sitting under a tree. Mike, his name is Mike. He's in bad shape!"

The words tumbled out as fast as I could formulate them.

"We already found him, Ashley. A helicopter spotted him in the woods about an hour ago, that's how we knew you were in the area."

"How?"

"I don't know the details, but someone called in a vehicle fire, a white van which turned out to match one we were looking for. But it sounds like he's going to make it. Don't worry, OK?"

I leaned back in the seat, dumbfounded, but relieved. I felt a hundred pounds lighter knowing Mike had been found and was getting the care he needed. I wondered next about his father.

"What about his dad? Did you find him? I think he's dead."

"No, they didn't find Mr. Pigliani. They found a pool of blood in the snow and tracks leading away from it, but so far it looks like he's still out there somewhere. Like I said, they found his burnt-out van stuck on the side of the road, but no sign of him."

"He's bad. Dangerous. Very angry." I said, turning to look at him.

"He's exceedingly dangerous. We've been aware of him for quite some time. Every cop in the state is out there looking for him right now."

Not knowing how to respond to this information, I said nothing, preferring to stare off into space. Now moving along the interstate at an alarming rate of speed, I realized I couldn't recall Officer Bentley putting the car into drive and setting off. One minute we were sitting still in the middle of the highway and the next we were in a completely different location, moving with dizzying speed.

"Ashley! Wake up buddy."

With great lethargy, I turned my head to look at him.

"I am awake. You don't have to yell."

"Okay, good. Just making sure."

"Did you know a bullet makes a sound as it zips by your head? I didn't know that." I mentioned.

"What? Uh, yeah, I did know that. I did two tours in Afghanistan, so yeah, I've been shot at several times."

As the interior of the car warmed me, I felt the strange sensation of fluid dribbling down my chin. With my still gloved hand, I wiped my chin and was unsurprised when it came into view covered with blood.

"Ugh. My nose is bleeding. Again. This is getting tiresome."

As though having a bloody nose was perfectly normal.

Swiveling his head in my direction to ascertain the severity of the problem, Officer Bentley' eyes grew wide as he pushed the car to even greater speeds.

"We need to get that bleeding stopped. Can you pinch your nose shut with your fingers?"

"Nope, no way. That'll hurt too much. Not going to happen. Sorry. You're going too fast for the conditions you know. You're going to get a ticket."

"Okay, no problem. What I want you to do is lean your head forward, put your chin as close to your chest as possible. Can you do that for me?"

"Yeah, sure. That'll be easy."

I did as he asked, lowering my head, attempting to get my chin to touch my chest. After about ten seconds I lifted my head and looked at my riding companion.

"How long do I have to stay like this?"

Blood continued to flow unabated, down my face.

"Until the bleeding stops."

"Huh. That figures."

Lowering my chin to my chest seemed like the appropriate thing to do.

Twenty-Nine

Officer Bentley received garbled instructions over the radio, answering them in a similarly garbled fashion before slowing to pull off the highway onto a narrow, bumpy road adjacent to a large field.

"Okay Ashley, we're here. Have you ever ridden in a helicopter?"

"What? How'd we get here? Where are we?"

Lifting my head, I saw a red and white helicopter, blades whirring, approaching the field not far from the car.

"We need to get you to a hospital as quickly as possible and the best way to do that is by helicopter. Don't worry, you'll love it."

Watching the helicopter as it transitioned from forward to vertical flight was astounding. The flashing lights on the helicopter's tail and underside blinked with enthusiasm, reminding me of the blue and red meteor shower I'd witnessed earlier. The helicopter, lights and all, disappeared in a swirling riot of snow thrown up from the blinding whir of the craft's main rotor blade as it neared the ground.

Shortly after touching down, two people exited the helicopter with what looked like a bright yellow table on wheels.

"Do you think owls are jealous of helicopters?"

"That's an interesting question Ashley. Umm … yeah, they might be."

Leaving the warmth of the car, Officer Bentley met the pair. They chatted as they approached, but from the warm confines of the police car and over the loud whirring of the helicopter, I couldn't hear any of it.

The three of them, accompanied by the yellow, wheeled table, walked briskly to the passenger side of the car. Officer Bentley opened the car door allowing a frigid blast of air to invade the peaceful cocoon of the interior.

"Okay Ashley, these two brave souls are going to strap you to the gurney here and off you go. Cool?"

"Umm, yeah sure. I guess."

My reply was laced with caution as I wasn't sure precisely what was going to happen next.

"It's OK, they'll take good care of you. No problem."

He stepped back, providing the helicopter crew room to approach. The two, dressed in dark blue uniforms with yellow script embroidered on the chest and wearing flight helmets closely mimicking the color scheme of the helicopter, bright red with white stripes, stepped forward.

"Hi, Ashley. I'm Officer Scott, the flight paramedic and next to me is Officer Blackburn, the flight nurse. We'll be taking care of you from here on out. Okay?" He raised his voice so I could hear him.

Gazing from Officer Scott to Officer Blackburn and back again, saying nothing, I nodded, experiencing a growing sense of apprehension about being put into a helicopter and flown to parts unknown.

"Have you ever flown in a helicopter before?"

"I've never flown in anything. Ever."

"Great! You're going to love it."

Easy for him to say, flying is a part of his job. I stared, wide eyed, at the two of them, wondering what flying would feel like.

"Uh huh."

"Ashley, I'm Officer Blackburn. Do you think you can stand?"

Officer Blackburn's piercing blue eyes and red hair and beard convinced me he had been a sea captain in a former life.

"Psshhh. Yeah, easy."

Officer Blackburn leaned in an unbuckled my seatbelt. Swinging my legs to the right and lowering them to the frozen, snow-covered ground, I stood up to face Blackburn and Scott, whereupon I immediately began swaying in increasingly wider arcs, left and right. With widening eyes, the fear of falling spread to all areas of my body as I attempted to raise my arms. As soon as I felt sure I was going down, Blackburn and Scott caught me by the shoulders and stood me up straight.

"How about we get you on this gurney here instead," Officer Scott offered as he and Officer Blackburn stepped in closer to steady me. When Blackburn felt I was secure and in no immediate danger of falling, he turned toward the bright yellow gurney and in one swift motion lowered it so that the underside was nearly touching the snow-covered ground.

"Alright, let's get you turned around and situated over the gurney," Scott said, gently turning me by the shoulders to stand next to the gurney.

"Okay Ashley, I want you to slowly bend your knees and sit on the gurney. Blackburn and I will help you every step of the way. Okay?"

Without replying, I very gingerly lowered myself until I felt the gurney begin accepting my weight.

"That's great. Now we're going to swing your legs over so you can lie down," Scott said.

They did as he instructed and before I knew it, I was being strapped snuggly into place. With Blackburn at the head of the gurney and Scott at foot, they lifted the entire apparatus so that it stood high above the ground, and we began the short trip to the helicopter. Officer Bentley walked alongside Scott, talking to him about something, but, as before, I couldn't hear a word of it.

When Scott and Blackburn had me loaded inside the helicopter, they boarded and began the process of making sure everything was secure. From my limited vantage point, sitting low inside the helicopter and staring at the ceiling, I could see strange blinking lights, clear tubes attached to oxygen bottles, and switches and buttons everywhere. Even though it was very businesslike and serious, it was a feast for the eyes. I imagined the helicopter had a very distinct smell, but with my nose in the broken state it was in, I couldn't smell anything.

Blackburn closed and secured the helicopter door, sealing us inside and insulating us from the loud exterior pandemonium of the engine and the biting cold. I could just see Officer Bentley as he smiled and gave me a confident wave and thumbs up. He then turned and, in a crouch, carefully jogged back to his patrol car. I was sorry he had left without giving me a chance to thank him.

Thirty

Scott and Blackburn donned headsets enabling them to talk to one another and the pilot. After Scott had given me a quick nod of his head, we were airborne. The alarming sensation of what I could only guess was a very momentary feeling of weightlessness flooded over me as my stomach did a loop. By the time my eyes had widened in response, the feeling had passed, and we were skimming over the treetops as the helicopter gained altitude. As excited as I was about my first ride in a helicopter, I struggled to keep my eyes open, instantly overcome with fatigue. Consciously, I tried to focus on anything that would hold my attention, anything to allow me to ward off the coming storm of sleep, to experience the thrill of heavier than air flight for the first time. Despite my efforts focusing on everything from the name on Blackburn's flight suit to the dancing rhythm of the clear tubing that led to a panel on the wall of the helicopter, the battle was lost.

Waking to a sharp, burning sensation in my left arm, I looked around, unsure of where I was, unable to make sense of the strange gathering of sounds and bizarre physical sensations created by the finely tuned, almost imperceptible vibration created by the helicopter's engine and rotor blades. Everything became clear as Officer Scott put the final piece of tape on the IV he had just placed under the skin of my arm. To protest such a thing would prove fruitless, the IV was there to stay whether I liked it or not.

Strapped to a gurney in a helicopter, flying at who only knew how fast and how high, once again, no longer in control of what happened, a feeling of helplessness assaulted me. I was reminded of the despair I felt during my first hospital visit and again while being held by Mike and his dad. I began to cry, tears rolling freely down my cheeks, doubtless moistening the pillow beneath my head. In an ordinary circumstance, I would have valiantly fought against the rushing tide of emotions, but on this occasion, I didn't bother. With so much going on in my life, I could no longer constructively deal with it as incredible amounts of pain, exhaustion, hunger, thirst, and fear all fought for my attention.

I thought of the people in my life and how important to me they were: Koko, Riley and Niki, Greg, Marni and Detective Sharply, I even thought of Fred, but mostly I thought of my mom. As difficult as my ordeal had been, I considered that it was most certainly just as difficult for her. I missed her terribly. I also wanted to be happy, expecting to be overcome with boundless feelings of elation and joy at being far away from the Piglianis. I felt none of these things. I was confused, and all I really wanted to do was crawl into a hole and disappear forever. I was torn, once again, from the relative clarity of consciousness, by fatigue as it grabbed hold with a vice-like grip, dragging me into the darkening depths of sleep, a place I desperately didn't want to go.

Opening my eyes, the confusion of unfamiliar surroundings was becoming a familiar occurrence as I stared up at stark, white ceiling tiles, evenly punctuated by bright fluorescent lights. The steady, rhythmic beep of an alien looking machine hanging next to me kept the time, which I guessed was the machine's interpretation of my heartbeat. The beep was calm and steady, betraying the chaos my life had become. Focusing on the clinical sound of my own heartbeat, the muted sounds of voices gathered in considered conversation could also be heard, though I couldn't ascertain who they were or what they were talking about.

Desperately wanting answers for the myriad questions that were attempting to form in the folds of my foggy, sleep deprived brain, I drew on my previous hospital experience and looked for the handheld controller that was sure to be close by. Scanning left, the familiar long plastic rectangle hanging on the shiny stainless-steel railing of my hospital bed came into view. With little thought, I reached for it only to be painfully reminded of the IV needle still imbedded in my arm. Gritting my teeth through the sharp pain, I grasped the controller and saw the familiar buttons for the TV: on, off, volume, mute, channel selector. I knew there had to be one that summoned a nurse, but I just couldn't find it. The concentration required to locate the correct button was giving me a headache.

Utterly frustrated, I gave up, dropping the maddening puzzle onto the bed. When the pain had subsided to a manageable level, I tried again. And there it was, the nurse call button, centered right at the top of the rectangle, blue with a blocky white interpretation of a nurse emblazoned upon it. Feeling completely ridiculous for having missed it in the first place, I pressed the button and waited.

In no time at all, a fuzzy form filled the doorway to my room and entered. Through blurry vision, I tried to focus on the approaching apparition, but my eyes wouldn't cooperate.

"What can I help you with?"

"My hands and feet hurt. What's wrong with me? Where am I?"

"As strange as this may sound, that's a good thing, it means the blood flow to your extremities is returning. But, yes, it's going to be painful. You were suffering from hypothermia, so the fact that you have feeling in your hands and feet is a good thing. I'll give you something for the pain."

She looked at her watch.

"Hold on, I'll be right back."

Not wanting to be alone, I began to object but stopped when her blurry outline disappeared. I closed my eyes and waited for her eventual return. When I opened them again, she was administering some kind of drug, presumably a painkiller of some sort, into the clear plastic tube of my IV.

"There, that ought to do it. You should start feeling better soon."

"How long have I been here?"

"Umm, I'm not sure. I just started my shift and I know you weren't here yesterday, so, less than 24 hours for sure," she replied. "But once the doctor makes sure you're OK to travel, you're going to be transferred to St. Peters. Shouldn't take too long if I had to guess."

Pondering this new information, I started to feel the undeniable effects of the painkiller coursing through my system. I began to feel, ever so slightly, like I was floating a few inches above the bed. I was also fading fast, which I didn't want to do, as I had too many unasked questions bouncing around in my head. I fought for consciousness, trying to focus my attention on the blurry face of the nurse at my bedside.

"Wait. What's your name?" My visual acuity continued to deteriorate. Her mouth moved in answer to my question, but I couldn't hear the words. I was frustrated and no longer able to feel my hands and feet. Again, I was fighting a pitched battle with sleep, a battle I knew from experience I could not win. Sleep will win every single time, and it did.

Upon waking, I was bombarded again with an overwhelming sense of confusion. The room was vibrating and noisy and from my bed I could see a bright blue sky streaming in from the window. It took me awhile to figure out I was in the cramped confines of a helicopter again. There were lights, tubes and wires attached to seemingly every surface and the whole ensemble hummed with the finely tuned oscillating precision of the helicopter's powerful engines. I sighed, pondering my luck. Here I was, on my second helicopter ride, too tired and too doped up to be able to take it all in. Desperately, I wanted to enjoy this unbelievable experience, but sleep, the silent assassin, had other ideas; my vision faded to black once again. I didn't even try to fight it.

Thirty-One

I was walking, led by the hand by someone I couldn't see. The pace was slow and steady, calm. Stopping, my guide turned me ninety degrees to the right, whereupon a blindfold was removed from my eyes. Standing before a large rectangle, slightly longer than it was tall and bordered on all four sides with a band of gold, appeared to be a painting, one composed of a bright, bold, blue background with splashes of orange, brilliant reds and greens and the muted earth tones of tan and brown. Unable to make sense of what I was seeing, I turned my head to the right to face my companion. Someone was there, someone familiar to me, but they were as blurry and jumbled as the picture hanging before us. I tried to speak, to ask one of the many questions swirling around in my head, but when I opened my mouth, no words came out.

Without thinking, I turned back to the painting and stared, waiting patiently as the image slowly came into focus. In front of me was the powerful image of a proud First Nation warrior sitting atop a horse. Facing me, the warrior gazed upon something unseen and slightly to his left, appearing to look at something located behind my right shoulder. Held high above his head by the sinewy muscles of his right arm on his lean, tan frame was a coup stick. The stick was impressive, brightly colored, with an alternating pattern of red and off-white beads with many feathers of black and white hanging from the shaft. This warrior had successfully counted coups many times.

The horse, a mottled mixture of white and brown, with ears that stood straight and tall and spoke of a bright intelligence, was magnificent. The warrior sat bareback with no saddle or blanket: a true horseman. There were many things about the warrior which were impressive, but it was his countenance that made the difference. His look was not one of defiance or pride, but confidence. His appearance spoke of someone who understood his place in the world and who he was within it. The warrior and his horse were perched atop a large hill covered with tall, green grass that flowed in the wind like waves. Beyond him, in the distance, tall, dark mountains loomed, the peaks of which were covered with a blanket of snow. I turned again to look at my guide and was surprised to see Koko standing next to me. Turning to look at me, he smiled wide, an expression I had grown to admire. He smiled not just with his mouth, but with his dark brown eyes that sparkled with life as he silently nodded, placing the blindfold over my eyes again.

Walking in silence and darkness, it was some time before we stopped again. Instinctively, I turned ninety degrees to my right, waiting for Koko to remove the blindfold. With the veil removed, I opened my eyes to see the same First Nation warrior, this time he sat near a glowing campfire. It was nighttime and the dancing flames of the fire cast a warm orange glow on the dusky outlines of a group of teepees behind him. Above, a blue-black sky dotted with more stars than could possibly be counted was segmented by a wispy band of the Milky Way. The warrior was smiling wide, surrounded by a group of people I instinctively understood to be his family. On his right, his wife, wearing the same wide, freely expressed smile of her husband. Her dark eyes reflected the rich, warm light of the fire as she gazed upon the children playing around her. Most surprising was the vast number of people in the painting. The warrior sat at the center, surrounded, not just by his immediate family, but by his entire family, his tribe. Around the fire were parents, grandparents, brothers, sisters, aunts, and uncles. No one was left out. Everyone was smiling, enjoying the company of the most important people in their lives. At the edge of the gathering stood a tall, strong figure, hidden in shadow. I was unable to obtain a clear image of his face, but he seemed important.

I had never witnessed a group of people so happy to be alive and in the presence of those they loved. I was unaware that times such as these were even remotely possible, and it warmed my heart to its very core to witness this moment in time, captured forever on canvas.

When I felt the time was right, I turned my head toward Koko, letting him know without words that I was ready to continue. Smiling and gently placing the blindfold over my eyes, he placed his right hand on my left shoulder as we continued our journey. While I was aware of walking for quite a long distance, I never noticed the passage of time. I didn't tire or grow bored and listless. In fact, I was consumed by a peacefulness and calm I had never experienced.

At the appropriate time and place we stopped, resuming the ritual as I turned and waited for Koko to remove the blindfold. This new painting, just as large and vibrant as the previous ones, depicted the ethereal moments in the sky at dusk, the elusive phase in between day and night, possessing the attributes of both but being neither at the same time. The clouds in the distance, a mosaic of deep oranges, pinks, and grays foretold a coming storm. In the center, the same warrior, now lying flat on his back atop a large rock outcropping. The skin on his once smooth face was weathered and lined with the wise wrinkles only old age can produce. His long dark hair, now thin and gray, lay comfortably around his ears and shoulders. Though I quickly realized I was witnessing the warrior's funeral, I wasn't saddened.

Surrounding the warrior were many, though not all, of the same people present in the previous painting. Near the center was the unmistakable image of the warrior's wife, her hair, now a mixture of black and gray, appeared to have been hastily braided giving her a disheveled look. Her face, covered in white paint, was weathered and lined, much like her husband's had been, framing eyes still possessing a youthfulness time could not erase. She was sad, that much was clear, but there was something else in her appearance I couldn't put my finger on, something I didn't yet understand. Allowing my eyes to wander around the painting, she had at her side her now grown children. Her grandchildren, hanging close by the sides of their parents, waited patiently for the ceremony to begin.

There was a tight knit closeness among the attendees, a familiarity that can only be achieved through relying on those around you. Again, at the periphery of the gathering, was the tall, strong figure I had seen in the previous painting. Though not hidden in shadow, his identity remained elusive, almost as if that portion of the painting had been purposefully blurred.

The people in the painting were more than just individuals gathered to remember the fallen warrior; they were more than a tribe; they were family. Standing, taking in all the details of the painting I could, I wanted to remember everything, not just the brilliance of the colors and the images they produced, but the feelings. I wanted to remember the subtle nuances on the faces of the people and what they must have been feeling in the moment. Most of all, I wanted to remember how all of those things made me feel. I was shellshocked that a painting could create such an emotional impact on its viewer. Until now, paintings, and art in general, were just things, but I now had a new worldview, as I understood that things had meaning and emotion far beyond what was revealed on the surface. The three paintings I had just been shown were dynamic, living forces of nature.

A solitary tear escaped the corner of my left eye as instinct told me it was time. Turning to Koko to thank him for taking me on this unbelievable journey, I gazed into the depths of his brown eyes as tears streamed down my face. I realized he had taken me on a brief, yet infinitely profound, exploration of a world I didn't even know existed, crossing the threshold of a world I understood, had grown comfortable in, and into a world where everything was new. It felt like opening my eyes for the first time. In knowing silence, Koko smiled and nodded.

Without opening his mouth, he said, "You are welcome, Ashley. And thank you."

Slowly, he reached out and placed the blindfold over my eyes.

Thirty-Two

My surroundings, appearing as a blurry smear of colors while my eyes struggled to open and with my brain slowly recognizing the rhythmic beep of a heart monitor nearby, seemed oddly familiar. There was the vague memory of a helicopter ride, so I was likely back in St. Peter's Hospital. Breathing in and out, I waited while my lazy eyes resolved the confines of my room. Looking around, expecting to see my mom, and, perhaps, Koko, I was gifted instead with deafening silence. Not a soul to be seen, not my mom, not Koko, not a single nurse or doctor. A multitude of get-well cards and flowers had been placed on the bedside table, along with flowers occupying every bit of space on the windowsill. In fact my only companion was the clinical, rhythmic beep of my heart monitor. Propping myself up on my elbows, I immediately collapsed as my head, ribs, and right arm simultaneously erupted in pain. Looking at my right arm, I discovered the source of at least some of the pain taped to the inside bend of my elbow, the protruding tubes of an IV. Blowing out an exasperated sigh, I waited for the pain to subside to a more manageable level before deciding what to do next.

Feeling reasonably confident I could engage my brain again without passing out, I slowly looked around the room, spotting the small plastic control panel hanging on the left rail of my bed. Easily within reach, I grabbed it without having to jostle the IV in my right arm and, without looking, pressed the nurse call button.

Less than a minute later, the door to my room opened.

Marnie glided into the room, beaming her infectious smile.

"Hey there, Ashley. You'll do just about anything for attention."

"Hi Marnie."

My voice was so scratchy and raw it surprised me.

"Boy, am I glad to see you. How are you feeling?"

Confused, thirsty, in pain, exhausted, and hungry, I didn't know how to respond. Not knowing where to start, I searched Marnie's face, looking for a clue.

Sensing my confusion, her smile never faded.

"What's the first thing that comes to mind?"

"Where is everyone?"

"Don't worry, everyone is here," she calmly stated before pausing.

"The waiting room is bursting at the seams with people wanting to know how you're doing."

Precisely as Marnie finished her sentence, Dr. Albermarle quietly entered the room.

"Hi Dr. Meg."

"Hi Ashley. Ugh, it's so good to see your smiling face. How about next time it's not under these kinds of circumstances OK?"

"Yeah, OK."

"How are you feeling?" she asked, checking my temperature and flashing a bright light in my eyes.

"Thirsty, exhausted and hungry. Where's my family?"

Immediately, I recognized this as the first time in my life I'd used the term 'family' in this context. Before today, family simply meant my mom, so I would just say, 'Mom,' whenever someone asked about my family. But this time, I meant 'family' in the same way everyone else means it when they use the word. To me, family now encompassed not just my mom, but Koko, Marnie, Dr. Greg and Dr. Albermarle, and even Fred the cat. My family consisted of all the people that cared about me, whether they were related to me or not. Prior to now, it would have seemed awkward, nearly impossible, to consider anyone other than my mom, a part of my family. Now it seemed essential, it seemed natural.

"They're in the waiting area. I wanted to make sure you were fit to have visitors before letting anyone in to see you. There's a bunch of them out there, too. You're popular around here."

"Huh. Okay."

"So, what do you think? You up for some visitors?"

"Sure. Can't wait."

"Great. I'll be right back with some crushed ice too."

Shortly after Dr. Meg left, the door opened, and my mom walked into the room. As soon as our eyes met, we both started to cry, the tears falling freely and without struggle for both of us. It felt like I hadn't seen her in ages and in my mind's eye, she appeared much older than when I last saw her. Reaching my bedside, she leaned over and kissed me on the forehead.

"I'm sorry, Mom." I said in a sobbing, scratchy voice.

"No. No, honey. You don't have to be sorry. What do you have to be sorry for?"

"For putting you through this."

"You didn't put me through this. None of this is your fault. You are not responsible for what happened."

"Why did this happen?"

"I don't know, Ashley. Sometimes, incredibly horrible things happen to people with the kindest souls. This is one of those times."

"I don't want to be afraid anymore."

Tears streamed down my face and onto the pillow beneath my head.

"You don't have to be, sweetie. As soon as you don't want to be afraid, all you have to do is decide not to be. It sounds simple, and in a way, it is."

"I don't understand."

"In time, you will. It took me longer than I care to admit until I was able to wrap my head around it too. But for me, it happened shortly after your father was killed. After the trial and all that mess, I was terrified. I had no idea how I was going to go on without him. I was afraid of my own shadow, but one day the realization came to me, fully formed, that I was either going to be a victim of fear for the rest of my life, or I was going to get in the game and forge ahead despite it. I had a decision to make, victim or victor. I chose victor."

After a few moments of silence, the door opened, and Koko entered the room looking completely exhausted, wearing a serious look on his face. It was the first time I had seen him not smiling for any length of time.

Approaching my bed, he stopped just to the right of my mom, took one look at me, and began to cry, tears escaping his brown eyes, tears he made no attempt to hide. He sniffled, wiping the tears from his face as he stood. The raw, unfettered display of emotion surprised me.

"I am sorry Ashley. I am just so very happy to see you."

"That's OK. You don't have to apologize. I'm very happy to see you as well."

Looking at Koko, my mom smiled, turned and pulled out a chair that had been resting against the nearby wall, offering it to him. Koko cracked a halfhearted smile and sat down, his hand shaking noticeably as he pulled a small red handkerchief from his pocket to dab the tears on his face.

"How is Fred?"

"Mr. Fred has not been himself lately. He is not eating and has spent quite a lot of time howling. I am certain he can sense the stress of the situation you were in."

"I can't wait to see him. Maybe he'll start eating again soon?"

"Yes, I hope so. He will be happy to see you, I am sure."

Dr. Meg entered the room, handing me a small, plastic cup of crushed ice after rounding the foot of the bed.

"So, how's it going? You feeling, OK?"

"Yeah, OK, I guess. I'm more tired than anything else. And my face hurts, quite a lot."

"That's to be expected. You have a broken nose and those tend to be rather painful. Eat some ice, take it slow, maybe it'll take your mind off the pain a little."

Until I put the first few pieces of ice into my mouth, I had no idea how thirsty I was. The melting ice was a wonder and I found it astonishing a few small pieces could so drastically lift my mood.

"Well, I hate to break up the party, but Ashley needs his rest, so visiting time is officially over," Dr. Meg announced.

"Aww, we just got here."

The exclamation came from just outside the room. Filling the space of the open doorway were Riley and her mom, both wearing looks of disappointment.

"Alright," Dr. Meg answered, glancing at her watch, "just a few more minutes."

"Cool," Riley replied.

An excited smile replaced the disappointment on her face as she walked around to the right side of the bed to stand next to Dr. Meg. Wearing a large, puffy, white jacket, blue jeans, with her hair pulled back in a ponytail and held in place by a black bandana that likely doubled as an ear warmer, she looked as terrific as usual. As wonderful as she appeared, there was more than a hint of exhaustion in both her and her mom.

"Hey Riley, how are you?" I asked with a painful smile.

"Pretty good. The more important question is how are you doing? I've got to be honest; you don't look so good."

"Oh this?" I motioned to my face with my left hand. "Yeah. I'm going with the rugged look, trying to change my image a little bit. What do you think?"

"Umm. Okay, it's not really working. I prefer the old fashioned, not beat up version."

"Me too. The rugged look might work for some people. I'm just not one of them."

I took a moment to catch my breath.

"Besides, it's painful to pull off successfully."

"It looks that way," Riley's mom added, cringing.

"Okay, that's it. Everybody out. Ashley needs his rest and by the look of things, so do the rest of you," Dr. Meg announced.

"What? But..." Riley began to object.

Dr. Meg interrupted.

"Nope. No buts, no exceptions. Everyone must go."

"Ugh. Okay. Sorry, Ashley," Riley said, dejected.

"That's OK. I don't think I'm going anywhere."

"True. Can we come back tomorrow?" Riley asked, turning to look at her mom.

"Sure. If it's alright with Ashley?"

"Absolutely!" I exclaimed with a bit more enthusiasm than intended. "I mean, yeah. That would be great."

Blushing with embarrassment, I hoped my bruised and swollen face hid the evidence.

"Okay. See you tomorrow." Riley smiled and stared at her shoes before she and her mom turned and left the room.

"Well, I guess I have to go too, honey." My mom sighed, appearing far more composed and at ease than she had when entering the room.

"I love you, Ashley."

"I love you too, Mom"

"I must go as well Ashley. But we will come back tomorrow," Koko said, with emphasis.

"Yeah, OK." I said, unable to hide my disappointment as they turned, heading toward the door.

"Koko?" I asked as my mom crossed the threshold of the room to enter the hallway.

"Yes?" He turned in the doorway to face me.

"Sometime soon, can we talk?"

"Yes. Absolutely, Ashley. Are you OK?"

"Yeah. But I need help sorting some things out in my head. I had a weird dream, and I can't make sense of it."

Koko's look changed from concern to serious contemplation.

"A dream? Yes, we can talk about that if you like."

I nodded my head. Koko nodded in response and with a smile, left the room.

Thirty Three

Waking early the next morning to a throbbing headache, I was thankful the room was dark, the window shades having been drawn closed at an earlier time. Without looking, I reached for the remote control, pushing the nurse call button as if it were second nature. About a minute later, Marnie bounded into the room, her comfortable sneakers squeaking on the smooth tile floor, with her usual amount of enthusiasm, which is to say, a lot.

"Hey Ashley. What's up? What can I do for you?"

"I have a terrible headache, and I'm so thirsty I can hardly stand it."

"Okay. Hold on, I'll be right back."

Spinning on her heels, she quickly left the room.

Returning several minutes later with a glass of water and two small white pills, she gently placed them in my left hand, waiting for me to put them in my mouth before handing me the small cup of water.

"These are your basic, run of the mill aspirins. Hopefully, it'll do the trick. I can't give you anything stronger until Dr. Meg comes in later."

"Thank you. I think it may be that I'm dehydrated."

"Yeah, probably."

"What are you doing here? Weren't you here last night?"

"I was. But it's already early afternoon. You've been asleep all day."

Even through my bruised and swollen face, Marnie could apparently see my shocked reaction.

"Don't be too surprised. You've been through a lot. I'd be alarmed if you weren't sleeping most of the time."

"Wow. I thought it was early morning."

"Nope. It's..." She paused to glance at her watch. "... just after two o'clock. Oh, and Jack, umm ...Detective Sharply, called and said he might stop by later to see how you're doing."

She turned away in an unsuccessful attempt to hide her blush.

"Jack? Who's Ja—? Wait a second, you guys are on a first name basis. I thought you found him detestable in every way possible."

"Wellllll, he may have, you know, asked me out. It happens."

A sheepish grin appeared on her face as she slowly backed her way toward the door.

"He asked you out? Detective Sharply? The same Detective Sharply you tried to kick out of my room? The obviously color-blind Detective Sharply? Well? What did you say? Are you going to go out with him?"

Offering no response, Marnie quickly turned, practically skipping out of the room.

"Hey, you can't leave me hanging like that." I yelled as the door closed.

"Friends don't leave friends hanging. It's not right!"

Marnie's muffled giggles echoed off the dull, off-white hospital walls as she walked away. Detective Sharply and Nurse Marnie? Shaking off my disbelief, I spent the next half hour flipping through channels on TV, trying, unsuccessfully, to find something interesting to watch. As if predetermined, I turned the TV off, placing the remote next to me, when the door opened to reveal Koko.

"May I come in?"

"Hi Koko. Sure, come on in. I'm awake."

Pulling out the chair next to my bed he sat down. During this short, seemingly innocuous display of entering the room and sitting down, Koko's fluid, effortless movements made scarcely a sound. I couldn't help but marvel at the grace with which Koko carried himself.

"Ah, good. I was afraid of waking you. How are you feeling?"

"Aside from a pretty ridiculous headache I actually feel OK."

"Good. That is excellent news. Well, except for the headache part."

Looking at Koko, I made a rather surprising and sudden realization as a wry smile slowly widened on my bruised and swollen face.

"Koko, what time is it?"

"It is…" He raised his left hand, glancing at the watch strapped to his wrist. "…2:35."

"Uh huh. When are visiting hours?"

"I am not entirely certain. Sometime later this afternoon I would guess."

He said this as a simple matter of fact, squaring his shoulders, smiling wide, the smile of someone who knew exactly what he was doing. He was breaking the rules, and he knew it. Just like having Fred living in his apartment, Koko occasionally saw no reason to adhere to what he viewed as the arbitrary norms placed upon him by society.

I made no attempt at hiding my delight at witnessing Koko's subversiveness.

"Did you sneak in?"

"No, I walked in like I did yesterday. No one paid any attention to me. The trick is appearing like you belong wherever it is that you are. It is not hard."

"You're not much for following rules, are you?"

"Well, rules are fine, I guess. But I have little use for rules that are needless."

"Like visiting hour rules?"

"Precisely. If I arrive at 2:35 instead of 4:00, either way, I am still here. Besides, I was not consulted when the rules were implemented in the first place."

"Yeah, that makes sense."

"You said last night that you wanted to talk about something. I figured it might be better if we get straight to it. Is that alright with you?"

"Sure. The sooner, the better right?"

I was initially reluctant to confide in him about my dream, worrying he would consider me a complete nutcase. But, as he sat with me, I understood he would listen without judgment or the slightest hint of criticism.

"The night before last, I had a dream. Everyone dreams, but I almost never remember mine. Every once in a rare while, I might remember a small bit of one, but it's more of a snapshot than anything else. This dream, though, was completely different."

Staring into my eyes for what seemed like an eternity, Koko slowly, almost imperceptibly, looked down and to the left, appearing to search for the right combination of words with which to respond.

When ready, he took a deep breath, and smiled. As per usual, not at all what I expected.

"You're smiling. Why is that?"

"I will explain shortly. For now, though, I would like to hear about your dream. Do you remember most of it?"

"That's the weird part. I remember all of it, down to the smallest detail. I can still see the faces of everyone in the dream, the vivid colors of the clothes they were wearing, even what they were feeling at the time. The stars in the night sky twinkled, and I saw them. How could I possibly remember all that?

"Dreams can be very powerful, Ashley. Tell me what you remember. You do not have to go into minute detail right now as I'm afraid we probably do not have enough time."

Taking a deep breath, I began, hitting the high points to be as brief as possible, relating to him the basic, most important details of the dream as I understood them. Upon completion and shifting my focus back to him, I was surprised by the look on his face, eyes wide with amazement, as if seeing something that was literally beyond explanation.

"So, what do you think?"

"Well. That is quite a dream. Let me ask you this, have you ever done any research into Blackfoot burial ceremonies?"

"No, never. Why?"

"Because some of what you described, especially the warrior's burial, closely mirrors that of an actual Blackfoot burial. It is not an exact depiction down to the last detail, but some of it is remarkably similar."

"I have no explanation for that. In fact, I'm stunned. All of what I know about the Blackfoot Nation is what you've told me."

"I am at a loss for words right now. There are aspects of your dream I would expect you to have no knowledge of. Strange. But you have confirmed what I initially suspected, which explains why I was smiling before. What you have experienced is less of a dream and more of what First Nation people call a vision."

"A vision?"

"Yes. Sometimes it is referred to as a vision quest, which we can talk about later. For now, it is important for you to understand that a vision, such as the one you described, is usually meant as a vehicle to help a person understand the meaning and destiny of one's life. Everyone that has ever lived has a purpose for which their life is created. A vision is used to help them determine what that purpose is. Do you understand?"

"I think so. But why on earth would I, of all people, have a vision? I mean, I'm not of the First Nation."

"True, but a vision can happen to anyone, at any time. Nowhere is it written that visions are the sole realm of the First Nation people. We tend to be more in tune with the natural world, Mother Earth some call it, than most and perhaps that makes a difference. Am I surprised you had the vision? Yes, very much so. Unfortunately, I am completely unqualified to help you interpret it. I could tell you what I think it means, but that would be unfair, as you are the only one who can properly and accurately interpret the deeper meaning of what you experienced."

"Can you at least explain the blindfold? That doesn't make any sense to me."

"Sure. It is a valid question. I suspect the blindfold is perhaps a way for the universe to not so subtly say that you cannot be privy to all that life has to offer before you are ready."

"I guess that makes sense." Maybe, I thought.

"Do you have any idea who the tall figure might be? The one whose face you could not see?" he asked.

"No, I really don't. I feel like I should know who it is, but the more I think about it, the farther away the answer seems to get."

"I have an idea you might try. Close your eyes."

With some reluctance I closed my eyes and waited.

"Picture the individual in your dream with as much detail as you can remember. Do you have a clear picture of this person?"

"Sort of. I can see everything except for his face, it's still blurry."

"Great. I want you to imagine your vision is seen through a very precise camera lens. Try to adjust the focus of the image, back and forth, in and out, until the face of the individual becomes clear."

I did as he asked, adjusting the focus of the image in my mind by moving the lens of the "camera" in and out. Initially nothing happened, the image remained just as blurry as I remembered it, but then, on my third attempt, something miraculous happened. The once blurry image resolved itself into one defined by sharpness and color and I instantly recognized the face as that of my father.

Without being prompted, my eyes opened, and I turned my head to stare at Koko. I was stunned.

"Ashley, what's wrong? Who did you see?"

"My father. The tall figure is my father."

"Wow. I did not expect that."

"Neither did I, but I'm sure it was him. He was smiling, which is strange because in almost all the pictures of him I've ever seen he's in his Navy uniform and not smiling at all. I'm not certain, but I think in the dream he was wearing combat fatigues."

"He was with the Teams, right?" he asked, using the informal title for the Navy SEALs. His use of this term surprised me as few people outside the military are familiar with the Teams as a moniker for the Navy's special forces unit.

"He was, for ten years."

"Well, I must admit that I am wholly unqualified to interpret your vision. It would be irresponsible for me to even attempt it," he admitted, lowering his head.

"So, what do I do?"

Koko took a deep breath.

"I know someone who may be able to help, but only if you are willing to speak with him."

"Certainly. I need all the help I can get."

"I have never told you about my brother, have I?"

"No. I didn't know you had any siblings."

"Yes, an older brother, Sinopa. Sinopa is the Blackfoot word for fox."

Koko's wisdom lined face displayed what appeared to me like the wistful remembrance of a difficult time. He didn't tear up, yet somehow the look in his eyes changed ever so slightly.

He continued, pausing to catch his breath or perhaps collect his thoughts, though I couldn't be sure which.

"My apologies for having not mentioned him until now. In any case, when Sinopa was a young boy, maybe four or five, he began having seizures. The seizures happened infrequently in the beginning, but their frequency and severity became progressively worse. Eventually he was diagnosed with epilepsy and put on medication. The medication helped, but he would still have an occasional episode, as our mom would say. Because of the seizures, he was bullied unmercifully, not to the extent you have experienced mind you, but still, it was severe."

"Did you try to help him?"

"Yes, I did. Early on, I wasn't much help because I was simply too small to make a difference. As we got older, I was able to deflect some of the bullying, easing his pain to a small degree I suppose, but I always regretted not being able to do more. Well, to make a long story short, Sinopa grew up, eventually becoming what Western culture calls a shaman, though that term is somewhat misleading. More accurately speaking, a shaman is what is known as a medicine man or medicine woman. These individuals are often the healers and spiritual leaders in the tribe. While my brother's peers bullied him because of his seizures, the tribal elders looked upon them with great reverence and respect. Because of this, they groomed him from an early age to use his seizures as an asset so that he might help people seek harmony between themselves and the world around them. In a very real way, Sinopa's seizures became an asset to the entire tribe."

"So, he uses his seizures and the bullying to his advantage?"

"No, not really. He has never sought revenge or retribution; those emotions are detrimental to the tribe. He utilizes the seizures and bullying in ways that help others. In fact, many of those that bullied him when he was young, now look to him for guidance. He has never turned anyone away. Sinopa is one of the most selfless people I have ever met, is one of the most respected people of the Blackfoot Nation and is a tribal elder." Koko stated with obvious pride.

"Wow, that's cool. I guess he didn't see that coming, did he?"

"No. Had you told him when he was young, that he would be where he is now, he never would have believed it. He could not see past his immediate pain, as most people cannot. Growing up was remarkably difficult for him, but it has made him the strong person he is today."

"Do you think he might be able to help me?"

"Oh, yes. Forgive me, I got slightly offtrack. Yes, I think Sinopa will be able to help you interpret your vision. I will talk with him soon."

"Thanks, Koko, I appreciate it. Maybe he could talk some sense into Mike, too. Although I doubt that's possible."

"Oh, I think it is possible. Unlikely perhaps, but certainly possible. People are capable of incredible change if they are open to the possibility. Speaking of Mike, I heard two people talking about him in the elevator just a little while ago. He is in a room on this floor, not far from here, from what they were saying."

"What? Mike is here? In this hospital?"

I had difficulty processing this new information.

"Yes, I believe so. Room 1408, if I am not mistaken."

A tiny seed of thought entered my brain, growing so quickly I had trouble keeping up with it.

"I have to go see him. You must help me. I mean, will you please help me?"

I blurted the question out.

Koko sat up straight, as if he had received a shock.

"I am sorry, you said you want to go see him?"

"No. I don't want to, I have to."

Reaching for the tape that held the IV to the inner bend of my right arm I carefully prepared to remove it.

"I'm not even sure why. I just know I must do this before I lose my nerve and change my mind. Can you help me? Please?"

Looking up into Koko's perplexed face and taking a deep breath, I grasped the exposed end of the IV needle with my left index finger and thumb, pulling firmly, not stopping despite the pain. With the needle free, I dropped it onto the side of the bed, closed my eyes, and exhaled. When I opened them a moment later, Koko had already rounded the end of the bed and was standing next to me, presumably waiting to see what I was going to do next.

"Wow, that was painful. Okay, I need to get out of this bed. That's probably going to hurt too, but there's nothing I can do about that now."

"Are you sure you want to do this? I am sure there are many rules against such things, especially considering the history between you and Mike."

Koko's attempt to change my mind was halfhearted at best.

"You're here well before visiting hours, and you're lecturing me about breaking the rules? Koko, what would Fred think?"

Koko cocked his head ever so slightly to the right and grinned.

"Touché."

Thirty-Four

"Okay, how am I going to do this?"

Gaining a better angle by propping up on my elbows only served to produce incredible amounts of pain throughout my body.

"Here, let me help you."

Offering his support, he grasped my shoulders with both hands.

"Can you lean forward? We can move you to the edge of the bed, then you can rest a bit."

I looked directly into Koko's eyes.

"Yeah, just don't let go, OK?"

He nodded, and a moment later I pushed with my arms as my legs swung over the side of the bed. While Koko provided positive physical assurance, I opened eyes I didn't remember closing to see myself successfully sitting up in bed, albeit slightly hunched over.

I looked at the heart monitor I was still attached to.

"Uh-oh… what do we do about that?"

He eyed the machine and its never-ending red, blinking eye.

"I failed to consider that."

"Can't I just disconnect myself from it and leave it here?"

"No, that will not work. As soon as you disconnect, the machine will stop reading your vital signs, which will alert the nurses down the hall."

He leaned forward to examine the machine more closely.

"What are we going to do?"

"Well, it is on wheels, why not just take it with us?" he asked, shrugging.

Looking toward the floor confirmed Koko's observation, the sinister machine was sitting on tiny, black wheels.

"Yeah, that might work."

Koko placed his right hand on my left shoulder.

"Ready?"

"Not remotely. But it's now or never, so we might as well get to it."

Slowly shifting my weight forward, I gently slid off the side of the bed until I was in a standing position.

"Take a moment to get a feel for it. We will go only when you are ready."

That seemed like a wise and necessary strategy. I stood motionless for a time, gaining confidence in my balance and ability to remain upright.

"Okay, let's go."

Looking toward the door, with one hand on my left shoulder and the other holding the heart monitor, he nodded. My first tentative steps, more abbreviated shuffles than anything, were pain inducing, evidenced by the creaking and groaning of muscles and joints.

We slowly traversed the floor of my room, stopping just short of the closed door.

"Mm, hold on. Are you able to stand on your own? I need to check the hallway. We do not want to get stopped by a nurse or doctor that happens to walk by."

"Yeah, sure. I'm good."

I sounded far more confident than I felt.

Tentatively, Koko released his hold of my shoulder and walked to the door, carefully peering through the tall, narrow window above the door's shiny, steel handle. Quickly looking left and right, he placed his right hand on the handle and opened the door, freezing instantly when its hinges squeaked in protest. Ten long seconds of waiting to determine if the sound raised the alarm of anyone in the hallway ensued. Confident to continue; he lifted the door handle to change the pressure exerted on the hinges. It worked, as he swung the door open without a sound and peered into the hallway, making sure our journey could begin unnoticed.

"Clear, no one in sight. Can you make into the hallway while I hold the door?" he whispered.

"Sure. Piece of cake."

Pulling the heart monitor beside me, I shuffled toward the open door. Resisting the urge to peer through the threshold of the doorway to make sure the coast was clear before venturing out, I passed into the hallway without pausing, knowing that by pausing and looking, Koko might think I doubted his abilities in our decidedly clandestine operation. Shuffle-walking without breaking stride, I stopped and waited for him to quietly shut the door behind me.

Koko surveyed the hallway in both directions.

"I am fairly certain we need to go left."

My ability to scan the hallway was limited to the direction I was facing because turning around required too much effort.

Detecting the faint din of conversation from a hallway on the right, likely nurses at their station, I knew the moment for action was upon us.

"Alright, let's go."

We turned left, slowly forging ahead toward room 1408 and Mike Pigliani. I was so focused on the task before us, I completely ignored the various art prints hung sporadically along the walls.

Arriving at the end of the long hallway, Koko peered right, around the corner, holding up his right hand. Instinctively and immediately understanding this gesture to mean stop, I did. Turning to look at me, he mouthed the word 'nurse.' Nodding, I cautiously turned around to look down the hallway we had just walked. No longer could I see the door marking the entryway to my safe and secure room. Even with Koko as my guide, I felt completely exposed. We were breaking all kinds of rules and as much as I wanted to feel excitement at such a prospect, a feeling of cold dread washed over me instead. Turning back to our direction of travel revealed Koko still staring at me. Wondering why he was still looking at me instead of keeping a watchful eye on the nurse around the corner, I cocked my head to the left, silently signaling my confusion.

He mouthed the word, "breath."

My eyes widened while my brain came to the realization that I had, indeed, been holding my breath. Silently exhaling, releasing an alarming amount of built-up tension, was precisely what I needed. Inhaling, filling my lungs, as much as the pain would allow, with sweet, new air, gave me a renewed sense of purpose.

Koko, having peeked around the corner again, turned toward me, a look of concern washing over his face.

"There is a nurse in the first room on the right. Can you walk past quickly? I will shield you, but you need to hurry, if you can."

"I can do this."

Proceeding around the corner, my eyes immediately shot to the first door on the right, which had been left open, I expected the nurse to exit and witness Koko and I slinking down the hallway. We couldn't afford to have our cover blown, so I quickened my pace as Koko moved to my right side, putting himself between me and the open door now just a few feet ahead. Despite not informing Koko of my accelerated pace, he didn't miss a step. He was in a place that I'd seen him inhabit only once before, on the rooftop of our building as he walked in the snow. As silently as he walked through the snow on the rooftop, here, he was equally quiet. His stealth was complete, absolute, seamlessly entering another realm right before my eyes and I never noticed the transition.

Passing the door, again my instinct was to peer into the room to see if I could spot the nurse that had temporarily halted our journey. Instead, I put my head down and shuffled forward, ignoring the urge to peek. With the open doorway passing through my peripheral vision, I slowed my pace accordingly. Not having reached room 1408, I was already breathing hard, surprisingly out of breath for the short distance traveled.

"Ashley, are you OK? Do you need to rest? Do you want to go back?"

"No, there's no way I can turn back now. I won't be able to forgive myself if I don't do this. I, I mean we, we must keep going. I'm just a little winded."

He nodded, scanning the empty hallway ahead. If I allowed my thoughts to stray in the direction of what it would feel like to face Mike, I would almost certainly lose my nerve and turn around. Instead, I consciously focused my mind on maintaining my balance and steady breathing. Inching ever closer to my goal, I was counting coup.

Continuing, Koko scanned the hallway ahead while checking the room numbers for 1408, which was where we believed Mike to be. Koko stopped, looked at me and, moving only his eyes, indicated an obstacle ahead of us. Following his silent direction, a uniformed police officer stood at the end of the hallway, chatting with a nurse I didn't recognize. Unsure what to do, I froze in my tracks as my heart rate increased substantially. The officer was facing away from us, so we were staring directly at his back. All he had to do was turn around and we would be discovered.

"I believe the police officer is here to guard Mike's room, to make sure he doesn't go anywhere,"

Koko whispered, giving me a look I interpreted to mean that our next move would be entirely up to me.

With no idea how to handle the situation if we were spotted, I went with my gut.

"We didn't come this far just to turn back, did we?"

Koko's reply was a wry, knowing smile and nod. We continued, each step increasing the odds of being seen.

We crept forward, inching closer to our goal at the same time we inched closer to the police officer. Koko abruptly stopped and turned to look at me.

"This is it, 1408. Are you sure you want to do this?"

Terrified of what lurked on the other side of the door, I nonetheless nodded. Racing beads of sweat trickled down my forehead as I placed my right hand on the cold, metal door handle and pushed down. A faint, metallic click pinged through the hallway as the inner workings of the latch released their hold. Cringing at the sound, I looked to my left, convinced the police officer was striding forcefully toward us. To my astonishment, he was still confidently chatting with the nurse, unaware of our presence.

Koko's eyes appeared as wide as mine felt as I refocused my attention back to the door of Mike's room and said,

"Well, here we go, into the lion's den. I just hope he isn't hungry."

"It is not the hungry lion that is the most dangerous, but the wounded one," he cautioned.

Inhaling deeply, I turned the handle, pushed the door open, and stepped inside.

Thirty-Five

Despite the clinical odor permeating every corner of the hospital as well as my broken nose, I instantly recognized Mike's distinctly unique smell, the aroma reminding me of the inside of the van he and his father had forced me into. The smell, a musty combination of sweat and filth, not nearly as concentrated as it had been in the van, still hung in the air, saturating everything it touched. With my damaged nose, I was surprised I could smell anything. I fought the urge to retch as I felt Koko take control of the heavy door, easing it closed so quietly after following me through, I wondered if he closed it at all.

Quietly shuffling into the room, the lights were on, and shades drawn, while high in the far corner, opposite the door, the muted TV displayed the latest sports news courtesy of ESPN. My heart thumped a steady drumbeat as I turned my head to the left, gazing upon the prone figure of Mike Pigliani motionless in bed, asleep. There were no get-well cards beside his bed, no flowers on the window sill, no indication at all that he had been visited by family. Aside from the possibility of profound terror, I had no preconceived notion of what I expected to feel when I saw him. But, as I stared at the person who had tormented me in every way a person could be tormented, I was overwhelmed with a profound sense of pity and sadness.

Mike, noticeably gaunt, his skin pulled tight across his broad skull, and severely chapped lips was a mere shell of the monster I had made him out to be in my mind, had no idea he was no longer alone. Reaching the side of his bed, I watched his massive barrel chest slowly rise and fall as he breathed. He, too, was connected to a heart monitor and an IV. The stress and physical exertion of our shared ordeal had taken a considerable toll on both of us, that much was clear. What I didn't expect to see when I looked at his right leg was that it was no longer there. It had been amputated just below the knee and was now heavily bandaged, much of which had been soaked through with blood.

Sensing Koko behind me, I guessed that he, too, was taking in the scene before us. Did he notice the same things? More likely than not, he noticed far more, as he often did. No doubt he was aware of the gleaming steel handcuff attached to Mike's right wrist; its companion cuff unceremoniously clinked shut around the stainless railing of the hospital bed. Despite the handicap of his leg, the authorities weren't taking any chances. Turning to look at Koko, I was surprised to see his eyes looking as big as mine felt after taking in the sight of Mike's amputated leg. Unsure what to do next, I did the only thing that came to mind.

"Mike, wake up."

My tone, flat but firm, had no effect as he continued his slumber. Defiantly standing my ground, silken tendrils of doubt began invading my consciousness. While I was on the verge of making the decision to leave, Mike opened a heavy eyelid on the right side of his face before I had the opportunity to inform Koko. I stood, transfixed, as Mike attempted to focus through the obvious haze of painkillers to make sense of what he was seeing.

"Half Breed, if you're not out of here in under five seconds, I'm going to beat you to death."

His voice sounded as rough as an old dirt road as his left eye struggled open to assist the right.

Knowing Mike's threat of violence to be a hollow one, I remained. Though unsurprised by his defiant attitude, it angered me. I ignored the insulting nickname, deciding it no longer held any power over me.

"I'm serious. Get the hell out of here."

His threatening intimidation was far from convincing as I doubted he had the energy to get out of bed.

"No."

My reply was a simple matter of fact. Outwardly trying to project an air of confidence, on the inside, I was a trembling mess. Try as I might, I was unable to understand the conflicting sea of emotions swirling around in my head as I faced him. Secure in the fact he was completely incapable of harming me, I should have felt calm, even relaxed, knowing beyond doubt, he couldn't hurt me. Still, I was terrified.

"Come on, man. I have a splitting headache and I'm in no mood for a friendly chat, so take yourself and Chief Wahoo and get out."

"His name is Koko, and you owe him an apology."

"Not gonna happen. Don't let the door hit your worthless ass on your way out. On second thought, make sure it does, it'll give me something to laugh about."

With no idea where this exchange was headed, I stood, glued to the spot, determined to find out.

After a long, awkward silence, he looked toward the ceiling, letting out a resigned sigh.

He brought his eyes back to bear on me.

"Fine. What do you want?"

"You know, I'm not sure. I guess a part of me wanted to see how you were doing."

It was the most honest answer I could come up with.

"Well, how do I look to you? They amputated my leg."

Trying to yell at me, all he could manage was a slightly raised voice.

"Yeah, I saw that. I'm sorry. At least you're still alive."

"You're sorry? Are you kidding me? Listen asshole, it's your fault they took my leg. You're lucky I can't get out of this bed."

His face was red and twisted in anger.

Instantly furious, it took all the self-control I could muster to not bombard Mike with a fusillade of angry shouting.

"My fault? How on earth is any of this my fault? Who kidnapped whom? Wasn't it you who kicked me in the face? Wasn't it your dad who shot at me? Multiple times? Did you expect me to just let you do those things? Did you think I was going to just sit there like a stone and not try to escape?"

He made no attempt to respond to my questions.

"Mike, I'm asking you direct questions. What did you expect me to do?"

"I don't know. Nothing? That would have been ideal."

"Well, you didn't get what you wanted did you? Get used to it."

"It's time for you to go."

He reached for the remote control to summon a nurse at the push of a button.

"Where the heck is that—"

"Right here." Koko answered, lifting his left hand to shoulder height, enough to allow Mike to see he held the remote control far from Mike's considerable reach.

"Gimme that." Mike demanded, licking his dry, cracked lips.

"No. Not gonna happen" Koko replied, mimicking words Mike had used against me only moments before.

So involved in my conversation with Mike, I hadn't noticed Koko pick up the remote. He had, evidently, seen the handwriting on the wall and silently made sure Mike would be unable to call for a nurse. He didn't miss a thing.

Mike gave up and closed his eyes. Whether trying to deal with the pain, or his exasperation with the presence of Koko and I, I couldn't tell.

"So, why did they amputate your leg?" I asked, attempting to steer Mike's mind away from his isolation and helplessness.

"I don't know. Something about it being too badly damaged. Infection? I don't remember. I just know that they didn't waste any time with it. I arrived at the hospital and in nothing flat was rushed into surgery. When I woke up my lower leg was gone."

His reply was void of emotion.

"Wow, sounds pretty serious."

Mike opened his eyes again and stared at me.

"Yeah. I don't remember much, but the look on the doctor's face kind of said it all."

"Does it hurt?"

I was surprised Mike was allowing the conversation to continue.

"Yeah, that's the weird part. It hurts like crazy, but the pain is in my ankle and foot, and they're gone. How is that possible? How can my foot hurt? It's not there anymore."

"It is called phantom pain, very common with an injury like yours. The pain will gradually diminish with time, but it will take a while. My mother had her left leg amputated just below the knee, like you, and she experienced the same thing. It is temporary, you will get through it," Koko replied.

"It can't happen soon enough, Chief."

My head whipped around to gauge Koko's reaction to Mike's insult, but he offered nothing in return. I turned back to Mike.

"Really, Mike? What is your problem? Is it impossible for you to open your mouth and not insult someone? Have you ever done one kind thing for anyone in your entire life?"

"You really think you have me pegged, don't you, Half Breed? You think you know all about Mike Pigliani and what makes him tick, don't you? You don't know anything about me. Do you honestly believe I enjoy being like this?"

He paused, his body tensing while a flash of pain coursed through him.

"I'm miserable. Okay? I wake up every single day of my life and I hate myself. I hate who and what I've become. You're no better than everyone else at that worthless school. 'Here comes Big Mike,' everyone says and immediately you judge me, deciding who I am and what I represent. Well piss off!

A coil of spittle ran down his chin as he finished his tirade.

"OK, enlighten me. Who are you? Give me something to go on." I asked. He faced me, and without so much as a blink, he spoke.

"Seen, but never seen.

Less than the shadow behind.

Nothing in between."

I stood there, shocked, unable to believe what I had just heard. In my mind, silently repeating what he had said, I counted the syllables with the fingers of my right hand. Five, seven, five, and as much as I loathed to admit it, it tracked perfectly, a haiku. Not just any haiku either, a deeply profound one, its execution perfect and brilliant.

"Wait, what? That was a haiku, wasn't it?"

"Yeah. I don't know. Maybe. Who cares?"

"I care. Where did you come up with that? Who wrote it? It's phenomenal." I opined.

"Who? Me, you stupid, little shit. I wrote it. And I can tell by the look on your face you don't believe me."

He was right. My first inclination was a refusal to believe he was capable of such eloquent prose. But my instinct knew the truth as much as my brain attempted to deny it.

"How did you come up with something like that?" I asked, wondering if he detected the jealousy in my question.

"I have a thing for haikus, OK. I don't understand how it works. The words arrive in my head at random times so I write them down. Sometimes the words appear in my vision, fully formed. I dream about haikus. It scares me. Anyway, I've got a binder full of them at home."

Immediately, I felt ashamed at how completely I had misunderstood and underestimated my enemy. Though to be fair he hadn't given much to work with.

Silence followed as he winced in reaction to the phantom pain, then he said,

"Okay, play time's over. You and your Indian friend can leave now."

"No."

"Half Breed, I'm serious. I will crawl out of this bed and pound you into the floor!"

He gritted his teeth tightly together in pain as he propped himself up on his elbows.

It was then I understood why I was here, why I had come to face him. Leaning forward, well within the powerful reach of my nemesis, I stared straight into his eyes.

"You don't get it do you?" My voice was barely a whisper. "It's over. The days of you treating me like your personal punching bag are finished. No more calling me Half Breed, no more kicks to the face, no more kidnapping. From now on, you're going to leave me alone."

Still and calm on the outside, my voice steady and even, on the inside I was boiling and trembling with rage.

"I'm not afraid of you anymore. You're not allowed to threaten or intimidate me ever again. If our paths ever cross in the future, you may call me Ashley. Understand?"

Staring into my eyes, he said nothing. His only response was to exhale and look away. I thought about pressing him further, demanding he acknowledge me, but the look on his face and his body language indicated he was done talking. With nothing more to say, I stood up as straight as I could and began to turn around to leave. Turning in place, my eyes panned down to the small table to the left of the bed. On it, sitting near the corner, strong and silent, was my small red and gray marble bear. Midturn, I stopped and advanced the few steps to the table, reaching out to pick it up. I looked at Mike, walled off in the solitary prison of his mind. Closing my hand around the bear, I turned around, slowly shuffling toward the door. Once there, I turned to look at Mike one more time before leaving.

The Mike Pigliani I saw lying handcuffed to the hospital bed, leg amputated just below the knee, was the thin, cracked shell of the person I feared. There was no joy, or even relief, in finally facing up to my tormentor. Witnessing the new Mike Pigliani, the embodiment of a person with a shattered soul, was akin to reading a book to its final chapter but finding no absolution.

Thirty-Six

Opening the door to Mike's hospital room, I entered the hallway, making no attempt to avoid the policeman Koko and I had seen earlier. Fatigue and pain had taken over to such a degree, I no longer cared if we were discovered. With Koko steadying me every time my balance showed a sign of wavering, we retraced our steps back to my hospital room.

"Are we close?"

As hard as I tried, I couldn't remember which room was mine.

"Two doors down, on the right."

Entering my room, Koko assisted in helping me climb into bed, our journey, my mission, leaving me completely exhausted.

"Thank you for going with me Koko, for helping me along the way. I couldn't have done it without you."

"Oh, I think you probably could have."

"Well, I'm glad I didn't have to."

"He had your bear. Did you give it to him?"

"Yes, sort of. I let him borrow it. When we were out there in the snow, he was in bad shape, physically and emotionally. He admitted he was scared. He didn't need to say it, but it was obvious. So, I thought of the bear, what it represents, and why you gave it to me. In that moment, Mike needed the bear far more than I did. I explained the meaning of the bear, but he kind of scoffed at the idea though I noticed he was clutching it tightly when I turned to leave. I thought it might help. Pretty stupid, huh?"

Across the wise, weathered lines of his face, a serious, contemplative look appeared.

"Stupid? No, not stupid at all. What you have done is truly remarkable. It is wonderful."

His serious expression began to change.

"Do you know what the greatest weapon in the world is?"

It seemed an odd question, given the circumstances.

"Nuclear bomb?"

"A powerful weapon to be sure, but no, not even close I am afraid."

"Ideas?"

"You are on the right track my friend. Good." He smiled. "The greatest weapon the world has ever known, the only weapon that cannot be defeated, is the weapon of peace."

"Peace? I don't understand."

"If I ask you to list as many famous warriors as possible you can think of you could probably come up with quite a few rather easily, right?"

"Sure. There are hundreds, probably thousands of them. Patton, MacArthur, Washington, Grant, Lee, and those are just the Americans in two wars. There are loads more from other countries and other times."

"Exactly. Now, do the same thing, only this time, name as many warriors of peace as you can."

"Okay. Jesus, Gandhi ..." Two names in and already I was hesitating.

"Oh, Mother Theresa. This is hard."

"Yes, unfortunately it is. Now, which group do you think is more revered throughout history? The admirals and generals or the peacemakers?"

"That's tough to say, but I think that it'd be the peacemakers."

"I think so too. Why do you think it is so much harder to remember who the warriors of peace are?"

"Peacemakers, overall, have had a greater positive impact on society. But they're not seen as strong until they're gone most of the time. Maybe that's why. It's a shame there aren't more of them."

"Yes, I agree. My point in all of this is that you, in your own small but significant way, have acted as a warrior of peace. You could have done any number of things in your dealings with Mike while you were in the forest. You could have simply walked out on him, leaving him for dead. You didn't do that. You went so far as to give him the marble bear to hang on to for strength. I do not think many people would have acted in such a way. Your father would be very proud of you, of this, I am sure."

Were my father still alive, I supposed Koko might be right. I'll never know. Koko remained with me until my mom arrived, leaving right around the time visiting hours were set to begin. The next few days passed without excitement as I was poked, prodded, and tested to the nth degree before being discharged from the hospital. Nurse Marni stopped in regularly but, to my disappointment, Greg did not. I was told he had taken some time off to be with family, which I could well understand.

Thirty-Seven

The ride home from the hospital was, in every way, uneventful as I dozed in the back seat of the cab during most of the ride, missing all the things I had previously noticed on my first trip home from the hospital. The same things were there, delivery drivers, snow, pedestrians walking here and there, bundled up against the driving wind and cold, but I didn't see them. Stopping in front of our building, my mom helped me out of the cab while the intoxicating aroma emanating from The Java Coast down the street made me hunger for a fresh latte. I longed to sit in the warmth of the shop and just be, watching the world pass by the large window in front.

"I can smell the coffee shop."

She held the door of our apartment building open for me.

"I know, isn't it terrific?"

Slowly, we walked toward the elevator and were carried up to our floor. Stepping into the hallway after the elevator doors opened, I looked around, realizing that in front of me stood a whole new world. I began to sob.

"Ashley? Honey, what's wrong?"

It took a few moments to gather myself together enough to formulate an answer. Scanning the nauseating, faded blue-green walls, sobs escaped from deep within my soul.

"The walls, Mom. Look at the walls. I used to hate that color. That faded blue-green paint was sickening. I absolutely hated it."

I paused again, catching my breath.

"Now though … it's the most wonderful color I think I've ever seen. It hadn't occurred to me until just now that I might not ever see it again. Such a small thing, the color of these walls, and yet, now, it makes all the difference. It's huge."

"Come on Ashley, let's get you home."

Entering our apartment, I immediately detected the faint smell of recently baked cookies. Chocolate chip, if I had to guess.

"I think I smell cookies. Dr. Albermarle said it might take a while for my sense of smell to return to normal. But I can already smell cookies."

"That's great—positive steps. Park yourself on the couch, and I'll go get some."

I heard the familiar sounds of dishes and glasses being prepared in the kitchen. She emerged from the kitchen carrying a plate of cookies in one hand and a tall glass of cold milk in the other. I was in heaven. The cookies, a marvel of intricate tastes and textures I had never noticed before, melted in my mouth. I ate half of the first cookie before falling asleep.

The next several days were spent doing a lot of sleeping and trying to catch up on schoolwork. Dr. Albermarle didn't want me going back to school until after the holidays, cautioning me to take things slowly, not to push myself too hard. In the early evening, a few days before Christmas as I sat on the couch watching The Princess Bride for the millionth time, came a discreetly polite knock on the door.

"I wonder who that is?" my mom asked.

Rising from the couch, she walked the short distance to the door. Taking another cookie to ignore the imposition of the interruption, I paused the movie.

"Hi. Please, come in."

The enthusiasm in her voice was more than I expected. Shifting my attention away from the cookie to see who had disrupted the cinematic mastery that was The Princess Bride was a sight that immediately sent my head spinning. I dropped the cookie.

"Hi Ashley."

It was Riley, and her voice was the sound of angels singing. On a normal day, Riley was a vision of beauty, this evening, in my living room, she was positively radiant. Blinking my eyes half a dozen times to make certain what I was seeing was, in fact, real, I looked to my mom, confusion clearly written on my face.

"Ashley, are you going to say something?" she asked.

"Huh?" I replied, looking back at Riley, then, again, at my mom.

"Oh. Hi. Sorry. You kind of surprised me. Hi Riley. Hi. How are you? I can smell cookies."

Imaginary face-palm. I can smell cookies. Who says that? She was completely unfazed.

"That's great."

"Here, Riley, let me get your coat."

"Oh, thank you Mrs. Perault."

Removing her puffy white coat revealed she was dressed to the nines in what can only be described as formal dress. The form-fitting dress, black with a tan and pink floral print, hemmed to just above knee and sleeveless, was one I wouldn't have thought anyone could reasonably pull off. Riley did so with striking success.

"You look stunning."

The words escaped my mouth before I had time to think about them.

"Thank you, Ashley."

She blushed, handing her coat to my mom.

"Riley, would you like to sit down."

"Sure."

She walked into the living room, sitting next to me on the couch.

"What's going on?" I asked.

She seemed nervous, gently wringing her hands while looking at the floor.

"Well … I was wondering if you wanted to go to the Christmas Dance with me?"

A small smile appeared on her immaculate face. Without thinking, I looked at my mom as if she were going to confirm she was hearing the same thing as I.

"Hey, don't look at me. I'm too old for the Christmas Dance."

I don't think I've ever seen such a broad smile on my mom's face before.

"Yeah. I mean, yes. I'd love to."

I nearly shouted it, clearly in a state of shock.

"Hah, hah. Okay, great."

"Wait, I thought you already had a date. What happened?" I asked, despite it being none of my business.

"Oh, he called about thirty minutes ago, said he was taking someone else."

How anyone could stand up a girl like Riley was beyond my capacity to understand.

"That might be the most ridiculous thing I've ever heard. I mean, that's just wrong. How in the world—"

Riley cut me off.

"Yeah, it's not ideal, but I'd rather go with you anyway. Well, you'd better hurry up and get changed, we need to hurry or we're going to be late."

"Now? Uh, shoot, I don't have anything to wear. What am I going to do? I'm going to be so underdressed."

I was starting to panic.

"It's OK, Ashley, I think everyone will understand and I'm sure they'll be happy to see you."

"Okay, I'll be back in a minute. Well, give me a few minutes. Be right back."

Cautiously rising from the couch to walk to my room, I returned ten minutes later, dressed in khaki slacks and a cobalt blue, long sleeved shirt and my favorite red paisley tie. Riley and my mom talked while The Princess Bride played quietly in the background.

"Sorry. This is the best I could do. I hope it's OK. None of my clothes fit anymore because I've lost a bunch of weight in the last few weeks."

"That's OK, you look terrific. We better get going."

"Wait, not yet. You're not leaving until I get a picture," Mom announced, running to the back of the apartment to get her cell phone.

"Okay, well, I guess stand next to the door. That'll do just fine."

Riley and I took our places near the door and stood shoulder to shoulder, an awkward distance separating the two of us. With the pictures taken, we said goodbye.

Chatting easily as we walked the short distance to Yorktown High, the temperature was enough to take my breath away, but for the first time in my life, it didn't bother me. Among the dynamic, glittering streets of the city, we walked side by side for a short time, Riley slowed a little, looked at me with the kindest smile, and took my hand. Smiling in return, a completely unrestrained gesture, came with ease. For the first time in my life, I was comfortable in my own skin, perfectly happy being me. I was free. It was in that moment when I realized, I had been all along.

The End

About the Author

Born in New Jersey and raised in East Texas, Ian J. Harrison spent his childhood swimming (a lot), spending far more time outside instead of in, building forts, and surprisingly, not getting into too much trouble. A college athlete in swimming, he received an AA degree from Ocean County College in Toms River, NJ and a BS in Kinesiology from Texas A&M University in College Station, TX. He enjoys woodworking and restoring vintage motorcycles with his twin brother, Scott, and herding a staggering number of rescued cats as well as several dogs. He is an Eagle Scout currently living in Texas.